BILLY LIAR
ON THE MOON

Books by KEITH WATERHOUSE

JUBB

BILLY LIAR

EVERYTHING MUST GO

BILLY LIAR
ON
THE MOON

by
Keith Waterhouse

G. P. Putnam's Sons
New York

FIRST AMERICAN EDITION 1976

SBN: 399–11682–6

*Library of Congress Catalog
Card Number: 75-33571*

PRINTED IN THE UNITED STATES OF AMERICA

Chapter One

THE only place where you can get a vodka martini in Shepford is just by the M. 1 slip road, ambitiously described in the official guidebook as the Highway to Europe. Road maps are not much use to the thirsty traveler, it being the council's policy to keep one jump ahead of Geographia Ltd. Anyone needing a vodka martini that badly would have to take verbal instructions.

Driving west out of town through the shopping center—or, for that matter, driving west out of town while still looking for the one-way side street that is the only access to the shopping center—you come across three or four small brick factories, one of them also mentioned in the guidebook. (It makes plastic weather shields for offshore generators; thus Shepford, though eighty miles inland, plays its part in the quest for North Sea oil.) Then there is a patch of rubble where another small brick factory is about to go up or has just fallen down. Then there is the borough's surplus cache of sewage pipes, stacked on what used to be a grass verge. Then there is the road junction with its cluster of signs: this way to the Town Center, that way to the Abbey, this way to the Castle, this way, that way and the other way to the parking lots, and around the back doubles for the Highway to Europe. This route takes you to the site that was rejected, so they say, by Holiday Inns, but accepted by Heritage Motor Lodges of America.

The Heritage Motor Lodge complex, resembling a Nevada desert gambling resort that has run foul of the Las Vegas Planning Committee, was but four minutes from the town center when it was built and is but twelve minutes away since the one-way system was perfected. But it is sufficiently near the motorway to give the discerning visitor a last chance of reviewing the life-style to which he has been reduced by the profit motive, repacking his case of samples and heading back to London or any point north—in my case, Stradhoughton.

If only I'd left before the second martini, not only would the Helen problem have solved itself, but I could have been driving into the Bull Ring car stack by half past nine, throwing up a Chinese dinner by half past ten, and still have had ninety minutes to play with before exploring the question I'd often turned over in my mind since leaving Stradhoughton all those light-years ago—did the drunks still race all the way around the Town Hall while the carillon sounded twelve?

I couldn't afford vodka martinis, and neither, I imagined, could Shepford District Council, which paid for them in a roundabout way. I drank them as a gesture to my designer-decorated surroundings—to fit in, as much as possible, with the padded leather bar, the bowls of pretzels, and the old English crossbows on the bare stone walls. The illusion, for which I was grateful, was of being, if not in New York, then at the very least in downtown Albuquerque, wherever that turned out to be. And anyway, it was not much dearer than the so-called lounge bar which had lately taken possession of the soul of the King's Head in the Cornmarket, and anyway, vodka martinis were what Oscar drank too.

"Nearest place south of Birming-ham where they know how to fix the darn things, Bill. Lemme say this. You British can build the best boats in the world, the best suits in the world, and I'd walk a billion miles for an English teacake. But you bet your ass you've never yet built a good barman. No-way."

"Right."

Why Oscar spoke like an Australian actor playing an American bit part in an English television play was because he didn't exist. Sometimes he absolutely didn't exist, for weeks at a time, but he'd been useful with the Helen problem lately, and he was often a comfort in other ways, so the least I could do was stand him a drink occasionally. He was an oil-man at present, and I was doing him a big favor by introducing him to the only firm in Britain that could turn him out a plastic weather shield for his offshore generator by the end of the week; but usually he was in public relations, and if I played my cards right, I would be on Madison Avenue before I was forty. Or should I, I sometimes used to wonder in whimsical moments, especially when the Helen problem wasn't too pressing, turn Oscar into a six-foot rabbit, like Harvey? That would depend on future access to the vodka martinis.

Who did exist, to the point of occupying Oscar's barstool and embarrassingly asking for draft Bass, was Purchase, who called himself a colleague of mine and was said to shave his nose.

"You mean the hairs in his nostrils," I'd said to Hattersley, who had brought me this tidbit.

"His nose. From tip to bridge."

"Upward strokes? Sounds improbable."

"Bridge to tip, then. It's true! I caught him at it in the washroom—the night we were all going to Pisspot's birthday do. He puts lather all over his nose and then he shaves it."

"The only man in Shepford with a conk like a baby's bottom."

Also the only man in Shepford I didn't want to see in the bar of the Heritage Motor Lodge—or, to be fair, going rap-

7

idly through a rollcall of about two hundred names and putting asterisks against the dozen or so who might remotely land up there—the last man I wanted to see. Although Purchase could describe himself as a colleague only in the sense that, say, a BBC admin clerk can claim credit for the nine o'clock news—for he was in the Finance Department while I was in Information and Publicity—we were, at least on paper, in line for the same promotion. No-*way*, as Oscar would have said.

FOR IMMEDIATE RELEASE. Mr. William Fisher, 33, is to be appointed Information Officer and Director of Publicity for the District of Shepford at a commencing salary of about double what he is getting at present, plus entertainment allowance, office car, honorary membership of the municipal golf club, key to the Civic Center drinks cupboard, and freeloading facilities at most official functions. He succeeds Mr. R. V. O. "Pisspot" Rainbell, who is taking up residence in a home for alcoholics.

"Be a bit late tonight," I could hear myself saying. "Bloody mayor's reception. Bloody Japanese trade delegation."
I could even say the same thing to Helen, if the Helen problem wasn't solved by then.

Mr. Fisher entered local government in the West Riding Borough of Stradhoughton, where he had been employed as an undertaker's clerk until dismissed for petty embezzlement. After joining the Rates Office on forged references, he gained experience in several municipal departments before transferring to the then County Borough of Shepford for a motive he finds himself unable to discuss. Mr. Fisher has lived in Shepford for eight years, although it seems like eighty, and has been in the Information Office for the past five. He is part author of *Pageantry with Progress* (new edition), the official guidebook. Mr. Fisher resides either with his wife and widowed mother on the Fairways estate or alone in a mahogany-paneled turret overlooking the ancient Cornmarket with its many pavement cafés, brasseries and bustling restaurants.

But this was no time for counting golden eggs. If Purchase was still sitting here humming and hawing over what to drink as a substitute for draft Bass when Helen walked in ten minutes hence, there was nothing short of a good shove into the Civic Center paper-shredding machine that could prevent his account of the rendezvous reaching the Senior Appointments Selection Board. Plus, as a bonus, a breakdown of my vodka martini budget, with informed speculation on how it was balanced. I could already see his smudgy colored photograph in the *Evening Mail,* a news sheet that seemed to be put together by a hundred monkeys at a hundred keyboards, and the accompanying text:

> Mr James Pugchase, a meber of te District Treasurer's Department ang chairman of the Shepford Festival Committee ival Committe shrdlushrdlu has been appointed Mr Purchase, who is an old boy of Shepford Grammar Information Officer and Publicity Director School, Te case was adjourned until Thrusday.

"No draft beer of any kind?" repeated Purchase. The barman, Harry (a name he had been issued along with his white jacket when joining the Heritage Happy Family), had just said that to him, in so many words. Purchase did with other people's sentences what he did with figures all day long at his trestle table in the office next to mine—he checked them for possible discrepancies. I had once made a tape of him cocking up an interview on the local radio, and he had repeated, word-perfect, a question about the Shepford Festival consisting of fifty-eight syllables. No wonder they called him the human radish, or would do if I had anything to do with it.

"Lager, then," he said, taking a far bigger handful of pretzels than he was entitled to on such a cheapskate order. The room was too dark to stare at his nose, a spot check I carried out from time to time. One little nick, or even better, a strip of Elastoplast, would confirm Hattersley's story: I didn't believe all he told me.

"Don't often see you in this neck of the woods," I said, slipping easily into the council-clerk patois. (If I'd wanted an A for Effort, I would have said "this particular hostelry.") I cupped my hand around the empty martini glass, wishing I'd ordered it on the rocks so that it would have come in a tumbler and made him believe I was on gin and tonic. As it was, he would have to think it was sherry. With an olive.

"One of your haunts, is it?" A ninety-degree glance around the bar, as casual as a turtle with inflamed neck glands, to indicate that he's only making conversation. You don't catch me like that, Purchase.

"No, it's not really my neck of the woods." I shouldn't have said that twice; maybe I'm nervous. "I favor it with the occasional visit."

"But not often?" No, Purchase, positively not often. Let's hope you gather as much from the half smile, the deprecatory shrug, the shake of the head, the slight curl of the lip, and the expression "No."

"This on your tab, Mr. Fisher?" said Harry, the barman. He was English, but American-trained, you bet your ass. He'd worked on a liner, so he told me. It should have been the *Titanic*.

"No, no, no, wouldn't dream of it," Purchase protested, now showing further bad taste by digging into his pocket for tenpenny pieces, as if completing a round in a saloon bar. "Here, let me get you one. I insist."

He nodded to Harry, who, before I could mouth "Small medium sherry," commenced an exercise with lemons, olives, ice, vodka, vermouth and shaker that would have won

10

him ten points for style in an International Barman of the Year competition.

"Because," continued Purchase, after quizzically following Harry's progress for some time in the apparent hope that he was about to produce the flags of all nations out of his cocktail shaker, "if you *don't* come here often, you *wouldn't* often see me here, now would you?"

Go on, Purchase, let's have it. In a minute you're going to say, "Not that it's any concern of mine where you spend your evenings," in a tone that suggests it should be the concern of every right-thinking taxpayer in Shepford. "Nor is it any of mine where you spend yours," I could retaliate, leaving him the way open for some cock-and-bull story about being taken short or popping in for a book match and a packet of Mannikins. You followed me here, Purchase. You know it, and I know it.

But it wasn't what Purchase was going to say in a minute that immediately worried me; it was what he was going to say any second now when Harry, after pouring my vodka martini, placed his bill a discreet distance away on the bar counter, though not so discreet a distance that a trained accountant couldn't read it upside down. And it was what he was going to say, if not to me then to himself, and later to everyone listed in the Civic Center internal telephone directory, when Helen entered in about eight minutes.

"Nice and dry, just as you like it, Mr. Fisher," said Harry, who seemed hell-bent on identifying me as the Heritage Motor Lodge's most favored son. "And there's one lined up for her ladyship."

Thank you, Harry, but surely there are more subtle ways of arousing Purchase's interest? Why not a revolving illuminated sign in the courtyard: HERITAGE MOTOR LODGES OF AMERICA WELCOME WILLIAM FISHER AND HIS MISTRESS, MRS. HELEN LIGHTFOOT?

I shrugged him back to his racing paper. Purchase, who

had finished the pretzels and was reaching for a bowl of nuts intended for the future occupant of the next barstool but two, hadn't heard, or pretended he hadn't. His left buttock reconnected with the padded leather, which hissed its dismay, and he turned back to me.

"Not that it's any concern of mine where you— Good . . . God!"

He'd seen the bill. In dramatic terms, his cry of anguish should have been an offstage one, like a crash in a Laurel and Hardy film, and Harry and I could have cringed our shoulders in sympathy. But it wasn't bad as cries of anguish went— rather similar to the one I'd uttered myself on being introduced to my own first Heritage Motor Lodge bar bill. ("Hey, lemme take care of that," Oscar had said, but I'd already put my hand firmly over the bill, felt in my top pocket for the American Express card that I must have left in one of my other suits, and tossed my last fiver on the bar counter.)

"A pound?" the awestruck Purchase whispered. "A *pound?* A POUND?"

"It includes tax," I said. But not service. Odd that despite all my anxieties about Purchase's presence here, my main worry was that he would embarrass me by departing, if he ever got round to departing, without leaving a tip.

"All I can say is if you can afford to drink here, you must have better salaries in your department than we in ours," said Purchase, who knew to the penny what I earned.

What I could do was slip a few bob on the bar counter near his glass and pretend he'd left it.

"Easy come, easy go," I said. "It's not every day I come up on the football pools." You can do better than that, Fisher.

"You say you've come up on the pools?"

Yes, Rastus, I'se come up on de pools. "Only thirty-eight quid—fourth dividend." He's going to check that. "Or at least that's what I work it out at—they haven't coughed up

12

yet. Let me get you another." Six minutes before Helen was due: the lemming instinct was working well.

"Make it two lagers this time," I thought I'd better say to Harry. A mistake, probably. I can't drink beer quickly. I could spill most of it over Purchase's trousers, of course, but would that hasten his departure or postpone it while he dried off?

Maybe she'd be late. There was always a sporting chance of a traffic jam on the clearway.

"I'm glad I caught up with you," said Purchase, another rueful glance at his bar bill indicating that I could take that remark how I liked, "because I wanted a word in your ear about the Festival."

Although this was no time for delaying tactics, I couldn't resist playing Purchase at his own game: "When you say you're glad you caught up with me, does that imply you followed me here?"

"I caught sight of your car on the roundabout. I did want a word—it's rather difficult in the office."

If it's rather difficult in the office, it must be about Pisspot.

"It's about Mr. Rainbell. Some of us are *rather* concerned about his drinking."

"Concerned about him personally or concerned about his job?" Or after his job, even.

"I'm not in the slightest interested in his personal life." Only in yours, Fisher. Four minutes to go. "But when it comes to disrupting committee meetings, arriving late, falling about and having no idea what's going on, then it's very much my pigeon."

"The poor old sod's only got eighteen months to go," I said. "And so far as his work's concerned, Hattersley and I simply carve it up between us. So unless you're tired of picking him up when he falls down the stairs, I don't see what you've got to worry about."

"What I have to worry about is the Festival. As you know, it's very much my pigeon." (Making two pigeons so far. Well, it is and it isn't your pigeon, Purchase. You got the job only because your mother had it before you, when Shepford was a grotty little market town and the Festival was no more than a Sunday-school float and a couple of sideshows. A classic example of nepotism being all right so long as it's kept in the family.) "I don't see how we can get through our work if that drunken lout is allowed to disrupt committee meetings, arriving late, falling about—"

Yes, you've already said that, and my time is more valuable than you think. "So why don't you bar him?" I cut in.

"That's more difficult than you realize. The Festival Committee can't function properly without proper liaison with the Information and Publicity Department."

Now then, Purchase, you look like a sporting gent. For a fiver, see if you can say this without moving your lips: "Put properly by Purchase, Pisspot's proper purpose is publicity." Or rather:

"So Hattersley and I go through the minutes. That's what we always do anyway."

"There are a thousand questions involving Information and Publicity. The department must be represented at personal level."

"So Pisspot sends apologies for absence and Hattersley or I take his place. What's wrong with that?"

"I was hoping you'd say that, Fisher. And rather you than Hattersley, if I may say so."

I'd drifted off again. Oscar was saying, "Bill, I wanna put this on the line. One of our team has a drink problem. We have to let him go. Lemme ask you this. Can you telescope your present commitments and be at your desk on the thirty-fourth floor of the Madison Building by nine A.M. Monday? You have to make a decision now." I frowned Oscar into the

14

leather shadows of some unoccupied booth and looked at the bar clock. It destroyed the New York or Albuquerque illusion by keeping Shepford pub time and was ten minutes fast. By Shepford pub time Helen should have been here nine minutes ago and so would arrive any second. I knocked back my lager and heard Purchase continuing:

"Hattersley's a very good man in his way, a good organizer I believe, but we have all the organizing strength we need. What we do need, Fisher, is someone with your flair."

My flair? But you don't want my flair, Purchase. Considering that we're both after the same job, what you would rather do with my flair is take it out to the council rubbish tip and recycle it.

And another thing, stop calling me Fisher, as if you'd been to a minor public school.

"Let me say this." He can't have got that from Oscar. "If you can arrange it with Mr. Rainbell, we'd be very glad indeed to see you on the Festival Committee."

Curiouser and curiouser, as they used to say in light fiction. The only thing Purchase had going for him, when it came to stepping into Pisspot's gin-soaked shoes as information officer, was that he was chairman of the Festival Committee. Shepford Shows the Way, ta-ra! Exports up by eight point five percent on some figures we've just made up. He could claim, or certainly would claim, to run the Festival almost single-handed. Why, then, was he tailing me like a private detective with an office over a Soho brothel, only to give me half of the glory with Green Shield Stamps?

It was something I'd have to ponder on later. I had to get him off the premises at once. "I'll see what I can do," I said and, making a great show of settling my bill with a handful of silver rather than displaying a bulging money clip to Purchase's quarterly-audit gaze, I rose from my barstool, knowing that he would do the same. There was no risk that he was

15

going to sit here by himself, knocking back lagers at thirty-five pence a throw. And indeed, Purchase was also sorting out his loose change, and now he had produced a thin, imitation-leather wallet and was peering into it.

"Fisher," he said, as I saw Helen arrive at the entrance to the bar, take a step or two toward us, stare hard through the gloom and then disappear with commendable speed into the ladies', "could you possibly lend me a pound?"

The plan was simple enough. Wave good-bye to Purchase in the parking lot, trusting he hadn't registered Helen's bright-red mini parked a lovebird's-breadth away from my old Austin 1100; make a great show, all indicators flashing, of heading for the roundabout and the route home; turn through the back doubles and be back outside the Heritage Motor Lodge in about two minutes.

But no one driving in Shepford should formulate simple plans without consulting the Highways Department first. The lane running alongside the car was a one-way thoroughfare leading to a T junction which, to bring it in line with most T junctions in the district, had recently become a compulsory right turn. Suspecting that this route incorporated a tour of the sights of Shepford before bringing the bemused motorist to within fifty yards of his starting point, I favored a policy—and more so favored it now, since it would have the additional merit of shaking Purchase off my tail—of making an illicit left turn out of the lot and connecting myself with the obvious route to the roundabout. Disregarding Purchase's scandalized bellows of "Wrong way! Wrong way!" I did this now, only to find as I turned into the main road that I was confronted by a great scattering of plastic traffic cones, warning lamps, blue-and-white arrows, and a sign reading: TRAFFIC EXPERIMENT—DIVERSION. I was led through a bewildering maze of back streets, some of them derelict cobbled alleys that could not have seen wheeled traffic since the last inhabitant was towed away in a horse-driven cortege. As I drove into a reclaimed children's play street, I said aloud, "One thing, Oscar, we've shaken off that bastard Purchase." *Right.*

I found myself, in due course, in roughly the area I should have arrived at by taking the proper turn out of the car park. Pulling up at one of the sets of temporary traffic lights that festooned the streets of Shepford like Christmas lanterns, I saw that the Ford Popular in front of me contained Purchase. Instead of his following me, I was now following him. He caught sight of me in his driving mirror and gave me a stiff, puzzled wave. I returned the salute, followed him through an obstacle course of white-painted railway sleepers that had been arranged along this section of the route for no clear reason, and took the first available turning. This was a steep, freshly-tarmaced incline, hemmed in by new brick walls and vaguely familiar. It was only as I reached the top and saw the blue sign decorated with kindergarten silhouettes of knives and forks and gasoline pumps, and the legend: NEXT SERVICES: 37 MILES that the feeling of *déjà vu* completely registered and I realized that I was on the M. 1, heading for Birmingham.

Helen would be ordering her second martini by now. She would already have received a negative from Harry to the question "Didn't he say anything about coming back?" and there would be a little pile of twopenny pieces by her glass. On the third martini she would go across to the telephone booth at the end of the bar, ring my number, and hang up when Jeanette or my mother answered. She would repeat the process on the fourth. It needed five before she would press home a coin and deliver some breathless, garbled, drunken and altogether unconvincing message about Mr. Fisher being wanted at a Vestifal meeting—*Festival* meeting, at the Civensor. Civic Center.

In times of stress, Helen drank martinis at the rate of one

every eight minutes. I was already two miles up the M. 1. An unbroken length of crash barrier ran down the central reservation of the motorway: no prospect of a U-turn. There were no slip roads before the promise of knives, forks, and gas pumps was fulfilled in a transport caff disguised as a primary school thirty-odd miles farther on.

Keep driving, Fisher. A hundred and seventy miles more, and you'll be in Stradhoughton. Book in at the Midland if it's still standing, and chase yourself around the Town Hall on the stroke of midnight. You could be a Dick Whittington in reverse.

The image gave me an idea. Was it illegal to reverse down the fast lane of the M. 1? Never mind that: was it possible? I decided to have a crack at it, although modifying the attempt (since the rush hour was not quite over) to the slow lane or better still, in view of the oncoming convoy of juggernauts, to the hard shoulder.

As I backed diagonally across the middle lane, a black Cortina, the property of Shepford District Council car pool and driven in this instance by Councillor Percy Drummond, chairman of the Senior Appointments Selection Board among other senior appointments, skidded out of my blind spot, horn blaring and headlights flashing. A word of explanation seemed necessary. Even if he hadn't seen my face—and he'd had to slow down in order to avoid ramming the crash barrier—he must have registered the car and the council's SUPPORT SHEPFORD FESTIVAL sticker on the rear window. I leaned out of the window and bawled, *"Gears stuck!,"* realizing only as the words were carried into the wind how uncommonly similar they must sound to *"Get stuffed!"*

Owing to some further experimentation by the Highways Department—they had succeeded, at one point, in filtering traffic into a one-way cul-de-sac, a kind of motorized sheep

18

pen from which it was impossible to escape without technically breaking the law—it was forty minutes past the hour when I got back to the Heritage Motor Lodge. The bar was empty. It nearly always was; but for the hidden subsidy from the Shepford District Council, which I passed on twice or three times a week, it would have been converted into a conference lounge by now. There was always room for another conference lounge at the Heritage, which made its living corralling packs of young executives, all with lapel badges stating their names and rank, into compulsory working dinners. Helen and I, arguing in fierce whispers in the corner booth of the bar, had once surfaced to find ourselves in the middle of a seminar about packaging.

"About twenty minutes ago," said Harry.

I was about to ask, "And was she—you know?," accompanying this cryptic inquiry with a vigorous piece of wrist miming that would have suggested a meths drinker knocking back surgical spirit from an eyebath, when Harry handed me the bill which Helen had left for me to pay. At that price, she must have crawled out of the place on her hands and knees.

"Did she make any phone calls, do you happen to know?" I asked instead.

"She made two or three," said Harry.

And did she get through to anyone, do you happen to know? Why ask? I'll hear about it sooner or later.

"Oh, I forgot to mention, Mr. Fisher," he went on, mixing a vodka martini on the correct assumption that I looked as if I needed one, "that other gentleman came back."

"What other gentleman?"

"Your friend. Who you were talking to earlier. He wanted a copy of his bill, for some strange reason."

Oh, Christ.

He didn't see Helen, did he? He must have done. Even after being marooned in the Highways department sheep pen, and allowing that he'd think twice or three times before driving the wrong way down a one-way street, it couldn't have taken him twenty minutes to get back here.

All right, then, so he saw Helen. He didn't speak to her, did he? You're whistling in the dark, Fisher: he would hardly have cut her dead, now would he?

But he doesn't know her. No, but he's the kind of fellow who'd talk to anybody, provided they were wearing the right clothes. Exchanging a civil word, he'd call it.

All right, then. What kind of civil words did he and Helen exchange?

"Did he speak to Mrs. Lightfoot, as far as you know?"

"Did he not!" said Harry, who was quietly enjoying himself. He waited until, deliberately tautening my wrist muscles, I raised the brimming glass to my lips. Then, with what he must have thought was very good timing, he added, "They got chatting; then of course her ladyship asks him to have a drink. You know what she's like, better than I do. Oh, no, he wouldn't hear of it. 'Not at these prices,' he says."

"Yes. He would have done." At times like these, a vodka martini is meant to be swallowed, not sipped. I knocked it back in one, as Harry continued.

"'Ho,' she says, 'you don't think *I'm* paying for it,' she says. Of course, she'd had one or two by then. 'Have one on Fisher!' she says. 'Fisher always pays.'"

"Coughing better, Mr. Fisher! Let me get you a serviette."

Chapter Two

I had a whole country once: Ambrosia. Strange blue poppies grew there, and there were cities, fantastic cities such as no one has ever seen the like of, built out on platforms over the sand dunes.

Now there's only one town left, and even that has a slightly secondhand air about it. The sun glinting on the glass roof of the covered market: that's a straight pinch from J. B. Priestley. The trams swaying like galleons: same source. The semibasement cafés where countinghouse clerks and drapers (the salt of the earth, very probably) sit playing chess: that's H. G. Wells, I believe, or is it Bill Fisher when he thought of becoming H. G. Wells?

But the rest of the vision is my own: the Corn Exchange, the old Theatre Royal, the alleys packed with workshops, the Bovril sign in electric light bulbs, the aldermanic statues, the green dome of the Linen Bank, the golden orb over Rabinowitz, the jeweler's, and all the people hurrying along the wet streets with their carrier bags—that's mine. Mine, anyway, in the sense that I had a stake in it. It's Stradhoughton, before they commenced to pull it down. Whoever would have thought I'd miss it?

I was president of Ambrosia. Who am I now? The youngest mayor ever, top weight. Gentlemen, I have not become first citizen of this great borough to preside over its demolition. Or perhaps I'm Man o' the Dales of the Stradhoughton *Echo,* ruminating over a pipe and a schooner of sherry in the Wine Lodge. My world is shrinking, as old men shrink when they get older still.

It's not going to happen. It can't happen now. I'm thirty-three. It's too late. It's not too late. It's never too late.

But what was it that was going to happen? I don't think I know.

Helen didn't ring, after all, or if she did, she hung up. Which doesn't mean to say she's knocked off for the evening.

And is that all I have to occupy my mind? Yes. That's where the trouble is, Fisher. Life's become day-to-day, hand-to-mouth. It's nearly time for another clean break or, more likely, another messy one.

"Your mother was just saying," Jeanette was just saying, "Akerman's hasn't been open for over a week. We're wondering if they've closed for good."

"I believe they've gone bankrupt," I said automatically. Who the hell are Akerman's? The butcher's? The dry cleaners? The tiny L-shaped corridor of cardboard boxes that tries to pass itself off as a mini-supermarket? Or that place that keeps changing hands—what is it these days, a wool shop or a wine shop?

Akerman's, Akerman's. Why do they give all these shops names, as if we lived in a village? And on the subject of names, why does my wife go around calling herself Jeanette? It may be what she was christened, but does she mean to say there's nothing to be done about it? Negotiations have not been fruitful. She won't let me call her Jean, and I won't let her call herself Jeanie. Stalemate.

"Because I haven't seen that ginger cat of theirs for ages, what always used to sit in the window," my mother said. That rules out the butcher's, then; the wool shop, too, unless it's an unusually well-disciplined cat. "I'm wondering if they've

22

gone back to St. Albans, with Mrs. Akerman's sister being poorly again."

Mother, you don't know Mrs. Akerman's sister. You've never met Mrs. Akerman's sister. All you know about her is her life history.

She had many such vicarious friends. Since the old man had had his final heart attack—nature telling him to drop dead, I'd called it, and felt guilty and depressed when he did—she had cultivated a wide circle of nonacquaintances. We got regular news, for instance, of a family by the name of Baines who lived in Derby. Our only connection with them was that a girl called Barbara, whom I'd been briefly engaged to back in the Ice Age in Stradhoughton, had once met them on holiday in Portofino.

"Talking of cats," Jeanette said, "we haven't seen Mr. Pussy-paws for a long time."

No, you wouldn't have done, dear, seeing that Mr. Pussy-paws doesn't exist. I'd invented this cat in a spare moment, though not its name, which was supplied by Jeanette. (Not the best of names for a child substitute, I would have thought, but that was her business.) It was supposed to scamper up and down the eleventh-floor balcony chasing moths, and once, so Jeanette believed, I had seen it stretched up on its hind legs, trying to reach the bell push to summon the lift. Jeanette had heard about so many of these exploits that she'd begun to think she had witnessed some of them herself. Perhaps it's true what the psychologists say about life in high-rise flats: you go potty.

From the living-room window, but for its shroud of lace, it would have been possible to see halfway across the county: the gravel pits, the abandoned quarries, the rezoned factories, the doomed woods where the new conference hotel would be, the ribbon of wire netting guarding the pollution-free river, and, far off at the end of a long, straight road, the village of Mayfield with its flat-roofed maisonettes, its crescents and cul-de-sacs of clapboard-fronted semis, and its pebbled piazzas of ranch-style bungalows, including, assuming it was still vacant, the one I had christened Mortgagedene, where Jeanette wanted to live.

From the bedroom windows, but for the venetian blinds protecting my womenfolk from the attentions of peeping Toms hovering at two hundred feet, you could have looked down on an asphalt quadrangle of garages, pram sheds, and laundry rooms, connecting, via a subterranean arrangement of concrete pillars, with the shopping precinct—in other words, a row of eight lockup shops, including four empty ones permanently barricaded with corrugated iron and also including Akerman's, which was apparently about to suffer the same fate.

Akerman's had not been dropped into the conversation by accident. Neither had the fictitious Mr. Pussy-paws. They were twin themes in what, if I cared to listen, would soon develop into an overfamiliar fugue.

"It might have got lost," my mother said. "It gets into that lift with whoever's going down; then it can't find its way back up." (She too had delusions of having met Mr. Pussy-paws in person.)

"That's why I won't have a cat," said Jeanette, "much as I'd like one. It doesn't seem fair, when you're cooped up on the twelfth floor."

My mother came in counterpoint with: "It's all right if you're on the ground floor, because then it can come and go. Same as with that ginger cat of Akerman's—it went all over. *I* don't see them opening again, though."

"That'll be *five* shops that's boarded up. Out of eight."

"And even them what's left, they won't make the effort. Same as that skirt I took to that cleaner's on Tuesday—it came back worse than it went in."

24

"I know. Look what they did to that dark blue suit of Bill's—they just about ruined it. I think I'll start going to that Keen-to-Kleen place in Cripplegate."

"But it's so far into town, isn't it? And look how long you've got to wait for a bus."

"*And* the fares are going up again."

"Tenpence. It's shocking."

"I don't think it's fair to dump people out here and then leave them with no amenities. It's not as if the demand wasn't there."

"Ooh, I know, love, I know."

"You look at Mayfield. It's only been built two years, most of it, and they've got a Boots, they've got a Tesco's, Electricity Board showrooms, Chinese take-away, wineshop, that Baby's Boutique they've got—and they're nearer to Shepford than we are. You could drive to the office in ten minutes, Bill."

Not bad going, Jeanette. Even working on material far less obscure than the Akerman's and Mr. Pussy-paws combine—the size of the kitchenette, for example, or the need, one of these days, for a third bedroom, a sandpit and play school occupying rather more permanent premises than an abandoned builders' Nissen hut—I'd known it take up to half an hour's chitter-chatter before they got around to the subject of Mortgagedene.

We are not going to buy a house in Mayfield, Jeanette.

Because we're not.

Because you'd be pregnant before we crossed the threshold.

Because Helen lives in Mayfield, and it is very difficult to ditch your mistress if you are meeting her twice a week at wine-and-cheese parties.

Because I don't like wine-and-cheese parties, Sunday morning drinks, or candleli4 sixsomes with vintage-car table mats and water ice served in a scooped-out lemon.

25

And look at it this way. Even if I get Pisspot's job, we can't afford it. And if I don't get Pisspot's job, I shall be buggering off out of Shepford.

The discourse, both the real and imagined sections of it, got no further. The two-tone doorbell rang—bing-bong! The kind of doorbell they have in situation comedies about this kooky lady who lives next door to her permanently perplexed husband's ex-wife. She always primps her hair and says, "I'll get it."

"I'll get it," said Jeanette, primping her hair.

My mother, knowing that there has to be a line or two of dialogue before the little woman blazes back in followed by the ex-wife who wants to borrow her ex-husband to fix her fuses—"OK, OK, but this is positively his last and final appearance. And this time he fixes them with chicken wire"— filled in with: "I was just thinking, time marches on. The twins'll be four next week."

Barbara's. Exactly the kind of woman who *would* have twins. And who would file regular bulletins on their progress to her ex-fiancé's mother.

I could see Jeanette doing exactly the same thing, in happier circumstances. Just think, if she'd married Barbara's husband's twin brother, they could be living next door to each other in twin bungalows, both scribbling away on their crinkled blue notepaper to be first with the news of the head-on collision of two twin prams on the shopping parade. And Mr. Pussy-paws could chase Mr. Fluffy-tail up a tree.

"She showed a bit of sense, did Barbara. If you're going to start a family, start it early. Then, when they're grown up, the rest of your life's your own."

Oh, Mother, what can you be hinting at? And why isn't the rest of my life my own now?

I needn't have married Jeanette. I needn't even have met her. "It must have been fate," she used to giggle in our court-

26

ing days when, getting nowhere fast on the front-room sofa, I would try to work out the lengthy odds against our having been thrown together. Fuck fate: it was nothing more than a chain of tragic nonevents. If I'd uprooted myself and gone to London when I'd meant to, I would never have met her. If I'd stayed as an undertaker's clerk and kept my hands out of the petty-cash box, I would never have met her. If I hadn't gone and worked on the Stradhoughton Rates Office, I would never have met her. Or—given that it was part of the mysterious pattern of the universe that the Stradhoughton Rates Office beckoned me at that time—if I'd habitually used the front entrance instead of the back one, I would have by-passed the open-plan typing pool where she worked and never have met her. Or, since I was compelled by Nemesis to use the back entrance because I was always late for work, and so must inevitably have skirted the side of the typing pool in order to reach my desk unobserved, she could have been sitting somewhere else, and I would never have met her. It was because she was one of five typists sitting on the outside aisle, and because I was incapable of entering a roomful of girls without sizing up the talent, that as I walked through the typing pool on my first late morning, I thought, without thinking: "Not that one, not that one, not that one. That one. She'll do." And if she had been sitting somewhere else, someone else would have been sitting in her place on the outside aisle, and I would have thought: "Not that one, not that one, not that one. That one. She'll do." Or, if the someone else had been as ugly as the other four, there would have been the canteen, or the office dance, or some other department's office dance, or the social club, or a pub, or a coffee bar, or a bus queue, and I would have thought: "Not that one, not that one, not that one. That one. She'll do." Love at first sight, provided I can have the best out of five. And whoever it was, we would have got married because it was the only way I

27

could get away from home; and we would have finished up at my mother's because there was nowhere else to live; and I would have leaped at the job in Shepford with a subsidized flat thrown in; and my mother would have finished up with us because the house was too big for her, so she claimed; and the double of Jeanette and Barbara, looking puzzled, would at this very second be returning to her knitting and box of Maltesers with the message: "There's nobody there."

I could have told you that before you went to answer the door, ducky. The drill was this: Helen would by now be skulking by the lift, and in a minute or two she would creep back, or more likely stagger back, and ring again. This time I would be the one to answer it, pursuing my investigations around the bend of the communal corridor on the pretext of breaking some mischievous boy's neck. Helen would beckon me from the fire door, and we would have a hurried conference on the emergency stairs, arranging a rendezvous ten minutes hence by the vandalized cigarette machine down on the so-called shopping precinct. The last time Helen had pulled this trick she had slipped down a whole flight of stairs and twisted her ankle, so that in addition to finding an excuse for leaving the flat at nearly midnight ("I can hear a meowing noise. I wonder if that bloody cat's stuck up a tree?"), I'd had to smuggle out a tea towel soaked in hot water. I had been living in hopes that this experience would have cured her, but seemingly not.

"It'll be that Charles from the floor below. He's a right handful," my mother said. Another of her nonacquaintances, much given to breaking windows and getting into scrapes. Actually, I was pretty well sure that Charles was one of my own inventions, like Mr. Pussy-paws, and that I had called him into being to explain some early escapade of Helen's; but it was equally possible that my mother had over-

28

heard his name in the fish queue and now regarded him more or less as her godson. Real or not, I was grateful to him.

My mother had stuffed the communiqué from Stradhoughton back into her handbag. For some reason she would never mention Barbara's name in front of Jeanette, always referring to her as "that friend of our Billy's what married that accountant."

"I was saying to our Billy while you were answering the door, that friend of his what married that accountant, her twins'll be four next week."

Time flies, Jeanette will say.

"Time flies," said Jeanette, adding, as she always did if we were hovering around the topic of Mortgagedene, "Isn't that the one who lives in those new bungalows?" You can save your breath for blowing your porridge, my little pot of honey, because the doorbell's about to ring again.

"That's the one. They've done very well, considering they didn't get married till a year after you and our Billy. Because if you ask me, houses cost more up there than what they do down here."

And the doorbell rang, leaving Jeanette's next sentence ("For what we're paying out in rent and rates, we might just as well have taken the plunge when we first came to Shepford") somewhere between her larynx and her front teeth.

For what we're paying out in rent and taxes, may we be truly thankful.

The fire door leading to the emergency stairs was next to the lift, which was next to the staircase proper, which in turn was next to the rubbish chute—a convenient arrangement for an arsonist, I'd occasionally thought when toying with the idea of murdering Jeanette. That arrangement was at present more convenient than it had ever been, for the fire door wouldn't open. I rattled the metal handle, which, being of the required specification for one of Shepford's prestigious tower blocks, came away in my hand.

"Then when you complain, they put the blame on vandalism."

This was from an observer of life's passing show who, in tightly belted raincoat, hat, gloves and scarf, was waiting for the lift. He looked as if he were going out either to sell insurance or to rape somebody. My mother would have known the biographical details: I recognized him only as one of a multitude of rat-faced neighbors.

"I left my golf clubs inside the door," I said, in case he felt need of an explanation.

"Did you now?" he asked keenly. "When would that have been?" I'll have to give up this habit of making voluntary statements.

"Last night."

"Because there were definitely no golf clubs there at twenty past five this morning."

It was none of my business what a rat-faced neighbor was doing on the emergency stairs at twenty-past five in the morning. Waiting to flash himself at the paper boy, I shouldn't wonder. I pushed the door handle back on its spindle and waggled it about a bit.

"It seems to be jammed."

"No, it's not jammed, it's locked."

"Is it now?" Also, I'll have to stop picking up other people's expressions, like a verbal chameleon. What's it a sign of? Immaturity? Lack of confidence? Desire to ingratiate? Never mind. "I would have thought there was something in the fire regulations about that."

"I don't know about the fire regulations," said Rat-face. "All I know is it kept us awake from half past four till twenty past five. Didn't you hear it, in that gale? Bang-bang-bang, all night long. That's how the handle's worked loose." He pressed the bell for the lift, which, assuming he'd rung for it already before the start of this dissertation on banging doors, was a long time coming.

"So you got out of bed and locked it?"

"I didn't lock it, no, because I haven't a key. I wedged it with a piece of cardboard. See." He drew my attention to Exhibit A, a folded sliver of cornflake packet on the floor. "And I expect *that'll* be lying there until goodness knows when, before anyone bothers to sweep it up."

"But it's not wedged now," I said, taking my plodding tone from his. "It's locked."

"Yes, we know it's locked. I had the caretaker up, first thing this morning. It was the only way he could get it to close. Apparently the wood's warped with the damp. It needs planing."

So Helen wasn't skulking behind the fire door. Then where was she skulking? Either on the stairs or, putting aside the outside chance of her having dived down the rubbish chute, in the lift.

I joined Rat-face at the lift shaft and peered down through the flaking trellis gate.

"No sign of life."

"I'm wondering if someone hasn't left the gate open on the ground floor. It wouldn't be the first time it's happened."

If someone like Purchase had been standing where Rat-face was standing now, he wouldn't be wondering about lift gates being left open. He'd be wondering why, since I claimed to have set off to retrieve my golf clubs from behind the fire door, I had now lost all interest in them and was seemingly about to go for a stroll in my shirt sleeves.

I'm going down to ask the caretaker if he can shed any light on the mystery.

"These golf clubs of yours," said Rat-face.

"Yes, I'm just popping down to ask the caretaker what he knows about them."

"I should do. Because, as I say, they definitely weren't behind that door at twenty past five this morning. When did you leave them there? Last night?"

"Yes."

"About what time last night?"

For God's sake. Five o'clock. Six o'clock. Nineteen and a half minutes to seven. "About a quarter to six."

"That's strange. That's very strange. Because my wife often leaves the child's scooter behind that door and I take it in when I come home from business at six o'clock. Are you sure it wasn't later than quarter to six?"

"I don't know. It might have been."

"Because there were definitely no golf clubs there at six o'clock. You didn't see anyone hanging about at all? No strange characters?"

Let me see now. There was a one-eyed, humpbacked dwarf who dragged his left foot and had warts all over his face, but I just assumed he was one of the neighbors.

"No, nobody."

Rat-face, his insurance round or rendezvous on the canal towpath forgotten, had become totally immersed in the Case of the Missing Golf Clubs. To avoid further questioning, I took over the lift-summoning chore, jabbing savagely at the bell push. Simultaneously, a loud clanging noise started up from several floors below, indicating either that I'd somehow set off the alarm system, or that the martini-sodden Helen had got herself stuck in the lift and had set it off herself, or that the building was on fire. Bearing in mind Rat-face's complicity in the recent breach of the fire regulations, I looked hopefully for smoke.

"That is the fourth time this year, to my knowledge," observed Rat-face. "Then when you complain the lift needs overhauling, they fob you off with some cock-and-bull yarn about it receiving regular attention. If it received regular attention, why does it keep jamming?"

On the landings below us, other rat-faced neighbors could be heard scuffling about in their fleece-lined slippers and rhubarbing about the alarm bell, the alarm bell's culpability in waking up their kiddies, and the methods by which the alarm bell might be switched off. Sundry voices-off chimed in with plot lines: "There's someone in the lift" . . . "It's down there—halfway past the third floor" . . . "Keep calm, my dear, we'll have you out in a jiffy." A technical adviser offered the opinion that the traveling cable was out of true and had been fouled by some unknown obstruction, probably the counterweight. A shirt-sleeved traffic-warden type, even more rat-faced than Rat-face himself, bounded up from the tenth or eleventh floor, taking the stairs two at a time in his excitement. Ignoring me, he addressed himself to Rat-face, instinctively recognizing him as one of his own kind.

"The Lord help us if there's ever a real emergency in these flats. Where's the use of everybody running around in circles?"

"It's a job for the fire brigade, I would have thought," Rat-face said.

"The caretaker, more like! Who else has the master key? He'll have to make his way down from the fourth floor and haul her up through the trapdoor."

"It's a lady, is it? Not of any great age, I hope and trust?"

"We don't know who it is at this stage. All we do know is that the caretaker isn't on the premises, as usual. It's a question of ringing that workingmen's club on the trading estate. You know he has a part-time job there, don't you?"

"No, I didn't know that."

"Oh, yes! Part-time waiter, three nights a week."

"Then when you look for him at eight in the morning, he's

33

still in bed. No wonder," chuntered Rat-face. Presumably being the owner of a telephone, down which, I was ready to bet,
he made breathing noises regularly, he led Rat-face Mark II
off along the corridor, pausing to issue an instruction to me.

"You might tell them we're phoning for help, would you?"

"Piss off," I thought, and considered my position. The
trading estate was about three miles away—four, if they'd
opened up the new access road by now. Allow twenty minutes for the caretaker to get here and another five for him to
rummage through his large assortment of keys. Say fifteen
minutes to half an hour to get Helen out of the lift. Assume
the existence of a Rat-face Mark III, with experience in the
St. John's Ambulance Brigade, who would want to treat her
for shock: the process of sticking her head between her
knees, burning feathers under her nose, and giving her cups
of sweet tea could take another half an hour or so. It would
be quite late before Helen was at large again, by which time
her husband would be expecting her home and in any case
she would probably have had enough for one evening. I
couldn't, of course, rule out the outside chance of Rat-face
Mark III topping her up with a swig of medicinal brandy,
but if that hideous possibility refused to leave my mind I
could always disconnect the doorbell. Sod her.

I went back indoors where, having switched off the hall
light to discourage callers, I was surprised to find my female
entourage increased to three. Helen, looking only slightly
the worse for drink, was sitting between my mother and
Jeanette in the armchair I had recently vacated.

Chapter Three

This is no way to carry on at your age, was what skimmed through my mind, among other thoughts, but was I blaming Helen or myself?

Myself, most likely. One thing about Helen, she had never tried to pass herself off as mature and responsible. Although in calendar years she was slightly older than me—thirty-five next birthday—she was capable of carrying on as if she were four or five years younger. Taking the gloomiest estimate of my own mental age, this put her at about sixteen on some occasions, the present one being among their number.

The other thing was that I had known she would be trouble on first clapping eyes on her—or rather, on her polka-dot panties, for she was doing handstands at the time, in connection with some office Christmas celebrations in the upstairs room of the King's Head Doubles Bar. The party was that of CCC—Creative City Consortium—a gang of architects and other roving vagabonds dedicated to making Shepford the showplace of their balance sheet. Helen had worked for them once. I was there as deputy freeloader, representing Pisspot, who was freeloading elsewhere that night.

Helen being trouble was the main attraction. Long lunchtime phone calls while the office girls were sunbathing on the Civic Center roof: "Was anything said when you got home last night?" Short midmorning calls while they pretended to be painting their fingernails: "Can you get out for five minutes? I'm afraid it's urgent." At least one confrontation with her husband, Geoff: "I ought to knock you down, Fisher."—"Go ahead, if it makes you feel any better." Adult behavior.

Jeanette, my mother, and Helen were all looking at me, expectantly. The studio laughter died down. Oscar, in his pale-blue angora sweater and golfing slacks, was the staunch, neutered, bachelor friend, the one you can trust alone with your daffy wife. His grimace said: "Oh, boy, have you got problems!"

"Oscar, you keep out of this!"

"Jeanette, I didn't open my mouth!"

"You were *thinking,* though! You were thinking, 'Oh, boy, has he got problems!'"

"Bill, did it ever occur to you that your wife is a remarkable woman?"

"So my son has a remarkable wife, so what's so remarkable?"

"Mrs. Winklebaum, you keep out of this too. Bill, I want to know what this—this *creature* is doing in my home. There has to be some *explanation!*"

Oh, there was, there was. Helen hadn't got stuck in the lift after all. Finding the fire door locked, she must have followed the corridor all around the building until it led her back to her starting point. She would then, in her bemused state, have rung the bell again. My mother or Jeanette, on the way in to or out of the bathroom, would have been immediately on hand to open the door before she had a chance to make her getaway. Shocked into comparative sobriety, but not to the extent of reacting like any rational human being with the excuse that she had come to the wrong flat, she must have babbled some story and been invited in on a pretext yet to be revealed. So who was stuck in the lift? Mr. Pussy-paws.

"Mr. *Pussy*-paws? Is that the best you can do?"

"Oscar! Bill is my husband, and he is entitled to a hearing without any interruptions. Mr. *Pussy*-paws! Is that the best you can do? You are *pathetic!*"

"Sorry to have been so long," I said. "There's half the neighborhood out with ladders, trying to get that cat out of the lift."

"Poor thing!" said Jeanette.

"It's a gad job they're sapposed to hev nine lives, isn't it?" my mother observed, smiling at Helen and talking, for our guest's benefit, in what she thought was a Home Counties accent. A hopeful sign, that. Short of pouring Helen a cup of tea and asking if she took shagger, she couldn't have been more hospitable. Jeanette, too, had expressed her brief sympathy for the plight of Mr. Pussy-paws half to Helen, as if to draw her into the family circle. Whatever the confrontation, it was not to be on what's-the-meaning-of-this lines.

"This lady's from the Bedding Council," Jeanette said, adding to Helen, "And this is my husband—?" in that irritating way she had of leaving the sentence unfinished, on a rising note, as if there were several more introductions to follow, very likely a string of children with names like Barry and Kevin.

What bloody Bedding Council?

Helen's smile was a piece of artistry: a warm, yet detached social worker's smile that seemed to be appraising a new acquaintance of whom she had heard quite encouraging reports. She let her wedding ring catch the light from the table lamp next to her: shrewd thinking. The cleavage, I was relieved to notice, had been buttoned away under the navy-blue velvet jacket. She crossed her legs and tugged down her skirt: another good touch, for she was not normally one of nature's tugger-downers.

"The Bedding Advisory Council actually, Mr. Fisher. Or to

37

burden you with our cumbersome title, the Council Advisorying the Bedding and Mattress Industries. CAMBY." Don't
push it, baby. And don't slur your words. And for God's
sake, don't correct CAMBY. "Do I mean CAMBY?" she went
on. "No. Council Advisorying Mattress Bedding Industries.
CABMY. *CAMBY.*"

"Something about a questionnaire," put in Jeanette help-
fully. She was not looking in the least pissed off with Helen's
performance, looked, in fact, quite eager to have her subur-
ban life brightened up with a bit of consumer research. My
mother, who thought this kind of thing was compulsory by
law, had put on the intense, I-can-understand-long-words
expression she kept for insurance men and council officials.

"We're taking a random sample of two hundred married
couples in this area, and names are chosen by computer from
the electoral roll. No personal details are included in our reports, and the information is confidential, are you sure you
have no objection?" She had this bit off pat, having once
done a similar job for the Gas Board.

"No objection at all," said Jeanette.

"None at all," my mother echoed, looking as if she had just
been cautioned by a police sergeant.

"And it's not inconvenient?"

Just bugger off, Helen. There's no need for this at all.

"Not in the least. We were just sitting here talking."

"Thank you. It won't take long."

It had better not. And when you go, Helen, you go for
good. This is it. It had already been it before she had started
this stupid rigmarole, but at least I had been ready to meet
her, explain, face it out. I had even, in a way, been looking
forward to the scene: telling your mistress it's all over may be
painful, but it's a responsible thing to do. I could have done
with the credit. Not now, though. Quite definitely sod her.

She had pulled a wad of yellow papers out of her handbag. Her first mistake. I had an idea what they were: handbills for the amateur operatic society where, according to what she told her husband, or at least told me that she told him, she was supposed to be understudying some ratbag or other in *The Yeoman of the Guard* on evenings such as this. They certainly looked nothing like market research forms, but my mother and Jeanette, both moistening their lips as if being auditioned for First and Second Village Maiden, seemed not to notice.

"Now the first question is about bedrooms. Would you say you had one bedroom, more than one bedroom, more than two bedrooms, more than three bedrooms?"

"Two bedrooms," whispered Jeanette, nervous. She cleared her throat and went on: "They're all two-bedroom flats."

"All in this block," my mother confirmed, eager to give evidence. "All two bedrooms."

"So more than one bedroom. And of beds in use, including spare beds but not convertible sofas or chesterfields, would you say you had one bed in use, more than one bed in use, more than two beds in use, more than three beds in use?"

"Er—more than two beds." Silly bitch. Trying to fall in with Helen's jargon, Jeanette had got it all wrong. She meant two beds; in other words, more than one bed.

"More . . . than . . . two . . . *beds,*" intoned Helen, scribbling. For Christ's sake, woman, do pack it in. "And if you don't mind my asking, you live here with your husband and this lady is—?"

Jeanette fielded this one to my mother with a glance indicating that her version of the relationship would carry more weight.

"I'm Billy's mother. Mr. Fisher's mother." I quite liked that

39

correction; it was the first time my mother had ever called me Mr. Fisher. I wished she could have done it with more style.

"So Mrs. Fisher senior would occupy a single bed in the smaller bedroom, while you and Mr. Fisher share the master bedroom?"

"That's right."

"In twin beds?"

To make it quite plain to Helen that I was having no part of this inquisition, I had picked up one of the women's magazines which infested the flat. My eye had fallen on the readers' letters page. "When I am not speaking to my husband I put his slippers in the deep freeze. Don't ask me why." Momentarily hypnotized by this, I had missed the significance of Helen's question, only realizing, as I looked up to see Jeanette's blank expression and Helen's social worker's smile, that something had been said that would have been better left unsaid.

"In twin beds?" insisted Helen, and I felt an alarming spasm of pain under my left ribs. Was I too young to be having a heart attack? More to the point, was I too young to *look* as if I were having a heart attack, if I keeled over this very second?

We hardly ever had sex because of Jeanette's headaches, and we slept in twin beds: that was what I had told her. And absurd as it seemed even at the time, I had immediately realized that there was another reason why the thing with Helen couldn't go on, for one of these days Jeanette and my mother would take themselves off to a wedding or a christening or a meat tea or something up in Stradhoughton, and Helen would get to know about it and insist on coming to the flat as a change from Shepford Woods or, if wet, the back of the car, and she would find out that I was lying about the twin beds.

Jeanette, with the slightly incredulous frown of a bright

40

child whose sums have been marked wrong, was saying, "No-oh. We have one single bed and one double."

"You and Mr. Fisher? In other words, one of you sleeps in the single and the other in the double?" *Cow.*

Jeanette, utterly perplexed, turned to me for guidance; decided, obviously, that domestic conundrums were outside the man's domain; and switched the appeal to my mother, who, from her vast experience of household trivia, came to the rescue.

"You see, Jeanette, where I think you're getting this lady confused is, you said more than two beds."

Helen looked apologetic: what-a-little-nuisance-I-must-be. "That's the answer I've ticked. More than two beds."

"Oh, I *see!*" Jeanette exclaimed, her face clearing. "I should have said two beds, shouldn't I?"

"More than one bed."

The cleared face clouded over again. "That's right, Jeanette," my mother said, soothingly. "Two beds *is* more than one bed, isn't it? More than *two* beds would be *three* beds."

"I suppose so."

Helen, ball-point poised, beamed from one to the other. "So more than one bed. One single and one double. And obviously Mrs. Fisher senior has the single while you and Mr. Fisher sleep in the bubble. Double."

She was pissed out of her mind. Why had I thought she had sobered up? Why had I thought, or even hoped and prayed, that she was going to get away with it? The countdown to disaster, I suddenly realized with a lurching in my stomach, had already begun: it was irrevocable.

As Helen made an elaborate show of correcting her notes, I repeated to myself, like a mantra: "When I am not speaking to my husband I put his slippers in the deep freeze, don't ask me why, when I am not speaking to my husband I put his slippers in the deep freeze." And the ridiculous thing was

41

that in this moment of panic I was staring at her legs, where the light threw a sheen along the dark-blue casing of her shins, and fancying her.

"Now, if we can just move on. This question is about attitudes to bed. Do you think of your bed as primary—pri-*mar*-il-ly—a place to sleep, or would you say it was a center for various activities?"

Jeanette and my mother exchanged telegraphic glances. Is this woman going too far? Don't know yet. Over and out.

"Such as reading," added Helen, intercepting the message.

I could get to my feet and tell her to go. "I'm sorry, I'm afraid these questions are altogether too personal." But I couldn't see myself saying it; it wasn't my kind of phraseology. And what would Helen think? It would be like a mask coming off—Bill Fisher, exposed as husband, householder and taxpayer. Your John Bull act, she would call it, when we met for just one more time because I fancied her. Do your John Bull act.

I could get to my feet and say something, anyway. Wing it. "It's getting late," or something. I half rose, looking at my watch.

"You've dropped your soup," said Helen, kindly.

A packet of powdered watercress soup, FREE with this Super Spring Issue, had slipped from the pages of the woman's magazine on my lap. As I stooped to retrieve it, Jeanette driveled on in released vein about all of us being big readers, her own preference being for the works of Georgette Heyer. The moment had passed or, more accurately, not yet arrived.

"So a center for various activities. In fact"—although Helen's tone was light and casual, I noticed with alarm that she no longer dared look Jeanette in the face—"the usual activities of a happily married couple."

"Well." Jeanette's embarrassment returned, manifesting itself in a short laugh, a slight shrug, and a flush around the throat. "Yes."

"And would you say these activities took place less than once a week, more frequently than once a week, more frequently than twice a week—"

"Excuse me, young lady!"

My mother's lips had been pursed for some time and had not become unpursed even during the red-herring interlude about reading matter. She now extended her repertoire of disapproval by folding her arms. "If you don't mind my asking, just exactly what is all this in aid of?"

With a timid flickering of relief I saw that Helen was losing her alcoholic overdrive. She was swaying slightly in her chair, and a faint mustache of sweat had appeared on her upper lip. If she asked to use the bathroom, it would be easy to shuffle her out of there. I had stopped fancying her.

"I'm sorry, I thought I'd made it clear," she said indistinctly. "National Federation Bedding Councils—"

"Yes, we know all about that, but where's the point in asking what you've just been asking? I mean, you haven't even shown us any credentials. You could be anybody, for all we know."

Jeanette, anxious not to be identified with rudeness on quite this scale, said, half-conciliatorily, "Have you got a card, or something like that?" Helen, now looking quite ill, began to rummage aimlessly through her handbag. My mother maintained the folded-arms posture.

"And you, our Billy, I'm surprised *you've* had nothing to say. Do *you* think it's right, people coming into your home and asking your wife that sort of thing?"

But it's only a game, Mother! It's only a bloody *game!* Didn't you ever play games? No, we know you didn't. And you frighten me when you say "your home" like that, pronouncing the aitch, and "your wife." You make it sound as if

43

everything's real, as if it matters, as if it's serious. For God's sake, look at Helen—*she's* married, *she* has a home, she cooks breakfast, vacuums, remembers to take her pill, has a bank account, all those grown-up things, and just bloody well look at her!

They did, and Helen had passed out.

We had got her around by shaking her quite roughly, Jeanette's suggestion of black coffee being firmly vetoed by the other interested parties. "I *thought* she was squiffy when she first came in," my mother observed. It seemed to wrap up the episode to her satisfaction.

We had steered her across the living room—not without some fear on my part, as she blundered into the sideboard, that she would forget where she was and address me by name. We had got her into the hall. Relieved of helping hands, she leaned against the wall and resumed the vague expedition into the depths of her handbag.

"They shouldn't send them out in that condition," my mother said. "You'd think they'd inspect them first."

"Have you got far to go?" asked Jeanette anxiously, addressing Helen as if she were stone deaf.

Helen had fished out her driving license. She waved it triumphantly, in answer both to the immediate question and to the earlier one about credentials.

"She's never driving in that condition!" my mother exclaimed.

Jeanette was examining the license. "Rookwood Crescent, Mayfield. Do you think you'd better run her home, Bill?"

All right. One last blazing row as we cross town, dump her car by the phone booth at the end of Rookwood Crescent, radio cab home, and sod her for all time. I opened the hall door, to be confronted by Rat-face and a young man of about my own age who was wearing a light overcoat and trying very

44

hard to look like a plainclothes policeman who was trying not to look like one.

"Ah, there you are! Run to earth! I thought this was your flat, but I wasn't absolutely sure! This is Detective Constable Carpenter."

"You're very kind, but I'll catch a bus," said Helen, once more blessed by a sudden bounty of clearheadedness. "Good night." Excusing herself to our newfound friends, she weaved off along the corridor.

"Good-bye," I said pointedly.

"Take care," Jeanette called.

"Sorry to disturb you, we're looking into a series of petty pilferings, I believe you're missing some property?" said Detective Constable Carpenter. "Is that lady all right?"

"That's what *we're* wondering," my mother said darkly.

I said hastily, "She'll be all right; she's just had one too many. No, I don't think we've missed anything."

"I understood you had."

"Golf clubs," said Rat-face.

"He doesn't have any gold clubs," said Jeanette.

"Yes, I bought a set secondhand the other day. They weren't worth much."

"If I could just have the details," said Detective Constable Carpenter.

Chapter Four

Turning into the Cornmarket from the winding alley by the Clock Tower, the visitor may well imagine himself in Brittany. The bustling market place, dominated by Alfred Waterhouse's magnificent Town Hall (see p. 16) is enclosed on three sides by a lively promenade of cafés, brasseries and open-air restaurants. The spacious Café Billard, with its red plush booths and marble-topped tables, is a favorite of Shepford's artists and writers, while the beveled mirrors of the Relais des Voyageurs next door reflect the town's leading luminaries, such as Councillor Percy Drummond and Detective Constable Carpenter, as they sip their afternoon mazagrans. No need to inquire too closely why Shepford's hosteliers have little trouble with the licensing laws!

The question most asked by tourists is how this outpost of Bohemia came to be established in an English market town. The answer is an interesting one. During the Napoleonic Wars, French prisoners were billeted for a time in Shepford Castle. Among them was a certain Henri Gaspard, a pastry cook. . . .

"Anything for the printer's?" asked Hattersley. *Pageantry with Progress* (new edition) was shaping well to become the department's greatest publishing fiasco since Pisspot's celebrated *Shepford Events* three years ago, which had promised chamber music on the Uniplex sports ground and five-a-side football in the Little Theater. Yellowing corrected proofs and yellowing uncorrected proofs hung from bulldog clips all around the office walls; no one could remember which was which. Photographs of civic landmarks, historic churches, and copper-based alloy factories were stacked on every available flat surface, though many had slithered behind the filing cabinets; no one could remember which buildings were scheduled for demolition before the new guidebook was published. A vital block of the lord lieutenant opening the Maternity Unit of the Aneurin Bevan Hospital had been missing for two months; it was to be discovered that Pisspot was using it as a paperweight. The quarter-page advertisement for the Shepford Brick Company still read "Pricks Are Our Business"; we had not yet decided whether to let it through or not. Without a good deal more effort, and some of the overtime that Jeanette thought I was doing already, there was little hope of *Pageantry with Progress* hitting the streets in time for the Shepford Festival, and that, I supposed, could cast some doubt on my ability to hold down Pisspot's job.

I tossed Hattersley a batch of captions: "This monument originally marked the spot where Sir Thomas Bell was killed during the Civil War. It was resited outside the new Olympic-length swimming pool when Bell Lane was widened for traffic improvement." "And there's all that balls about Opportunities for Industry. Where are those bloody girls? They should have had it typed up days ago."

"Powdering their arses," said Hattersley. "Give them a chance, it's only ten to eleven."

And when they reemerged from the bog, he, although he was technically my junior, would be the one to tell them to get cracking. "For your information," they would say, "we haven't stopped since half past nine." "Yes, and for *your* information, the covers are still on your typewriters. Get on

47

with it." I couldn't do that. The style I had chosen for my dealings with the girls was banter with what I hoped were mildly sexual undertones; I would have found it difficult to switch character. Hattersley, on the other hand, could be discussing their knockers in one breath and making them retype his letters in the next. It bothered me. Perhaps he had a flair for leadership that I lacked.

"Seriously, though," he added; and that was something else. He would clown around as if the job didn't matter, and then he would buckle down as if it did. Another schizophrenic tendency I found disturbing; you got it in subalterns who played leapfrog in the mess all night and then led their men over the top at dawn. I work hard and I play hard, was what they said in later life, after they had become chairmen of great industries.

"Seriously, though, we'd better stop pissing about and get this guff organized." I should have been saying that to him.

"Don't panic; it's getting done." He should have been saying that to me.

Turning into the Cornmarket past the builders' hoardings surrounding the Clock Tower, the visitor may well imagine himself in a large car park. The arrangement is only a temporary one, however, for as soon as the cobbled marketplace has been tarmaced over, the council has it in mind to redeploy it as an overspill bus station. The car park, dominated by the old Town Hall which is now largely used as a linoleum warehouse, is enclosed on three sides by a seedy collection of disgusting pubs, do-it-yourself shops, fried chicken take-aways and electrical appliance establishments, all architecturally undistinguished except the Old Snuffe Shoppe which is about to be pulled down. . . .

"One of these days," observed Hattersley, looking over my shoulder, "some of that shit's going to find its way to the printer's. Then you'll be in it."

Yes, particularly as the printing firm, up in Birmingham, was owned by Councillor Drummond's brother-in-law, so Helen had once told me. Presumably he had declared his interest when the contract was dished out. (Or possibly he hadn't. "I'll tell you exactly why you're going to recommend me for Pisspot's job, Drummond. I happen to have paid a little visit to a certain printing firm in Birmingham. . . .")

The two secretaries, Sheilagh and Patsy, who always made their frequent exits and entrances together, like Siamese twins, came into the office carrying mugs of coffee; their first appearance that morning so far as I was concerned, for I had arrived half an hour late. It was pushing it a bit to call them secretaries—they were office girls, according to their official grading—but I liked to think of them as such. My secretary. I'll get my secretary to book a table. You can always leave a message with my secretary. If they had been born eight years earlier and had found themselves in the Stradhoughton Rates Office, I could have been married to either one of them by now.

While Hattersley chuntered on about there being such a thing as a fair day's work for a fair day's pay, I winked solemnly at Sheilagh to show that I personally did not give a bugger. I could just about equally have winked at Patsy, for with their long hair, long legs, big eyes and big mouths the two girls were as interchangeable as Cindy dolls, but Sheilagh was slightly ahead on points in not wearing a bra. Slipping back in the time machine to the three-and-nines at the Odeon, Stradhoughton, I sometimes dwelled pleasantly on the scope that would have been afforded by a braless girl. On the debit side, however, she would have been wearing tights. My mind skipped over a succession of fiancées, steadies, and blind dates, all Maidenformed like armadillos above the waist, yet as vulnerable as a whale's underbelly below it. For back-row punters, there must have been a dramatic shift in erogenous zones over the years, a revolution that had passed me by. The thought should have made me melancholy but didn't: I felt like old men who could remember when you got change out of a pork pie for fourpence. Much-needed proof that I was older than I used to be.

Contemplation of Sheilagh's boobs made me feel randy; for a second or two we were surfing off Malibu beach. Oscar, in tartan Bermuda shorts, was Patsy's. Both girls liked older men; we had an air-conditioned Lincoln Continental, a duplex off Sunset, and a string of credit cards. We could show them a good time.

They would want to dance barefoot to a combination of voices that somewhat postdated the Ink Spots. I could only do the quickstep. Where was Helen?

"Any messages?" I asked.

It was now three days since Helen had rolled up at the flat. So far there had been urgent calls from a Mrs. Hetherington, a Miss Springer, a Mrs. Mooney, and—an ingenious one, this, better even than her recent pose as an assistant at the reference library, offering me a map of old Shepford for the guidebook—a voice purporting to be that of a television researcher in Birmingham. I had not yet rung back and had no intention of doing so except when my resolve was weakened by Sheilagh's braless bosom.

"Councillor Drummond's secretary rang," said Sheilagh. A likely story.

"Was it, er—" I did some eyebrow work, intimating to Sheilagh that we were partners in a conspiracy. So far, touch wood, Purchase had been unexpectedly discreet about his encounter with Helen at the Heritage Motor Lodge. Perhaps he had filed it for future reference. Meanwhile, I didn't mind Sheilagh suspecting that an affair was going on or had until lately been going on, so long as she didn't know whom the affair was with. We had never discussed Helen's phone calls, although it was pretty clear from the odd warning nudge when I walked into the office sometimes, that they got freely discussed with Patsy. "*—sounds like a right nut case,*" I had heard Patsy saying on one of these occasions. Walk tall, Fisher; you have a reputation.

"No, it was her, truly, I know her voice. She's got that stuff typed out, if you want to pop over for it."

I am not a bloody errand boy, my flower. If there is any popping over to be done, it is for those of popping-over rank to sort out among themselves. On the other hand, half an hour in the King's Head Lounge Bar on the way back would not be injurious to health. Quandary.

"Oh, and there was another call from Central Police. Would you ring that detective constable before noon?"

Christ.

"What does he want now?"

"Just said he wanted another word with you."

Christ.

"Get him on the line, would you?"

Is it possible to experience three sensations at once, one of them pleasurable and the other two not? Yes, it is, for I was fully conscious of and able to isolate and identify my mixed batch of emotions—which, if I wanted to include this analytical process as a sensation in itself, rather than a by-product, brought the count up to four.

The one that ought to have been predominant, but wasn't, was a small wave of panic at the prospect of another interview with Detective Constable Carpenter; subsidiary to that was mild anxiety about my mental stability, this having been stimulated by a feedback from information collated by the isolating and identifying department, which had quickly spotted that whereas my whole mind should have been filled with apprehension, a large portion of it was in fact filled with something else, this something else being the great bubble of delight that always swelled inside me whenever I said to Sheilagh, "Get him on the line, would you?"

I have a secretary. I ask her to get me people on the line,

and she gets them on the line. I ask her to make tea, and she makes tea. I dictate letters.

I have a check book. I have a credit account with a firm of tailors. I have an Access credit card. If I want to, I can go into betting shops. Landlords do not ask me my age when I buy a drink. I drive a car; I drive a car so unself-consciously that fellow motorists do not stare at me, and sometimes I can drive for fifteen or twenty miles without thinking, "I drive a car." I have keys on a key ring. I have a desk diary in which my secretary writes appointments. My secretary is getting on the line a detective constable who wishes to talk about golf clubs. It does not seem strange to him that I walk into secondhand shops and buy sets of golf clubs. He believes I play golf; if I told him I played bridge, too, he would have no reason to doubt my word. He will call me Mr. Fisher—probably even sir.

I lit a cigarette. Look, Mummy, I can smoke.

"Mr. Fisher?"

"Good morning." I can make conversation.

"Many thanks indeed for ringing back. I'm sorry to be troubling you again. I'm wondering if you've had any more thoughts about those golf clubs since our telephone conversation yesterday?"

Yes, that when I saw Rat-face wondering why I wanted to open the fire door, I should have left him wondering.

"Well, as I explained the other night and as I think I said yesterday, they were no great loss. In fact, they were in such a tatty condition I can't see a professional thief bothering to take them away." I can talk man to man with detective constables, but my voice tends to break a little on long sentences.

"You reckon it was one of the local lads, do you?" He knows how to talk like a detective constable, but shouldn't he be calling me sir by now?

"It could have been." And shouldn't I be calling him officer? He would probably enjoy that: him calling me sir and me calling him officer. I remembered our initial interview at the flat after Helen had gone, when he fished out his notebook with some pride and was clearly playing at detectives. To oblige him, I played at witnesses. We were of roughly the same age: if I called him officer and he called me sir, we could do wonders for one another's ego.

It could have been, officer. It could easily have been the young scallywag Charles, the terror of the Fairways estate, if only I could remember whether I had made him up or not.

"It could have been. I don't know. I'm just saying the job wouldn't have been worth a professional thief's while." *The job.* V. good.

"You'd be surprised, Mr. Fisher. You see, we're judging these stolen goods by what you paid for them. You might have got a bargain. They know the market, some of these characters. You'd be surprised."

I didn't involve myself in the logic of this, if indeed there was any logic. I was waiting for the opportunity to call him officer, which, for the moment, had become my main ambition in life.

"Quite," I said, for "Quite, officer" would not have rung true.

"So if you *could* give us more details, especially if you could remember where you bought your golf clubs, it would help us greatly."

"I'll most certainly try, but at the moment I don't think there's anything I can add to the statement." I could have done it then. I could have said, "I'll most certainly try, officer." And I shouldn't have said "the statement." I should have said "my statement" or "my previous statement."

"Ah, now that's mainly why I'm ringing, Mr. Fisher, because technically you haven't made a statement yet. Not that there's any need to at the present moment, but it would save

paperwork later on if we could get something down on, er—"
he's trying to avoid saying "paper" again—"If we could get
something written down."

"Any time you like." I could have slung in an "officer"
there, but for the feeling in the balls, consistent with having
been hit in them with a padded ping-pong bat, which affected my thinking. Does a voluntary statement count as perjury?

"There's no great hurry," said Detective Constable Carpenter's voice easily—too easily for my liking. Have a cigarette, laddy, and let's go over this yarn of yours again from
the top. All that gauche stuff about not being able to say "paper" again was a blind, in order to lull me. If there was no
great hurry about taking my statement, why was it his main
reason for ringing?

"Meanwhile," he said, "if you *do* remember the name of
that second hand shop." That was his main reason for ringing.

"If I do remember, I'll certainly call you back."

My voice was working on too many fronts at once: it was
trying to sound normal to myself, trying to impress Sheilagh
and Patsy with its sexiness, trying to show Hattersley—who
was listening, although pretending not to—that calls from
the police were to be taken in my stride like calls from the
town clerk when Pisspot was out, trying to convince Detective
Constable Carpenter that he was talking to an innocent party. The overloading on the system was caused by the entry of
Purchase from his rabbit burrow in the Finance Department
next door. I saw him pause at Pisspot's desk, as if expecting a
flaccid hand to wave at him drunkenly from one of the dra-
wers; saw him look at me and register me unavailable for immediate consulation; saw him turn to Hattersley as last in order of seniority and hold a murmured conversation with
him.

"I wish you would, Mr. Fischer," Detective Constable Car-

54

penter had said; and I heard my own voice, in a choirboy's treble, responding, "I will indeed—officer."

I regretted at once saying officer. I had self-consciously put verbal quotation marks around the word, making it sound like a foreign expression. Purchase looked at me as if I had mispronounced something from a French menu. Hattersley looked not at me, but at Purchase, with a slight cringe of the cheekbones suggesting that elocutionary fastidiousness was perhaps a taste they had in common. Sheilagh and Patsy looked at no one, for they were hammering away at their typewriters as though being clocked by a time-and-motion consultant. Drop in more often, Purchase—you seem to inspire productivity.

Detective Constable Carpenter was saying, "The thing is, Mr. Fisher, what I find a bit puzzling is, there aren't all that many second hand shops in Shepford," and I, after wondering fleetingly if it was too late to shift the whole used golf-club market to Birmingham or preferably to the larger Midlands conurbation, was saying, "More than you'd imagine, officer," in the choir boy's falsetto range; and he was saying, "How many would you say exactly, with your knowledge of the borough?"; and Purchase, accompanied or rather escorted or more exactly ushered by Hattersley, was proceeding to Pisspot's desk, opening the bottom drawer on the left hand side, and extracting from it the olive-green file containing all the department's expenses dockets since the start of the financial year.

Christ and double Christ.

"Difficult to say offhand, officer." Stop calling him officer. "Ten or a dozen. Probably more."

"As many as that, would you reckon, Mr. Fisher?"

To hospitality at the Heritage Motor Lodge for Mr. Oscar Seltzer of Time-Life Inc. (London Bureau), in connection with revival of local wood-carving industry: £3.60.

"Oh, easily. Especially if you include tht little junk market in the old abbey ruins."

To hospitality at the Heritage Motor Inn for Mr. R. Horniman and Mrs. G. Lichfield, BBC representatives, to explore possibilities of TV coverage at Shepford Festival:£5.20.

"But you did recollect you hadn't bought your golf clubs at the junk market, Mr. Fisher. Didn't you recollect that yesterday?"

"Oh, quite. Exactly."

To hospitality at King's Head for Detective Constable Carpenter of Central Police, in connection with publicity for road safety campaign: £1.00.

"So that narrows down the field quite considerably."

What I will have to do is bluff it out. Admit nothing. Look Mr. Purchase, all I know is he *said* he was from *Time* magazine and he had an American accent and of *course* I didn't ask for his credentials, why should I? After all, whoever he was, he wasn't a bloody Russian spy. As for the BBC people, if you doubt my word, it's quite easy to check by ringing round the various studios until you find them.

Entertaining Detective Constable Carpenter was a mistake. *Hospitality, which must not be excessive and which must be authorized in advance by a responsible officer of the council, is strictly limited to bona fide visitors on official business (including commercial and industrial, housing, foreign deputations &c) where benefit to the borough might accrue. Hospitality may not be extended to other servants of the council, tradesmen, industrialists &c, except when officially receiving bona fide visitors as above.* Yes, I know the rules backwards, Purchase, I just bought the poor sod a drink, that's all. Here—there's a bloody pound note. Now we're quits.

Talking of pound notes reminded me that he still owed me one from our recent outing to the Heritage Motor Lodge. I remembered his anguished yelp when he saw his bill and wished that my own bill for that evening was not now clipped to my latest fiddle sheet, as evidence of entertaining the industrial correspondent of the *Daily Telegraph.*

"Are you there, Mr. Fisher? Hello? I was saying, we should be able to narrow the field down to about four or five shops."

"Yes. Could you hold on a second, officer? Somebody wants a word."

Uncradling the receiver from my hunched shoulder, where I was learning to nurse my telephone calls like a junior executive, I covered it with my hand. Purchase, brandishing the incriminating file, was hovering by my desk. Punctilious bugger. Mr. Rainbell is head of the department and, in his absence, Mr. Fisher, and, in Mr. Fisher's absence, Mr. Hattersley. If I had been sitting in the bog with my trousers around my ankles, he would have been waiting outside, cracking his knuckles.

"Shall you want a signature for this?"

"I should think Rainbell will. It's his file."

"It's the council's file, Mr. Fisher. I understand Mr. Rainbell is on sick leave. As acting head of the department, I'm asking you if you would like a signature."

No, no, Purchase. What you mean is, I am asking you, as acting head of the department, if you would like a signature.

When the judge sentences me to fifteen years, adding that he wishes it were within his power to make it twenty, I shall be standing in the dock correcting his grammar.

"Look, I'm on the phone as you can see. Can you hang on a minute?"

"We all have our business to attend to, Mr. Fisher. I'm quite fully authorized to inspect these accounts. I'm asking you again if you require a signature."

"Forget it."

"Then I shall send over a pro forma receipt. Oh, and by the by—" He drew out the imitation-leather wallet and abstracted a clean pound note. "Many thanks."

"If you find any of those items puzzling," I said, "you'll find there's usually an explanation."

What I will have to do is acquire a set of golf clubs. If God's in his heaven and I can find a set in one of Shepford's few secondhand shops, I shall buy them, chuck them down a quarry, keep out of Detective Constable Carpenter's way for as long as possible, then tell him I've suddenly remembered where I got them and keep my fingers crossed that the shopkeeper won't recall the exact day of the transaction. If God is not in his heaven and there are no secondhand clubs to be found, I shall have to buy a new set, jump up and down on them a bit, sell them to a secondhand shop, go back the next day wearing a false mustache and buy them back—no, wait a minute, don't fall into that trap: wear the false mustache when *selling* the things and remove it when buying them back, in case he gets asked for a description—and then follow the routine as above.

Purchase had departed with his trophy and I was back on the telephone with Detective Constable Carpenter.

"Anyway, Mr. Fisher, I won't keep you, and as I say, it's not all that important, but if you *do* happen to find yourself near any of those secondhand shops—"

"Excuse me. Sorry about that." The telephone receiver, back in the crook of my shoulder, had become dislodged and fallen clattering to the floor, dragging the whole instrument with it. I retrieved it and this time held it in the conventional manner.

"—was saying, there aren't all that many of these secondhand shops, so if you *do* find yourself in the neighborhood of one or two of them, and anything *does* jog your memory. . . ."

58

"I'll definitely give you a ring."

"And we'll keep in touch. Thank you indeed, Mr. Fisher."

"Thank you indeed, officer."

The receiver, as I put it down, had the damp imprint of my hand around it. I picked up a sheet of paper at random, saw it trembling like a prize essay being read out to the entire school plus the board of governors, and put it down again. I cleared my throat to dislodge the choirboy who was still lurking there, and said to Hattersley, "So what was all that about?"

Hattersley, it gave me comfort to notice, was as worried as I was. Not that he had need to be. Our worry quotient should have been in the ratio of roughly 5:1, if calculated to the proportion by which my expenses regularly exceeded his.

"Your guess is as good as mine," he said, shrugging too elaborately. "I suppose he fancies a bit of light fiction to read over lunch."

"But he's never looked at the swindle sheets before."

"There's always a first time."

"I'm not even sure he's entitled to. Why did you give him the file? Why didn't you tell him to wait till Pisspot gets back?"

"Why did you let him *take* the file? You're in charge," retorted Hattersley. "Anyway, he reckons he's supposed to see all expense sheets before we get reimbursed."

"No, he isn't. He gets a weekly chit from Pisspot, and so long as it's not above a certain level, it's none of his twatting business."

"Don't tell me, friend. Tell him."

While this edgy bickering was going on, Patsy was waving the tea-money tin under my nose. It was one of the office's jokey traditions that Hattersley and I were supposed to fork out a fivepenny piece every time we called Pisspot Pisspot.

"Ten pee, please. You said it twice."

"Not this time, Patsy. I need every penny I've got."

"He's thinking he'll have to start entertaining his lady friends out of his own money," Sheilagh said, rather surprisingly. I trusted that she was making a harmless joke rather than maliciously aiming to hit nails on the head.

"Have to start giving them luncheon vouchers instead." Patsy giggled.

"All right, that'll do!" said Hattersley sharply. Curious, come to think of it, that he had never made any oblique reference to Helen himself, since he was not averse to the odd snigger and must have twigged as much as Patsy and Sheilagh that something had been going on. It had crossed my mind more than once that he had his own extramarital problems on the quiet and that we were supposed to be observing an unspoken agreement to keep out of the arena of private lives. I could have been wrong, but there had been one or two mornings when I had arrived unexpectedly early at the office, to find him alone and still in his overcoat, making phone calls of the "Look, I can't talk now, I'll ring you at lunchtime" variety.

"Of course," he said to me, "you know why Purchase has it in for us, don't you?"

Yes. No change out of a quid at the Heritage Motor Lodge.

"Has he got it in for us, especially?"

"That story about him shaving his nose. It's got back to him."

"Not from me, it hasn't," I said. I had only told it to Ron Casey of the *Evening Mail,* hoping he could drum it up into an interesting paragraph. SHEPFORD MAN SHAVES NOSE.

"And you needn't look at us, either," said Patsy.

"I *am* looking at you," said Hattersley.

"Yes, I see you are. Haven't you ever seen a pair of boobs before? We've all got them, you know."

"If we told people outside this office all that we know," said

60

Sheilagh, who I hoped was still joking, "it'd fill the *News of the World*."

"I said that's enough! And if you've got nothing to do, I can find you something to do. In fact," Hattersley went on, deliberately addressing himself to the ceiling, "if we all worked a bit more and talked a bit less, we might get this guidebook out before Christmas."

Cheeky sod.

Turning into the Cornmarket from either of the access roads connecting with the shopping-center perimeter car stacks, the visitor will find himself in one of the oldest parts of Shepford. Until comparatively recently the commercial hub of an ancient borough that had changed little over the centuries, the Cornmarket has by now outlived its usefulness in a modern industrialized community. The spacious Civic Center on the edge of Bell Park has superseded the Victorian Town Hall with its drafty chambers and endless, gloomy corridors, while the twice-weekly open-air market has literally "moved with the times," for it is now housed in the combined wholesale/retail market outlet, with full cold-storage facilities and loading bays, conveniently situated near the new bus station. (A Green Arrow shuttle service between the bus station and the town center operates during normal shopping hours.)

Although the Cornmarket may have a neglected air at present, the visitor should not be deceived! Plans are well in hand to revitalize the area so that it may once more play a vital part in the ever-expanding business life of Shepford. In a three-phase program, all the existing shops will eventually be replaced by a linked shopping mall, also comprising offices, flats, restaurants, service areas, and underground parking facilities, that will be among the biggest units of comprehensive development in Europe. The Old Town Hall, at present subject to a Preservation Order, will be completely renovated and adapted to house the long-awaited Agricultural Museum. The market square it-self—the original Cornmarket, to be renamed Shepford Plaza—will, when paved and planted with trees—

The telephone rang. Sheilagh put her hand over the receiver.

"That woman from the BBC in Birmingham again."

"Who sounds like someone we know?"

She nodded.

"I'm out." I got up and threw the stuff about the Cornmar-ket, double-space typed on Planning Department letter-heads, over to Hattersley. Let's start pulling a bit of rank, Fisher. "I can't improve on this piss. See if you can. I'm going over to see Drummond."

Chapter Five

"Momma Winklebaum, will you please *lissena* me? I am asking why your son—*your son*—is filling my home with *galf* clubs!"

"My son. When there's galf clubs in the broom closet, he's my son. When he brings home his salary check he's your husband."

"Jeanette. Mrs. Winklebaum. May I have a word?"

"Oh, sure, Oscar, the floor is yours. You practically live here, anyway. As the saying is, *tee off.*"

"Jeanette, all I have to say is that when a normal, healthy guy like Bill takes it into his tiny mind to introduce fourteen sets of galf clubs into the family home—the *family home,* Jeanette, now don't you forget that—there has to be a reason."

"Oh, sure there's a reason, Mr. Oscar Henry Cotton Junior Seltzer, and maybe you can supply it."

"Now, Jeanette! Don't do that, Jeanette! You'll regret it for the rest of your life, Jeanette! Jeanette, put down the galf club!"

"I warned you, Oscar!"

"Jeanette! Never do that again. *Never* hit your husband's best friend with a Number three iron."

I smiled, twisted the lemon peel in my glass, raised the glass to my lips, sipped, and glanced in the frosted mirror opposite my red plush banquette. The mayor, the chief of police, *m. le président* of the Chamber of Commerce, the curé, and the owner of the wood-shavings factory who had collaborated with the Germans during the war—all fat, all with napkins tucked under their wobbling chins, all swigging the wine of the house, all sweating away at their Chateaubriands with *pommes allumettes* on the side—were no doubt discussing the scandal of the new public urinal out there in the Cornmarket. All was well. Except ye lord watcheth ye town, ye watchman watcheth in vain—the inscription carved in wood over the Old Town Hall doorway, soon to be picked out again, no doubt, by Arts College students busy with the gold leaf. Phase one of the three-phase program. And while they were tarting up the front, they would be dismantling the great organ in the Grand Hall and trundling it into a plain van around the back. But all was well for me.

I had been to see Councillor Drummond. Besides being chairman of practically everything it was possible to be chairman of and as well as being the mayor-elect, he was one of the town's leading solicitors with an office in Shepford's only remaining Georgian terrace on the other side of Bell Park from the Civic Center. Getting there was something of a rhododendron-hopping adventure, for Helen, who was between jobs, had taken to lurking in the park on the off chance of seeing me. She had once worked for Drummond's outfit—there were few establishments in the town where she hadn't worked—and I would not have put it past her to have persuaded his secretary to give Sheilagh the popping-over message with the object of waylaying me.

All clear. She was probably sitting at home, either ringing my office under one of her numerous aliases or waiting for me to ring back. I got safely to Drummond's chambers and was shown into a pleasantly furnished first floor room overlooking the park, hung with photographs of its occupant bowing and scraping to minor royalty at civic functions and

64

dominated, so far as I was concerned, by a set of brand-new golf clubs in the corner by the drinks cabinet.

" . . . bound to say struck me piece *rather* dangerous driving," Drummond was saying. He was a difficult person to follow at the best of times: he liked to think he had a reputation as a busy man, and he approached his sentences as he approached his appointments—at the trot, the pronouns and prepositions scattering behind him like dropped memoranda. At present, as he galloped through his reminiscence of my backwards-drive across the M. 1, he was even more difficult to follow than usual, for I was mesmerized by his golf clubs.

I pulled myself together and mumbled a few fragments of my well-honed story about the gears having failed, at the same time wondering, as I always did with Drummond, how he managed to make me feel like an inky little office boy.

"Yes. Yes. Yes. Yes. Accept advice, keep off motorway thorough overhaul competent mechanic." He dismissed the subject from the agenda with a clap of his hands and turned to the next item.

"Now. Rainbell. What can tell about him?"

"I'm not sure. What want know about him?"

"Drinking. Is getting worse, is getting better?"

My eyes, of their own accord, had swiveled back to the corner. Stop it, Fisher. You are not going to steal Councillor Drummond's golf clubs. You are making a simple problem into a complicated one. Besides, it is not a practical proposition.

Mistaking my silence for a decent reluctance to shop Pisspot—of which there were, in fact, small traces—Drummond prompted: "Can speak freely."

"Well," I hedged, "what can say? At least he doesn't drink in the office."

"Know doesn't. Never *in* bladdy office."

65

Poor old Pisspot.

"Tell truth, think he's slowing down bit lately," I lied. "Stopped drinking so much lunchtime, good sign."

"Hadn't stopped drinking lunchtime last Festival Committee meeting. Tight bladdy owl. Tell frankly, Fisher, want Rainbell off that committee."

"So Mr. Purchase was saying."

You servile sod, Fisher. Why Mr. Purchase? Why couldn't you call him Purchase or better still James Purchase or better still Jimmy Purchase? And why can't you call your doctor by his first name, as Hattersley does?

I switched my eyes from the golf clubs, met Drummond's, which stared at me unwaveringly, and returned to the golf clubs in some confusion. I know why he makes me feel like an inky little office boy. Because he's a genuine, card-carrying adult, he's not just playing at it. Anyone who can wear a black coat and striped trousers without feeling a prat, or even looking very much a prat, must have been a genuine adult since the age of fourteen.

"Believe you Purchase had words." A row, does he mean? No, words. *"I'll have words with my master."* Officer-class talk.

"Yes, there was some idea that I should substitute for Mr. Rainbell at the committee meetings, if we can find some way of—"

"Yes. Yes. Yes. Yes. Wish would. Had word with him yet?"

"With Rainbell?" Well done, Fisher. The *Mr.* fell away like orange peel that time. "No, he's on sick leave at moment."

"Sick leave arse, three-day hangover more like. Well, how manage it own affair, but tell frankly, don't want see bladdy man that committee again. Like bladdy walking brewery."

How manage it might be own affair, but how *would* I manage it?

I would get Pisspot pissed. Come committee meeting day, I would lead him to the King's Head Lounge Bar at half past eleven in the morning, force-feed him with gin and prize

66

him into a taxi home at three o'clock. Then on to No. 4 Committee Room on the fifth floor of the Civic Center, the new Shepford Festival whiz kid whose ideas shoot off like fireworks, yet at the same time has a firm grasp of bread-and-butter detail. Sorry, Pisspot, but if it wasn't me, it would be Hattersley. What is it that Oscar says? Somebody loses, somebody wins, somebody wins, somebody loses. That's how you play the game, kid.

But I felt a twinge of shame. Perhaps I wouldn't get Pisspot pissed after all. I would simply refrain from discouraging him getting pissed on his own initiative.

"By by, not problem that direction self, have you?" Drummond asked.

Come again?

"Keep staring drinks cabinet. Golden rule this establishment: sun over yardarm."

"Matter fact, looking at golf clubs," I said hastily. I would need an accomplice. I would need Helen. She knew the routine of Drummond's office: when he would be out to lunch, how to get to his room by the back stairs, thus circumnavigating his secretary. Then one of us would keep a lookout while the other snitched his golf clubs.

But wouldn't that land me with Helen again? I mentally kicked myself. One stupid remark to a rat-faced neighbor, and I am saddled with a mistress I don't want, except when I fancy her, and a bag of stolen golf clubs which are the property, furthermore, of the man on whom I depend for my promotion.

"You'll have to stop telling all these lies, Billy," my mother used to say, all those years ago. Yes, mother. It's just that I'm a slow learner.

"Play?" Drummond asked.

"Knock ball round sometimes," I said.

"Where play? Must have few holes on Sunday morning."

"Love to," I said, astonished; then added quickly, skipping

over the issue of where play, "Trouble is, golf clubs stolen. Bladdy nuisance, big expense buying more."

You see, Mother, if I hadn't told one white lie to a rat-faced neighbor, I would have been at a loss for a ready-made excuse when Drummond nearly called my bluff by inviting me to play golf. There is method in my madness, if you hang around long enough.

But never mind that. Drummond was inviting me to play golf. This adult in his black coat and pinstripe trousers was inviting the inky little office boy to play golf. Why?

He must perceive in my makeup something that I cannot yet perceive myself. He must recognize a coming man when he sees one. He would be able to spot my potential where I couldn't, he having the adult gift of insight.

I would learn to play golf. Having stolen Drummond's golf clubs, then jumped up and down on them a bit and sold them to the secondhand shop, then bought them back and thrown them down the quarry, then made certain that Detective Constable Carpenter found them before anyone else—such as the scallywag Charles, if he really did exist—I would reclaim my property at the police station and play golf with Councillor Drummond. Except that Councillor Drummond couldn't play golf because his clubs would have been stolen.

I decided not to steal his golf clubs and to have nothing more to do with Helen, who could only be an encumbrance on someone recognized as a coming man.

"Back subject Rainbell," said Drummond, having shunted the golf invitation into a cul-de-sac of vagueness. "Between four walls, think time closely approaching put pressure consider resigning director information. Simply not up to job expanding town this size."

Yes, Councillor Drummond. That's Purchase's line, too. No doubt you'll put the skids under Pisspot between you, him taking one leg and you the other.

"I would have thought as he's only got eighteen months to

68

go—" I began, but Drummond swept on as if I weren't even in the room, let alone as if I hadn't spoken. Should I put a pencil behind my ear and *look* like the office boy?

"Brings me question successor. Premature ask, of course, but must have considered putting own name forward."

Me? *Me?* Well, yes, of course I bloody have, but—

Sorry, Pisspot, I'm going to have to get you pissed. I shall lace your gin with white rum.

I am sitting in Councillor Drummond's office, and first he has asked me to play golf with him, and now he is asking if I have considered putting my name forward for Pisspot's job. There is a catch here, and he wants something from me. Or there is not a catch, and he wants nothing, but he has marked me down as the best man for the job. I will wear a black coat and striped trousers, Drummond, old man. I will send Oscar packing and I will finish with Helen—I *have* finished with Helen—and I will have Mr. Pussy-paws run over and I will not steal your golfclubs.

But what about Purchase? Drummond, obviously, could not yet know that the second favorite was in possession of my swindle sheets. He could know, but apparently didn't, that his ex-secretary Helen had reeled into Purchase at the Heritage Motor Lodge and informed him that the drinks were on Fisher, thus not so much opening up a field for speculation as planting one with land mines. All Drummond did know, and seemed to approve of, was that Purchase had asked me to take Pisspot's place on the Festival Committee, thus doing himself in the eye. There was something that didn't add up here, but I was in no mood for making an audit of Purchase's motives. I was the Shepford District Council director of information in black coat and pinstriped trousers, pacing my paneled office where a proper secretary rather than a jumped-up office girl—Helen?—sat with crossed legs and poised pencil while Mr. Fisher thanked the Lord Lieutenant and Lady Breezley for their kind invitation to a reception at

Breezley Hall on the fourteenth to meet Her Majesty the Queen Mother, but regretted that he would be unable to attend owing to his absence from Shepford on the official council visit to the City of Prague to examine new methods of industrialized system building.

"By by, this Prague beano," said Drummond, as if reading my thoughts. While I had been having some of them, he had gone on to say that went without saying were several other candidates field, and I had said of course appreciated that, and he had passed on to any other business, *i.e.*, the Prague beano, with the encouraging remark that didn't see why job shouldn't go most qualified man already several years' experience council publicity work.

"This Prague beano," he said, standing up to indicate that I should do the same and be ready on the starting line directly he had invited me to piss off. "Like it played down press, if all possible."

Yes, I'll bet you would, you crafty old bugger. The habit of various councillors of swanning off to exotic places such as Prague, Dar es Salaam and Paris on freeloading trips had been getting them talked about in the *Evening Mail,* and Drummond's habit of invariably attaching himself to these expeditions had begun to get him singled out for special mention.

"See what can do," I muttered.

"Course, trip not till September, some time after Festival. Hope Rainbell gone by then. Great clown, shouting head off, makes these affairs sound flinging ratepayers' money about bladdy orgies. Hope have responsible man by then, point out press these things fact-finding missions, nothing more. Bladdy hard work."

There *is* a catch, and he wants something from me. I know what you want, Councillor Drummond. You want a yes-man.

"Yes, Councillor."

70

Chapter Six

And now the Café Billard was filling up with the lunchtime crowd. I hissed at Henri to fetch me one more aperitif—the last one, and then I ought to be getting back to work. No, buggeration to that—I *was* working. I glanced at the sheet of foolscap which Councillor Drummond had given me—the original point of the popping-over expedition. It was his introduction, as Shepford's next mayor, to *Pageantry with Progress* (new edition), and a fine anthology of platitudes it made. Links with the future just as strong as links with the past . . . town proud of its history but even prouder of its place in modern society . . . tiptop living conditions . . . spacious parks . . . factories second to none . . . thriving domestic plasticware industry . . . exciting plans . . . forward-looking . . . room for further expansion . . . to stand still is to go backward . . . "Needs tidying up, do with it what you will," he had said. I thought seriously about throwing it in the fire.

I slipped the document back in my pocket and toyed with my half pint of sticky draft lager. The plush banquettes and the mirrors had gone: I was sitting on a cane chair by a Formica-covered table littered with screwed-up crisp packets in a corner of the King's Head next to the electronic fruit machine that paid out in washers. With only a little more effort the King's Head could have been the foulest pub in Shepford; we used it only because it was marginally less foul than the other pubs in the Cornmarket, our reason for venturing into the Cornmarket in the first place being that the new brick shed housing the *Evening Mail* offices was close by, and we could ambush the *Mail's* reporters with invitations to visitors' day at the sewage farm.

Ron Casey and the rest of the *Evening Mail* patrol were forming their regular semicircle at the far end of the bar and talking loudly about football. They hadn't seen me yet, and I wasn't sure that I didn't mean to slide out through the side door that had once been the entrance to the public bar, before a wave or a grimace or the mimed uptipping of a glass beckoned me into their presence.

There had been a time, back in Stradhoughton, when I had scraped the acquaintance of newspaper reporters, hovering on the edge of their company and laughing at their oft-told tales of how the municipal correspondent came back from lunch and set his desk on fire. The *Evening Mail* boys were a dull lot in comparison, more like clerks: their drinking school was a timid affair of halves of bitter and shepherd's pie and plowman's lunches, and in the early evenings they folded up their unadventurous last edition with its green-and-orange photographs of people shaking hands or wearing knitwear suits now available at the Cripplegate branch of a third-cousin-twice-removed of the Bon Marché, Birmingham, and went home to wash their cars. Another thing: I had been given this impossible mission by my new patron Councillor Drummond, play down Prague beano press, if all possible. How was I supposed to do that? "Oh, by the way, I shouldn't make too much of that visit to Prague if I were you. They'll be traveling economy and taking packed lunches." Whatever I said, I could readily imagine the leading article—or "Viewpoint" as they preferred to call it—in the *Evening Mail:*

At a time when Shepford ratepayers are onc again steel-
ing hemselves form the shock of a further massife ingrease
qɒıpoqıpıpıqıpıpıqp os[ɐ sɐʍ ˙sǝ8pn[ǝɔ 8uoɯɐ os[ɐ sɐʍ ɯ-u ɐ 8uıɹɐǝM
qoise- set off on another of their expesive jaunts to far-
away place.

We repeat the uestion we put to Cllr Drudommn and his
colllleagues when they spent three tatepayers' expense: "Is
your jouney really day's at a de-luxe hotel in Ostend at he
matching acdessories.

An excited twittering reached my ears from the *Evening
Mail* corner—the dawn-chorus sound, like baby starlings
welcoming their mother with a worm, of apprentice drinkers
greeting a seasoned regular. Young voices trying to sound
hearty tried on such expressions as "Oh, not again," "Get
them in, Casey," and "Just in time, mate, it's your round." I
looked along the bar, expecting to see the entry of the *Mail's*
only hardened drinker, their crime man Jack Wilmott, perhaps treating them to a mock cringe and shielding his head
with one arm to feign elaborate concern about last night's behavior at closing time. Instead, it was Pisspot.

I felt, as I often did when he was sober, a quick surge of
what I had once thought was pity but which by now I had begun to recognize as affection. Later, when he was drunk, he
would be a bloody nuisance, lurching from side to side like
an old Stradhoughton tram as I steered him out into the
Cornmarket; thrashing his arms about and knocking tonic
bottles over as he made some argumentative point over an
absolutely irrevocably final double gin in Shepford's only afternoon drinking club; insisting, perhaps, on staggering back
to the office and collapsing in his chair, or worse still on the
floor, like a stranded, snoring walrus. But in the mornings,
with his glasses slipping off the end of his nose or pushed up
to his forehead, a pipe repaired with insulating tape smol-
dering in one tweedy pocket and a copy of the *Guardian*,

looking as if it had recently wrapped lettuce, stuffed in the other, and the strands of multicolored wool unraveling from his wrongly buttoned cardigan, he could look touchingly vulnerable—especially against the laminated panels, glass doors and silicone-finished vestibules of the Civic Center, where he spent the hour before opening time shambling anxiously up and down like a professor of ancient Greek trapped in a bowling alley. "The Shredded Wheat factory" he called the Civic Center; the redundant Town Hall, where he had served most of his time in local government, was "Hatter's Castle." I was fond of old Pisspot. I went across and joined him.

"The *motor*car," he was booming as I walked over, evidently to quell the excessively boring debate on miles to the gallon that was the *Evening Mail* crowd's only standby when the topic of Shepford Rovers palled, "the *motor*car has done more harm—more harm—to the fabric of this town than any intruder since Oliver Cromwell, with the possible exception of Messrs. Creative City Consortium Incorporated and Limited, and their blasted shopping precincts. And on top of that—on *top* of that, allow me to finish, young man, I believe I have the floor—what you lads won't realize is that the *motor*car is an instrument of repression. Oh yes! I speak among you! Every new mile of road, every lay-by, every car park is land seized from the common people! Yes indeed! If I had my way—if I had my way—if *I* had my way, do you mind, young sir—if I had my way, no motor car would be allowed in Shepford unless a Labor councillor walked in front of it, singing 'The Red Flag.' Ah!"

The diatribe was a familiar one and the dragged-in joke an old one, and Pisspot was already in danger of losing his audience. The "Ah!," addressed to me, was exclaimed in some relief. I, at least, would not desert him. There had been times, indeed, when I had been reminded tetchily that it was my job not to.

"Morning, Reggie." I grinned. "Enjoying your sick leave?" It was not yet noon, and he was already two-thirds of the way through a large gin and tonic. A bad sign that, for had he been bent on social drinking rather than serious drinking—not that the two categories were particularly distinguishable as the day wore on—he would have started with a couple of pints of bitter. Perhaps I ought to call Hattersley and warn him that I might be late back.

"Convalescence, dear boy, convalescence. And see—" he returned to the group at large, addressing them as ever like a large public meeting—"see what happens when I convalesce. Is Arsehole at his desk? No, Arsehole is not at his desk. Does Arsehole hold the fort? On the contrary, Arsehole does not hold the fort. Arsehole at eleven thirty this morning, I have no doubt, was gasping outside the doors of this very public house with his tongue hanging out, waiting for opening time!"

(He had been calling me Arsehole ever since it had got to his ears that I called him Pisspot. "Call me Pisspot if you will," he said. "I *am* a pisspot. I am a piss-ar*tiste*. But so long as you call me Pisspot, I shall call you Arsehole, for only an arsehole would refer to a friend and colleague behind his back as Pisspot. And should you cease to call me Pisspot, I shall nevertheless continue to call you Arsehole. You will be known as Arsehole for all time. You will be remembered as Arsehole. The name will be inscribed on your tombstone: *Arsehole Fishah!*" I was never quite sure whether he was truly offended or not.)

"He was here till closing time yesterday, Reg," joshed one of the reporters. "Over to the Lantern Club, back here at five," supplied another one. I let them work this joke to death and then, in case they had planted any small doubts in Pisspot's mind—not that he would have given a toss anyway—explained about my errand to Drummond's office.

75

"Ah! Bulldog Drummond, the Pooh Bah of Shepford! And did the *bar*stard mention," asked Pisspot, draining his glass, "that he is trying to get me fired?"

You sly old sod, you don't miss much, do you?

"Oh, yes! Drunk in charge of a publicity department. *And* the barstard wants me off the Festival Committee, so my spies inform me."

You've got friends, Reggie, that's what it is, and I'm one of them, truly I am. But I've got to get you pissed. Not today, though. If I get you pissed today, it is only because I'm your friend.

"Let me get a round in,' I said. "Big one, is that, Reggie?"

"Tonic water, dear boy," pronounced Pisspot important-ly—but then he pronounced everything importantly. And he did like his little joke.

"Large gin and tonic," I ordered.

"*Tonic* water. Slimline. . . . low calorie . . . Indian . . . *tonic* water. Containing nought three four calories per fluid ounce. If you please."

More guffawing from the *Evening Mail* lot as my mouth dropped: "Look at him, he can't take it in," "He's suffering from shock, give him a large brandy," etc.

"He doesn't drink, Bill," spelled out Ron Casey. "Didn't you read it in last night's *Mail*? We put out a special edition."

"Seen the error of his ways, haven't you, Reg?" said ano-ther as Pisspot bowed complacently, like an old-style ham ac-tor acknowledging his applause.

"Whether my ways were in error, young man, will even-tually be judged by a higher authority than ours. However, I am in a position to confirm Mr. Casey's announcement. You see before you, my dear Arsehole, a pisspot who is an ex-piss-pot. A lapsed pisspot. A reformed pisspot. I am on the pro-verbial wagon."

But you can't be, Pisspot! Don't you realize—I've *got* to get you pissed! I've got to get you pissed and wheel you home in a barrow and then take your place on the Festival Committee. And I've got to keep you pissed until they throw you out of the Civic Center and I get your job.

I said, too shaken to imitate his mode of speech, which I often found myself doing despite all my resolutions not to, "What's brought this on, then?"

" 'What's brought this on?' 'What's brought this on?' He is given earth-shattering news and he asks, 'What's brought this on?' Where is your sense of occasion, dear boy? Cause bells to ring! Put out more flags!"

And on and on and on and on and into the saga of Pisspot's conversion. Three mornings ago—the day he commenced his sick leave—he had awakened not in his bed but in the middle of the bandstand in a public park in Wolverhampton. He had been to an extraordinarily good dinner in Wolverhampton, the retirement dinner of an old colleague of his, as a matter of fact, but he could remember nothing beyond the loyal toast. As for claiming to be off with flu, he *had* been off with flu, having found himself drenched to the skin—the result, he surmised, of having waded through the boating lake at some point. Mrs. Pisspot had called the doctor, and the doctor had lectured him like the proverbial Dutch uncle, and in short he was on the wagon.

"Alcohol," bellowed Pisspot, "is a liquid paradox. It is a stimulant, yet a depressant. It is a food, but at the same time a poison. Now to a system such as mine, so I am informed by reliable authorities. . . ." And on and on. Most of the young reporters grew bored, as they often did after a few minutes of his company. They began to drift off to the plastic tables with their plates of shepherd's pie. I felt angry with them: the favorite uncle had amused his nephews for a moment with his tricks with pennies and playing cards, but now they were tired of him.

Soon only Pisspot, I and Ron Casey were left at the bar. Only then did Pisspot drop his voice a decibel or so, and the

77

public-orator style with it. "There's another angle to this, Ron," he said, "but I don't want it publicized at present. Agreed?" You *are* a sly old sod. You drove them away on purpose.

"Agreed." Ron Casey, the rising star, tried to look like the wise old moon. I wondered if I looked as cross-eyed when doing the same trick.

"You will remember my wheeze or scheme for taking early retirement? Cancel earlier message. Celebratory dinner postponed. No bodies will be found on bandstands eighteen months hence."

"Does that mean you're staying on, Reg?" Silly, stupid, wooden-headed, cloth-eared bugger, what do you think it means?

"I'm afraid I'll jolly well have to. Can't afford not to. I took the opportunity while on my bed of pain of peering very closely indeed into the Rainbell coffers. I did not like what I saw. I need the brass, the greenbacks, the *dow* as my Brummingham father used to call it. So I shall work out my full term at the mast, and you"—this was to me—"will have five years to wait before stepping into dead men's sodden shoes. Sorry about that, my dear old Arsehole, or may I call you Bill? Let me buy you a drink."

If I emigrated to the United States, would I have to take my wife?

Pisspot, having produced a fiver and waved it at the barmaid in a wide circular motion embracing practically everybody in the pub, continued: "So that is one more reason for the turning over of new leaves. With Master Drummond breathing heavily down my neck, I shall probably be best advised to step that little bit more carefully. Not that the *bar*stard could get me out of that office with a crowbar, if it came to a showdown."

I was reminded of something that the *bar*stard could do, or rather what the *bar*stard's sidekick could do. Excusing myself

78

to Ron Casey on grounds of private business, I murmured in Pisspot's ear.

"What? What? What? Speak up! Don't mumble!"

"*Pur*chase," I hissed. "In our office this morning."

"Ah! The phantom nose shaver! Did you know that Purchase shaves his nasal organ, Ron? Good advertising tie-up there: I shave my nose with Wilkinson Sword."

Covering my mouth and trying to make it look like a parody of Purchase shaving his nose, I muttered out of the side of my mouth, "He took the green file."

"What green file? Which green file? I have hundreds and thousands and millions of green files."

"*The* green file. *The one in your left-hand drawer.*"

"Oh, the swindle sheets!" roared Pisspot, completely unconcerned. "Good luck to him! Which reminds me. Prague," he went on, turning to Ron Casey, though why it reminded him, I had no idea. Perhaps sobriety was softening his brain. "You wanted facts and figures on Prague. Subject to audit, I would say it has the makings of our costliest beanfest yet."

Pisspot, you silly old fool, we're supposed to be playing it *down.* Or are we? *I* am, but only as a yes-sir-three-bags-full-sir favor to Drummond. Pisspot doesn't do that sort of thing.

"You do know," I said recklessly, "that Drummond wants us to nobble the *Mail* to get the whole thing played down?"

"Of course he does, dear boy. The man's not a total nincompoop."

"Bribes accepted between the hours of twelve and half past," said Ron Casey, producing his notebook.

Odd bits of paper, pound notes, pipe cleaners, newspaper cuttings, letters, bills, and toffee wrappers were showering to the floor as Pisspot tugged his pockets inside out, his usual mode of finding a missing document. He retrieved a memo stamped CONFIDENTIAL from the torn lining of his jacket and peered at it over his half-moon spectacles.

"Prague, city of, Shepford Council piss-up in, figures relat-

79

ing to," he announced. "And it goes without saying, this doesn't come from me."

Are you a rotten director of publicity, Pisspot, or a very good one? I suspected he was a better one than I would ever have been in what now seemed the absurdly unlikely event of my getting his job, a better one, anyway, than the town deserved. If he didn't give a toss, it was only because there was not very much in Shepford worth giving a toss about, but he had a kind of exasperated, exasperating integrity that I admired and looked in vain for in myself.

As Pisspot, giving a reasonable imitation of a town crier, dictated the juicier bits from his confidential memo, I leaned against the bar sipping draft lager and idly surveying the lunchtime drinkers through the bank of mirrors behind the bottle shelves. There had been a time when the original engraved mirrors of the King's Head, advertising gin, port and dinner ale, had put me in mind of the plush saloons of the Café Billard; but when it was tarted up into a lounge bar, they were sold to antique dealers, and now, in their place, hung cheap but faithful reproductions of the same mirrors, bought from a flash arcade in Birmingham. It was through the middle one, the one advertising Bass Blue Label, that I saw Helen entering the pub.

She was wearing a yellowish corduroy skirt, a white open-necked shirt, a row of rather unsuitable red wooden beads, and sunglasses, and she looked stunning. She spotted me at once, but I made a fractional motion of my head toward Ron Casey, moving closer toward him at the same time. Helen, displaying the great sense of which she was intermittently capable, walked to the other end of the bar. Even she, I rightly guessed, did not care to run the risk of Casey's "Shepford Man's Diary" reporting her as being ust god fiends with the popular Bill Fisher of Shepford's ifnormation and puglicity department.

80

She established herself at a table by the door, fiddling with her beads and sipping what looked to me like a very large vodka and tonic indeed. She would hover there until I left and catch up with me as I strode across the Cornmarket. Just five minutes, she would say, you do owe me that. What I wanted to do was get her across the table, now, and make the white shirt rather more open-necked than it was already, but I had more sense than that; I would leave when Pisspot left, taking him by the elbow and steering him to the office or to the pictures or home or wherever he wanted to go now that he was living his new life of no wine and roses. He would be my shield.

He had finished his conference with Ron Casey, who had pushed his glass away to indicate that no question of another round would arise, in his opinion. Pisspot was cramming the reclaimed litter of his recent excavations back into his accommodating pockets. Helen, ignoring the stares of the *Evening Mail* shepherd's pie set at neighboring tables, continued to play with her polished red beads, her sunglasses pushed up to her hairline and her eyes fixed on me. I shoved my own glass of washing-up liquid aside, partly to indicate to the management that it was washing-up liquid, partly to tell Ron Casey that if he wasn't going to buy a round, it certainly wasn't my turn, but mainly to hint to Pisspot that if he was ready, I was ready too.

"Well, my dear Arsehole, I have drunk enough slim-line—low-calorie—Indian—tonic water to launch a balloon. Do you propose to escort me to Shredded Wheat Towers, or is it your intention to be here when the towel is flung over the nonexistent barrel?"

God, I fancy you, Helen.

"Come on, Reggie. And by the way, I didn't say it before because I didn't get the chance, but I'm glad you're staying on."

81

"I should bloody well hope so."

You old rascal. By now you should be halfway to roaring drunk and I should be leading you into the Lantern Club and persuading them to make you a life member, if you aren't one already. And having launched you on a seven-day jag, I should be taking your seat at the Festival Committee, and thereafter your desk and your job, and telling Hattersley, my number two, that it's the luck of the game you didn't get your full pension. But I'm glad you're on the wagon, Pisspot, and I'm glad you're staying on.

He had little experience of leaving a public house sober, and he staggered automatically as he turned for the door. At the same time, Helen's hand tightened on her wooden beads, and they snapped and went rolling across the linoleum floor. I had taken Pisspot's arm with what he must have thought was patronizing solicitude.

"We are no longer an inebriate, my dear old boy." (It would have helped matters along no end if you were, my dear old Pisspot. I need you senseless.) He shook himself free, walked with exaggerated dignity towards the door, skidded on one of Helen's scattered beads, and fell very heavily on his back, knocking himself unconscious against the only remaining iron-legged table in the King's Head. Ron Casey rang for an ambulance, one of the shepherd's pie crew got a wet towel, and Helen drank up very quickly and walked out, while I, for the sake of appearances, knelt by my fat friend's side, doing nothing in particular and closing my eyes when I saw blood.

Chapter Seven

It was not often that my mother and Jeanette were to be found in the same room after midnight. The former having introduced the latter to nocturnal pursuits such as knitting bed jackets or doing tapestry work by numbers, they were neither of them early-to-bedders by inclination, but they had worked out a shift system whereby one voluntarily clocked off at about eleven, while the other kept the night watch with me.

These vigils gave each of them in turn a regular platform for personal statements of the type that embarrassment or a sense of delicacy might have inhibited with the other one being present. My mother, for example, had once begun a rambling discourse on the thinness of the walls, and we had discussed modern building methods for fully an hour before it dawned on me that what she was trying to get at was that the squeak of bedsprings sometimes disturbed her dreamless sleep. (You should have mentioned that to the lady from the Bedding Council, Mother, and then I could have pointed out that the only reason for bedspring squeaking on these premises is that we have a squeaky bed.)

Jeanette, for her part, would use up her allotted time in seeking advice on whether she should give up the Pill, her belief being that it brought her out in a rash (permission refused), or demanding assurances that I still loved her (confirmation postponed), or asking how I would react if by chance she found herself pregnant (dismissed as hypothetical question), and similar personal matters. She too would occasionally touch on the subject of the squeaking bed. She was even more conscious than my mother of the thinness of the walls, and two years ago, when her fastidiousness had begun to border on frigidity, we had switched operations to the bedroom carpet. The eroticism of this experiment had long worn off, and I supposed that I should have got myself down to Pillow-talk (Shepford) Ltd. and bought a new bed, but that, like signing the papers for Mortgagedene, would have been forging another link in a chain I wanted to break. The time would come when the bloody bed would fall in altogether, and then I would have to leave Jeanette.

The night shift generally went off duty at about half past twelve, and I would stay up on my own for a minute that became two hours, smoking and listening to the radio, lost in my own thoughts and my own world, a free man for a while and nobody's hostage. I enjoyed these sessions with myself more than any other part of the day, and it was with some irritation that I realized that tonight's was going to be seriously curtailed. It was my mother's turn on the bridge and Jeanette, according to the custom and etiquette of the house, should have departed for the squeaking bed an hour ago. Instead, she was aimlessly pottering about, sorting through magazine racks and making cups of cocoa, while my mother steered herself along one of her frequent exhausting rambles down Memory Lane.

"Then there was another time when his dad's monkey wrench went missing. And he wanted that monkey wrench for a special purpose, I forget what he wanted it for, but it was for a special purpose, he had to have it that day. Any road, he looks high and low, and *you* know what a temper your father had, our Billy, it was *b* this and *b* that, and oh, b h, where's that b monkey wrench, and guess where he finds it. *This* one had it squat away in his bedroom and what he wanted it for I do not know to this day. . . ."

You're rewriting history, Mother. You're making it sound like an amusing family anecdote, but there was a drumhead court-martial when the old man found that monkey wrench. And you're making it sound as if I was about eleven at the time and I wasn't, I was eighteen. And why did I take the monkey wrench?

"And that undertaker's shop he used to work for. All them calendars of Mr. Shadrack's what never got posted. I bet you don't remember them, do you, our Billy?"

"Mm." And thieving the petty cash and stealing coffin plates. "*Taking things,*" she used to call it, with the distaste of a maiden lady finding a French letter in her bed. "What's this I hear about you *taking things* from work?" She had to force herself to say the words and they sounded strange on her lips: they were words like "abortion" and "naked" and "buggery" and "French letter" that she would just as soon not have had in her vocabulary.

She can't be cauterizing old wounds, it was all too long ago for that kind of therapy. She must be expressing relief, heaving a big sigh now that it's all over. Yes, that's what she's doing; everything's turned out all right. I was a little devil in them days, but look at me now, all married and wearing a cardigan and settled down and paying the milk bill and the taxes and all grown-up. Fancy a game of golf on Sunday, mother? I'll put the green fees on my swindle sheet.

"He was a little devil in them days. Wasn't you?"

Jeanette had been taking little part in the conversation beyond the odd, barely civil monosyllable, and she had by now entrenched herself in an armchair, where she sat with arms folded, quite blatantly waiting for my mother to take herself off to bed. It was clear to me why she was jumping the

85

night-patrol roster: we were in for an emergency resolution, one of the major set pieces on the future of our marriage that, once every three months or so, supplemented the usual routine debate about birth pills and pregnancies.

"I'll see to the cups if you want to go up, Jeanette," my mother said in the heavy, flat-iron voice that she thought was her diplomatic one. (In her terms, the location of any bedroom, whether in house, bungalow, maisonette or flat, was always "up.") She too was plainly hanging about to table an emergency resolution, and I could guess from previous late-night sittings what it was. *Have you noticed how depressed your Jeanette's been getting lately? Well, it's none of my business, you suit yourself what you do, but if you want to know what I think, I think it's time she was starting a family. . . .*

"That's all right, I'm not tired," said Jeanette tightly.

Bugger the pair of them. I'll go to bed myself.

I got up, stretched, scratched my hair, yawned a bit, and was digging out the loose change that always slipped down the side of the chair on these domestic evenings when I saw that my mother had somehow allowed herself to be out-maneuvered. Perhaps Jeanette had told her to piss out of it in so many words and I hadn't heard, or more likely there had been a slight, rank-pulling frown; at any rate she had commenced to scoop up handbags, bottles of pills, hot-water bottles, trashy novels, and other bedtime accouterments, while Jeanette appeared to be saying, "I should let your mother use the bathroom first."

I deposited myself back in my chair and, as a gesture of exasperation, flicked on the radio at my elbow. Phone-in program: men who sounded like London taxi drivers and women who sounded like Croydon hairdressers, insomniacs all, discussing inflation. *"What I'm trying to get at ees, Dave, I aven't your gift wiv words, bat, bat, what my question ees, is this, which ees, if that's true what that gentleman jus sayed, if I unnerstan im correcly, what e says ees, ees, that this, where the Common Market is ac-*

*tually keepin prices down so he claims, them was is very words I'm
sorry Dave I am very sorry my old mate you don' mind if I call you
that only I bin lisseninga your program for a very long time since it
started in fact an what I'm trying to get at ees. . . ."* The dron-
ing, obsessional voice, echoing slightly and crackling with at-
mospherics as if being bounced by satellite from the suburbs
of the moon, induced a zombielike, chilly, three-in-the-
morning, fire-out-and-no-cigarettes feeling; my exasperation was replaced by melancholy.

I inhabit a suburb of the moon myself.

Nothing ever happens in this flat. Nothing has ever happened here, save that brief intrusion by Helen from my real
life. Nothing can ever happen here. It is neutral ground, no-
man's-land; it is a waiting room.

"Haven't seen Mr. Pussy-paws lately, I hope nothing's happened to him," Jeanette said, as she often did.

You have never seen him, my blossom. We are dealing
with a made-up cat. I made up Mr. Pussy-paws for the same
reason I stole the monkey wrench: to relieve the monotony
of living on the moon.

Was that a moment of perception I just had?

I didn't reply to Jeanette. She was only marking time until
my mother emerged from the bathroom, put her head
around the doorway to say good-night for the second time,
put the chain on the hall door, then made her last and absolutely final reappearance with the news flash that she has just
done what she had been doing every night for the last eight
years.

*"I mean what I mean ees, you know and I know Dave, y'know, I
mean y'know it is a definite fact, I mean you ave only got to look at
y'know all these different countries. . . ."*

"I've put the chain on the door. Good night."

Good *night*, Momma Winklebaum.

Jeanette got up and switched off the radio. She crossed
and closed the door which my mother always left slightly

ajar. She shut the window, which was letting in a small gasp of night air. Whenever Jeanette wanted a serious talk, she gave the impression that she was making preparations to gas herself.

It was very quiet. The radiator clanked once. There was an eerie *ping!* from the unplugged television as its electronic innards cooled down.

"You see," I said, "it *does* make a pinging noise."

"Bill. I want to talk to you."

Oh, Christ. I mean, it comes as no surprise, but oh, Christ, just the same. Come on then, get it over with.

She took a deep breath and stepped on the diving board.

"And I want a straight answer to a straight question. *Are you seeing somebody else?*"

Relief.

Are you *seeing somebody else?* What's all this I hear about you *taking things?* The same shame-tinged tone. And I could have laughed aloud. Jeanette, flower of my life, I have been seeing somebody else for the last three and a half years. I have been seeing her twice, three times, four times a week, evenings, lunchtimes, Saturdays, and Sundays when her husband was away, and you have never suspected a thing. I have come home at two in the morning stinking of scent, and you haven't dreamed I was seeing somebody else. You have taken a suit of mine to the cleaners containing a pornographic letter from Helen, and you have not known I was seeing somebody else. You have seen me covered in scratches, consistent with having spent the evening in a blackberry bush, and it has not crossed your mind that I was seeing somebody else. And now, when I have stopped seeing somebody else—as I positively have—you ask me if I am seeing somebody else.

"That's a funny question to ask."

"What's the answer?"

"You know what the answer is. The answer is bloody no."

Pause for a certain amount of wedding-ring twiddling and

some compulsive straightening of dead matches in an ash-tray. She went on in a low, level, over-calm voice: "This morning you said you wouldn't be home until about eight because you had to go and have a drink with Councillor Drummond to talk about your guidebook."

"Well?"

"You said you were meeting him at that wine bar in Cripplegate."

Mistake, that. Never say where you're going, only where you've been, and not even that if practical.

"Well?" She knows I wasn't there. That's all right: I met him somewhere else.

"I was in town this evening, Bill. Late-shopping night. And I saw that coat I've been looking for in Truelove and Verity's, but I didn't have enough money. *So.* I went into the wine bar, and Councillor Drummond was there, but you weren't. And he said he hadn't seen you."

Ah. Now this is a difficult one. The truth is, Jeanette, I was on an errand of mercy. I went to visit Pisspot in hospital. And if you don't believe me, you can get on that phone now, ring the Thrisby Ward at the Aneurin Bevan General, and tell the night nurse to wake the old sod up. And the only reason I didn't tell you where I was really going was that it would have been a waste of a perfect excuse. Because one of these evenings Helen is going to succeed in catching me, and we'll need a last drink to take us through the last argument, and that's going to take two hours minimum, and I'll come home and say I'm sorry I'm late but I had to visit Pisspot in hospital.

But you might have trouble in following that.

"I can tell you exactly where I was this evening. I was visiting Rainbell in hospital."

"Then why say you were seeing Mr. Drummond?"

"Jeanette. Let's establish where I was first. I was visiting Rainbell. And if you don't believe me, you can get on that phone now, ring the Thrisby Ward at the Aneurin Bevan

89

General, and ask the night nurse. I got there at half past six, and she came on duty at seven."

"And you weren't seeing another girl?" Another woman, the expression is, at our age.

"I was seeing Rainbell." I picked up the telephone receiver, one finger poised on the dial. "Do you want to check?"

"Don't be silly, of course I don't. What I can't understand is why you didn't tell me."

Then let me put your mind at rest. I *was* seeing Drummond, but he canceled at the last minute. Then I was going to call you only I remembered it was late-shopping night. . . .

Sod that. Tell her the truth. Tell her the truth, and you could be out of here by morning.

It was my turn to twiddle with spent matches.

"It's hard to explain."

"What is? What is there *to* explain?"

"Jeanette. Let me give you an example. Did you know I was taking Rainbell's place on the Festival Committee?"

"You never told me that. Is that why you had to see him in hospital?"

"No, it isn't why I had to see him in sodding *hos*pital. You're missing the point."

"What point?" Total bewilderment.

"Of why I didn't tell you. It's because I can't bloody *tell* you things. Anything! Anything at all! About anything!"

"But that's stupid. You *do* tell me things."

No, I don't, not unless I have to. I can't talk to you without rehearsing the words in my head first. Talking to you is like being interviewed for a job because you don't talk back, you ask questions. And I can't tell you that because I can't tell you things. And I want to leave you because I can't tell you things, but I can't tell you I want to leave because I can't tell you things.

"Is that what's wrong between us, Bill?"

"I don't know what's wrong between us, Jeanette."

There is nothing between us; that's what's wrong. I would be calling you Jeanie by now if anything had gone right, if we had any hope of making it.

"There's something, I do know that. There's been something for the last few months."

"There's been something for the last eight years." I didn't mean to say that aloud, but it was said now. Perhaps I can tell her things.

"What—you mean ever since we got married?"

Yes. We shouldn't have done it, Jeanette. We got married on the wrong terms: yours. I know why I married you, but your reasons were just as trivial: wanting a husband. And the deal was that I should behave like one, and if I did, you would become a good and loving wife. But you would have done that for any husband who came your way. And you love me now because you have the responsibility of loving your husband. And you'll cry if I go, but they will only be the mature, slow tears of a reasonable person. It's bloody unfair.

"Well," I said lamely, "it's not exactly been a ball of fire, has it?"

"Do you mean you're fed up of me?"

Yes.

"I don't know what I'm fed up of. The whole of bloody life, I think." I picked up the evening paper. THAT PRAGUE TRIP—CLLR ꓷNOWWꓵ牛ꓷ RELPIES. Go to bed, Jeanette. The moment's passed. No crisis this evening. I've got some things I want to think about.

I thought, as she rose, that she was taking the hint. Instead, she came and curled herself up at my feet, one arm around my knees. I stroked her hair, it having evidently been placed close at hand for that purpose. I was reminded of two old films: *Brief Encounter* and *Lassie Come Home*.

"Do you know what I think, Bill?" Go on, then. Let's have your analysis. Let's see if you can get within two thousand light-years of the true facts. "I think," she said with the air of having cracked the Rosetta Stone, "that you tend to over-dramatize."

I do, I do. And you, my poppet, tend to underdramatize, which is worse. Nothing ever happens in this flat.

I wonder what Helen's doing at this moment. Screwing her husband in the bath, very probably. "I'm faithful to you outside home," she'd once said. "But I can't help appetite."

"You think because we don't talk about—oh, world-shattering events, I don't know, that we don't talk at all. We do. We talk all the time. About *little* things. *They're* important, Bill." She made them sound like dwarfs. Come on, Snow White, we haven't got all night. "And you think because one day's like another, and we lead an ordinary life like the people next door and the people next door to them, you think it's dull. It isn't dull, Bill. *I* don't find it dull. I find it exciting."

You wouldn't recognize excitement if it chased you down the street.

"Exciting. How?"

"In all sorts of ways. Things to look forward to. Holidays. Outings. Going out for a meal sometimes. In fact, we're always on the go when you think about it."

"Yes. I suppose we are." Why am I giving her points? Because she is a good wife, who is ill used by not having a good husband. It's bloody unfair on her, too.

"And you know what your trouble is, don't you, old worry-guts? You don't know when you're well off. You don't, Bill, it's true. But just you look back to where we were when we started and where we are now. Nice job, good money, nice town to live in, nice flat—well I'm saying nice flat, that's because we've *made* it nice. And we can always move—I know you're nervous about taking on new responsibilities, but we'd have no trouble in getting a mortgage, and how many couples can say that? And I *know* we've got your mother to put up with, but it won't be forever."

Why not? Are we going to bury her in the back garden at Mortgagedene? I sometimes dreamed of getting rid of the pair of them like that. Weed killer, inspector? Certainly I bought weed killer. For my new rockery.

She droned on persuasively about the qualities still attaching to a slightly used marriage, reminding me more and more of the manager of Feet First Shoes when I had tried to return a faulty pair of chukka boots. I had stopped listening. Thinking of police inspectors had reminded me of detective constables. If I told Jeanette now why I had to find a set of golf clubs, she would look at me as if I were speaking German.

"Aren't we? Bill?"

"Aren't we what?"

"Bill Fisher, you're half asleep! I thought you wanted to talk!"

One of us did; one us didn't. "Sorry. Tired eyes."

"Well, at the risk of repeating myself—don't you agree that we're still good in bed?"

"Well. Let's say on the bedroom carpet."

She squeezed my leg and smiled up at me, shyly. I could have cobbled together a warm moment for us out of these ingredients if I'd wanted to. But I held back. I'm not signing anything else. No, we're not very good in bed.

Helen and I had once been supposed to go to a flat that she borrowed sometimes, from one of her friends in the operatic society she never went to; only something went wrong, and we couldn't get the key. The car was in dock, and it was pissing with rain, so to pass the time we sat in the bar of the Heritage Motor Lodge, drinking vodka martinis and working out, on the back of an old envelope, roughly how many hours we'd spent having each other in the last three years or so. And it came to about seven hundred hours or, worked out in days, roughly equivalent to the month of June, which it then was. The image of such a flaming June had not been far out of my mind ever since. I saw myself waking up on that summer morning, the first of the month, with Helen by my side; beginning to touch, explore, kiss, stroke, scratch, bite; through the long day, through the night, bathed in sweat, to the second and third and fourth of the month, through the week and the weekend, through Midsummer's Day, Whitsunday, Father's Day, and the queen's birthday, through the Test match and Wimbledon: neighbors go on a fortnight's holiday to Yugoslavia and return, a Middle East war is fought and finished, Fords of Dagenham have turned out fifty thousand cars, and the rhythm continues, this endless song—our faces astonished at what we are doing, as flowers bloom and die, the earth spins, and the moon passes through all its phases. It was a month of life, that was, and we were very good in bed. Sex is a powerful aphrodisiac.

"Well," said Jeanette in the fullness of time. "I'm glad we've got all that out into the open." The marriage had been given its periodic road test and granted a further certificate. Concessions had been made on both sides. I would tell her more things. She would ask fewer questions. I would be more considerate. She would be more understanding. I would stop leaving the dustbin for her to hump out on Tuesday mornings. She would stop taking the ashtray out of the bathroom. You wash, and I'll dry. Perfection.

I sprawled in my chair, defeated and depressed, while Jeanette detached from its card and popped into her mouth the pill that brought her out in a rash. She kissed me on the forehead and, with quite a successful attempt at huskiness, whispered, "Don't stay up too long, will you?"

I wouldn't, my little flower, if I thought I'd find you spread-eagled on the bedroom carpet. What are you doing in July?

Chapter Eight

"Apologies for absence, Mrs. Drew who cannot be with us, Mr. Rainbell who is in hospital recovering from a fall." The slightest smirk hovered on Purchase's thin lips, and I saw the image that must have formed in his mind of Pisspot still singing as he rolled down three flights of steps. "I'm sure we all wish him well."

Year year! from the hypocritical ratbags there assembled.

"Now the question arises of Mr. Rainbell's successor, or should I say Mr. Rainbell's proxy? We have a slight constitutional dilemma here—"

"No constitutional dilemma soever, greatest respect chairman. Standing orders clearly state one representative Information Publicity Department, nowhere specified which particular representative, send whom they please. Sit down, Fisher."

I had been kept hanging about like a spare part while Purchase sorted out his crisis of protocol. He would have liked to have had me in an anteroom, but as there was no anteroom available and he couldn't very well make me stand out in the corridor, I had been motioned to go and stand by the window, where I was absently watching two workmen in a cradle hosing down the streaked front wall of the Civic Center and trying to look as if I were not technically present.

There was one remaining vacant chair at the long conference table: presumably if the absent Mrs. Drew had been able to be with us after all, I would have had to squat on the floor. I moved toward it and was about to sit when Purchase, who was poring over some well-thumbed mimeographed sheets that must have been his precious standing orders, held up his hand.

"Before you take your seat, Mr. Fisher. With respect, Councillor Drummond, that's not quite the interpretation I would put on standing orders. Standing orders in fact require the Information and Publicity Department to *nominate* one member, and the member it has in fact so nominated is in fact Mr. Rainbell."

This piece of hairsplitting left me in a ridiculous posture, backside poised in midair, hands gripping the arms of my chair, as if I were about to do a spectacular forward roll across the table.

"Very well, then propose co-opt Mr. Fisher this committee."

Smart thinking, Drummond. That gets rid of any future appearance by Pisspot, doesn't it, unless we're both supposed to fight for the same chair?

"I'll accept that resolution. It should solve all our difficulties. It is proposed by Councillor Drummond that this committee do co-opt Mr. William Fisher as an additional member. Do I have a seconder?"

Nobody twitched a muscle. I remained hovering six inches above the seat of my chair in the attitude of a gorilla waiting for its next banana. Come on, you silly sods.

After what seemed like a full minute, a youngish man in a broad-striped shirt and biscuit-colored linen suit—Jack Dance, the main-fuse-box live wire of Creative City Consortium—slowly raised his gold pen to the angle of about ninety degrees.

"Seconded by Mr. Dance. Those in favor? Against? Then it is resolved that Mr. William Fisher be co-opted to the Shepford Festival Standing Committee. Welcome to these proceedings, Mr. Fisher."

Year year. Does that mean I can sit down now?

"I believe you may sit down now, Mistah Fishah," quavered a leather-faced old ratbag who sounded as if she had been gargling with gin all morning. I bared my teeth at her, nodded stiffly at one or two random faces, and sat, sweeping my agenda to the floor as I pulled in my chair. The smirk played a fleeting return visit to Purchase's face, and it suddenly came to me why he'd been so anxious to get me on his committee. He wanted to make me look like an idiot in front of Drummond.

"Bill," Oscar whispered in my ear as I retrieved my agenda, "he figures you're batting out of your league. Now lemme say this about that. You wouldn't have gotten this far if you hadn't been in the World Series class right from the start. Don't let me down, kid."

"I now call upon the secretary to read the minutes of the previous meeting," said Purchase.

The committee secretary, whom I had never met but who looked like retired bank-manager material to me, rose to his feet and in a monotonous gabble began to read *War and Peace.* I arranged my agenda, scribble pad, newly sharpened pencil and other paraphernalia into a pleasing pattern and took in the other faces. I knew most of them through having avoided them in the course of my job. Besides Purchase, Drummond and Jack Dance, there were a couple of parsons; an amiable councillor called Hopkinson, who seemed to be number two to all the offices that Drummond was number one in; the odd youth leader; a small collection of Rotarians; two bearded men and a mustached woman representing the arts, the distaff side otherwise being catered for by various ratbags from organizations such as the Women's Institute and the Townswomen's Guild. Most of them were fiddling

97

with their pencils, and so, even though it meant destroying the symmetry of my arrangement, I did the same. I began to lose my self-consciousness. Nobody was staring at me, wondering what a boy of fifteen was doing at such a gathering. I was unnoticed, unexceptional, adult.

I had been right to wear my dark-blue suit—my best one, the one in which the pornographic letter from Helen had once made its undetected journey to the dry cleaner's and back. All the men present, except Jack Dance in his smart linen job, were wearing dark-blue suits. I fitted in with them, melted into their company. I was willing to bet, though, that none of them carried in his inside pocket a document featuring the phrase, *"You do not yet know all the things I can do with my tongue."*

The bank-manager type droned on, and I felt restless. I patted my inside pocket to make sure that Helen's letter was still there. Although I had congratulated myself on my nerves of steel for keeping such explosive material in so hazardous a hidey-hole, I was in fact on solid ground. Jeanette lacked the instinct of curiosity, and she never went through my pockets; it was safer there than hidden in a drawer, where it might be found by accident, or locked in my office desk, which might be opened with duplicate keys. However, as I clutched feverishly at my jacket, probably confirming my adult status to the rest of the committee in that I appeared to be in the convulsions of cardiac arrest, I realized that I was not on solid ground after all and that Jeanette's deficiency in curiosity must recently have been remedied, for the letter had vanished.

Christ, double Christ, and treble Christ. ". . . *referred back to the musical events subcommittee,*" driveled our worthy hon. sec. Shut up, you silly old goat, and let me concentrate. Did I move the letter myself? No, I positively didn't. I checked that it was still there when the suit came back from the cleaners, and I haven't even looked at it since. All right, then: has it fallen out of my pocket? Impossible: stop clutching at straws. ". . . *exploratory discussion with Inspector Corcoran of the Police Band.*" Has my mother found it? Quadruple Christ. Unlikely, though: she never goes into our bedroom. Jeanette has found it, QED. Jeanette has got my letter.

I now, in retrospect, registered Jeanette's odd behavior of the last few days. With other things on my mind, I had been vaguely aware that she was acting strangely, without really taking it in. Usually, after one of her in-depth explorations of our marriage, she remained in a state of perkiness for some days, uplifted by all the promises of fresh starts. This time she had reverted quickly to a condition of broodiness and one evening had alarmed me by emerging from the bathroom red-eyed and puffy-cheeked. To my relief she had gone almost immediately to bed, although it was her turn for the night watch. But then the night watch as an institution seemed to have been abandoned lately. Even though Jeanette or my mother sometimes did still sit up with me, neither seemed to have much to say. That, as I now came to appreciate, was because unknown to me, we had not been on speaking terms for a week.

I would bluff it out. After all, the letter didn't have my name on it. "My darling" could be anybody. It could be Hattersley. Hattersley was having it off rotten with Sheilagh, and he had dropped her incriminating letter on the floor of the King's Head Lounge Bar that night when I had got home very late because of the Shepford Publicity Club meeting. We had been having a sandwich and a glass of beer before the meeting commenced, Hattersley had gone on ahead of me to switch his car lights off, and I had found Sheilagh's letter, signed in her middle name of Helen, which Hattersley always called her, on the floor. I had put it in my pocket to return to him, and then it had completely gone out of my mind.

Jeanette's hash settled, I returned to the business at hand, feeling that I had just been through a very white-faced peri-od indeed and wondering if the carafe of water was there for ornament or could you drink it? ". . . *by a majority of fifteen votes to one to protest vigorously to Shepford District Council, Councillors Drummond and Hopkinson abstaining.*" The panic was not over yet, I could tell by my heart thumping. It wasn't Jeanette, because her hash was settled; it was something else, some other nagging worry that I'd just been reminded of. Sheilagh. Something to do with Sheilagh. Yes. Sheilagh had taken yet another message from Detective Constable Carpenter, and would it be all right if he dropped into the office when he was passing this way?

Where was I going to find a set of golf clubs?

". . . *make final representations to the Arts Council with the ob-ject of extracting a definite yea or nay.*" I had tried every sec-ond-hand shop in Shepford (of which there was a far greater number, I might remind Detective Constable Carpenter, than either he or I had imagined). I had scanned the sales and wants columns of the *Evening Mail* which promised Welch dressers and encyclopdldlds as new, but not glof clubs. Finally, clutching my Access credit card (and pretend-ing it was the American Express card I coveted), I had ven-tured into the town's only sports shop, prepared to pay full price. They had had golf clubs on order from their depot, but a computer error had sent them cricket bats.

Recognizing an anxiety neurosis when I saw it, I was by now casting about in my mind for other things to fret over while I was about it. The Access card, which should have played only a walking-on part in these ruminations, seemed to linger in my thoughts. It was because I had not had the chance of using it lately; that was what made me feel guilty. I wondered if the Access people were offended. I saw two men at the Access headquarters, quite senior executives they would be, frowning over my statement and asking where they had gone wrong. "A man in Mr. Fisher's position, steady salary, you'd think he'd be glad of the facilities we offer, and yet he hardly uses them at all." I resolved to run up more credit, to please them. I would buy a biscuit-colored linen suit like Jack Dance's.

My brow cleared as I disposed of what seemed to be the major of all my worries and I saw that the readings from Tolstoy had ceased and that I was enclosed in a plantation of upstretched hands. I rapidly shot up my own arm, only to receive a withering look from Purchase.

"You must abstain, Mr. Fisher. Since you weren't present at the last meeting, you can hardly be expected to judge whether the minutes are correct or no."

Oh.

"Carried unanimously. Item two, venue. Now I think we must deal with this as a matter of urgency. Are we satisfied with the Cornmarket as the traditional focal point of the Festival, bearing in mind the run-down condition of the area, or do we wish to explore the site adjacent to the Central Bus Station, taking into consideration the difficulty of access from the town center proper?"

"Well, I may be a bit of an old sentimentalist," said one of the business types, who looked less of an old sentimentalist than Heinrich Himmler, "but I do rather look forward to standing on that Town Hall balcony once more, watching the procession go by."

"And after all, we shan't get the chance next year, way things are going. What say, Percy?" said Councillor Hopkinson.

Drummond shot him a look that seemed to mean something, I couldn't guess what. But then I frequently didn't know why Shepford men gave each other funny looks or what they were talking about half the time. I comforted myself that this was because they didn't know what they were talking about themselves, but at heart I suspected that I was not really well informed enough for my job, and certainly not for Pisspot's job, not that I would ever get it now.

The Cornmarket enthusiasts won over the bus station faction, I once more abstaining, this time on the grounds that it didn't matter to me if they held their Festival in the marshaling yards. There were one or two other items of business, equally uninspiring; then Drummond moved briskly, "Propose form selves usual working party," there were some relieved "Ayes" as the motion was put to the vote, and he and Purchase exchanged chairs. But of course: Purchase was nominally chairman, but it was really Drummond who was running the shop, and this was how he swung it. Well, at least we'd get on faster now.

"As chairman working party, must stress time running short, get down nuts and bolts without further ado. Item one, publicity. Believe our newcomer's pigeon."

A spasm of pain crossed his face as he pronounced the word "publicity," and he shot me a look containing a fairly high element of personal dislike. Possibly he was thinking of the non-playing-down of the Prague beano by the *Evening Mail*; that kind of publicity, he was sure to believe, would be newcomer's pigeon.

They had all got copies of some balls that Pisspot and I had slung together, largely concerned with fictitious plans to flood the world media with invitations and press passes. In reality, we had long ago stopped bothering, for no one ever came. A man from one of the Birmingham papers had arrived one year, but only, it turned out after we had given him lunch, to visit his sister.

Feeling more nervous than I had judged I would be when rehearsing my speech in the bog earlier that day, I proceeded to guide the ratbags present through the balls in front of them, becoming uneasily aware as I went along that I was doing little more than plow through the stuff verbatim. The meeting grew restive, and I was relieved rather than otherwise when Purchase cut me short.

"While on the subject of television coverage, Mr. Chairman, if I may interrupt, I believe I am not too premature in revealing that we are almost certain of a three-minute item in the BBC-1 newsmagazine from Birmingham, at quite a peak hour."

Cries of "Good!" "Excellent!," "Well done!," etc. The Women's Institute ratbag kept whinnying, "First clarss! First clarss! First clarss!" over and over again, until Drummond banged his gavel.

"I spoke to one of their research people only today about accommodation and so on," Purchase continued. I saw that he was giving me a crafty look, and after he had gone on for some time in self-congratulatory vein, it was revealed why. "There *is* one puzzling aspect, Mr. Fisher, speaking through the chair. This lady got through to me as Festival chairman only because she had no success at all in getting through to *you*, Mr. Fisher. She tells me that despite numerous telephone messages to your office over a period of several days, unfortunately you were unable to find the time to ring her back."

This didn't go down well with Drummond. It wasn't meant to. Well, you see, Mr. Chairman, I thought all those calls were from an ex-mistress of mine whom I am trying to avoid. Well she *sounded* like this ex-mistress of mine, according to Sheilagh, and Sheilagh should know, she's spoken to her often enough. And anyway, why is a research assistant at the BBC in Birmingham going around sounding like Helen?

I wonder what she looks like. I wonder if we can put her up at the Heritage Motor Lodge. I wonder if she likes vodka martinis.

Wait a minute. If Helen hasn't been calling me for the last

103

three days, disguised as a research assistant at the BBC in Birmingham, what *has* she been doing? A three-day silence: that's unusual. She's up to something.

But personal problems of that kind would have to wait: I had a personal problem. "I think I can clear that up, Mr. Chairman," I said, noting with satisfaction that the quaver had left my voice. "It's perfectly true I've been stalling these Birmingham people because we may have bigger fish to fry. The fact is that we've every hope of being featured on the *Nationwide* program from London, which of course is networked, er, nationwide."

More lawks-a-mussy cries from the gang; a nice line in foiled-again expressions from Purchase; and, more to the point, some congratulatory words from Drummond.

"—feather in cap, certainly would! How soon know one way other?"

"Question really sitting down hammering out details, Mr. Chairman. Thought good idea, committee agrees, go up town discuss personally with producer."

Most of the assembled ratbags were braying *Year year*, while those with business interests yapped excitedly about the need to show something of Shepford industry as well as the lighter side, and the Women's Insitute ratbag resumed her chant of "First clarss! First clarss!" and I saw that as well as doing myself a bit of good with Drummond—not that I any longer had much reason for doing myself a bit of good with Drummond—I had won myself a free trip to London.

Let Purchase pick the bones out of *that* when he saw it on my swindle sheet. And, when he had tired of the war of nerves he was undoubtedly waging, and it came to the inevitable inquest on the swindle sheets he had already impounded, let him also pick the bones out of *To hospitality at the Heritage Motor Lodge for Mr. R. Horniman and Mrs. G. Lichfield, BBC representatives, to explore possibilities of TV coverage at*

Shepford Festival: £5.20. I should have made it £8.50. How much, I wondered, could I sting them for on the London beano?

I would be able to take Helen. No I wouldn't, because I'd finished with Helen. And another thing, why was she avoiding me, and what the hell was she up to?

My moment of glory passed, and Drummond moved on to the next business, which was pressing need brighten up program, all very well usual sideshows, *Murder in Cathedral,* knobbly knees contest, egg-and-spoon race what have you, what wanted was something really original, really first-class tiptop original idea.

I decided at first to sit this one out, but then, it seemed, so did everybody else. At any rate there was a profound silence broken only by the sound of a furrow-browed, rat-faced youth leader snapping his pencil in two. He was probably plucking up courage to suggest naked wrestling.

Encouraged by my previous success, but more to say something than because I had anything to say, I opened my mouth and the words "dog show" came out. I had no idea why I was saying "dog show," which had entered my mind unbidden. I could equally have said "Bicycle bell" or "gas-stove" or "luggage rack."

"Dog show? Say dog show?" Drummond was looking at me with great distaste, as if I had suggested a ladies' shit-shoveling contest.

"Er—yes."

"Hardly an original suggestion," murmured Purchase, examining his fingernails.

All right then, buggerlugs. Let's *make* it original.

"I'm not thinking of the usual dog show," I said. Aren't I? What kind of dog show *am* I thinking of then? An *unusual* one, obviously. "This one would be different." Oh, yes? In what way?

105

"In what way?" asked the gin-gargling ratbag.

"Well." And more by a process of elimination than anything else, the idea burrowed desperately through my skull. If not an ordinary dog show, then an extraordinary dog show. If not the kind of hound you got at Cruft's, then the kind of hound you didn't get at Cruft's. If not saddle-faced dog trainers who all seemed to look like the gin-gargling ratbag opposite, then some other kind of trainer.

"A *children's* dog show," I said. "And any child who has a dog, or who can borrow a dog for the day, can enter. And there'd be prizes for the ugliest mongrel, and the spottiest spotted dog, and the most disobedient dog, and the silliest dog, and. . . ."

I tailed off. It was obvious that everyone present owned a best-of-breed borzoi. I had not so much lost my audience as never been within ten miles of it from the start. Sod them, then. Let someone suggest hoop-la.

And then the frozen silence was cracked by Jack Dance, speaking for the first time. "Like it!" he said. "Like—*it!*"

A buzz of interest. Having made about twenty million pounds in ten years, largely by pulling down most of the shops in Shepford and putting up car stacks to accommodate the anticipated rise in the volume of shoppers, Dance was widely respected as a man of vision.

"Mr. Chairman," he began in the mid-Atlantic twang he had brought back with him from a trip to New York a couple of years ago, "I have some experience of the media—or should I say I have some experience of avoiding the media." (Sniggers.) "But I know what the media want. And I am telling all of you present that a children's dog show, on these lines, with the ugliest mongrel and what he said, will hit every newspaper in Fleet Street. Think of the pictures! Five-year old Suzie Faffernackle and her cross-eyed pooch—first time it's ever won a prize! Mr. Chairman, you know me, you know

106

Jack Dance, and Jack Dance tells you, ladies and gentlemen, this is a *winner*."

As if getting instant playback on a tape recorder, I was repeating Jack Dance's speech word for word in my mind, but I, not he, was making it and I was on my feet in my biscuit-colored linen suit and receiving the *year years* and *splendids* and *first clarsses*, and Drummond was beaming at me (instead of at Jack Dance) and saying asked for tiptop original idea and by golly been presented with toptop original idea; and then the pandemonium was cut into by the Women's Institute ratbag, who pointed a trembling finger and screeched, "Good heavens!"

I followed her unbelieving gaze and saw Helen waving at me through the window. This was rather weird, because we were on the fifth floor.

Others looked too. Some rose to their feet. The one or two who were still capable of dashing dashed to the window. Those with their backs to the wall craned their heads around, just in time to see the workman's cradle in which Helen was precariously balanced being hoisted up out of sight. Fortunately all those who might have recognized her—Purchase, Drummond and Jack Dance, another of her many ex-employers—could only have caught a glimpse of her bottle-green trouser suit.

"What blue blazes that?" barked Drummond.

How did Helen know I was here? Easy: she rang the office and said she was a probation officer involved with the disappearance of my godson Michael, and how could she get in touch with me urgently? But Sheilagh or Patsy would have recognized her voice. Try this, then: she has been rampaging around the office and asking questions. No: because they would still have recognized her voice.

"I believe I can explain that rather startling interruption," I said. "I gave permission for a lady photographer from

107

Time magazine to go up to the roof to take some panoramic photographs of the town."

"Why devil didn't go up lift?"

"She's probably looking for an unusual angle, Mr. Chairman—the new Shepford seen with that builder's crane over there in the foreground. That's the kind of symbolic picture they like, and she couldn't have got that shot from the roof. I remember discussing it," I said, turning to Purchase and speaking quite weightily, "when I entertained the head of the *Time-Life* London bureau at the Heritage Motor Lodge recently. Of course, you know what these American magazines are like—it will probably come to nothing."

I know how she knows I was here: it's because she rang Hattersley. But Hattersley recognizes her voice too: he ought to, because he's taken one or two of those calls himself when the girls have been out in tandem making coffee or having a pee. But he's never asked me what's going on between me and whoever. Why not? Because something is going on between him and somebody, and we have this tacit agreement that we don't talk about it. I've caught him, often enough, and even more often enough in recent weeks, making mysterious phone calls and bringing them to an abrupt end when I've entered the office. So there's obviously somebody; how do I know this somebody isn't Helen? And when I talk about the office to Helen, why does she no longer ask after Hattersley though she always asks after Pisspot and Sheilagh and Patsy? "I'm faithful to you outside home, but I can't help appetite." But what if the outside-home supply drops? We haven't had each other for a month.

Stop this silly train of thought, Fisher, it's silly. But watch Hattersley.

The meeting went on: a very long discussion about first-aid tents and ambulance stations that appeared to grip the ratbags among us more than it gripped me. What was Helen doing? Did she intend to throw herself off the roof, or what? No, of course she didn't; but she had got a foothold on these premises. I would have to get her off these premises. If I didn't get her off these premises, she was likely to roam anywhere, into Purchase's office even, reminding him as he got back from the committee meeting that they had met once before, when the drinks had been on Bill Fisher. I would have to get up to the roof and confront her, alone and face to face at last.

"Other business?" intoned Drummond, closing his folder.

Yes. But it's personal.

It had been a very short interview with Helen, although not the very short interview I had had in mind when belting up the last flight of stairs and onto the roof with a view to kicking her off it. She had been standing on the very edge, facing me as I came out through the skylight door, and I really did think she might fall, if not jump.

"You do owe me five minutes," she'd said, as I knew she would. But her seriousness surprised and disturbed me after the prank she had just pulled. She was very sober: I didn't know why I had to assume that Helen must have been drunk to persuade the workmen to hoist her up here.

"All right then, five minutes. Come away from there, for God's sake!" (And I thought: when on roofs, people really do say "Come away from there, for God's sake!")

"We can't talk here, can we? Won't they be locking up the building soon?"

"Do you want five minutes or five bloody hours?"

"I'd like to see you at the Heritage. Do you mind that? After all, if it's to be the last time, I think you should let me choose where it's going to be. Isn't it the least you can do?"

Possibly. And I'll bet you've booked a bloody room there, under the name of Fisher. I didn't fancy her at all. She didn't know that I'd just passed a test: if I didn't fancy her now, on the roof, which would have been an erotic adventure, then I didn't fancy her.

She had her own car with her, very likely parked in the mayor's reserved bay, so we agreed to meet at the Heritage Motor Lodge in half an hour, give or take ten minutes for possible congestion on Route Four, a new expressway that had recently been bulldozed through that side of the town. I would have to tell Jeanette I had been visiting Pisspot in hospital.

We went down the lift in silence. I saw her safely out of the building and went back to my office to clear up my desk. Although it was not yet six, the two girls had skived off, Hattersley was missing also, but Detective Constable Carpenter was present, sitting in my chair and skimming through the dummy copy of *Pageantry with Progress* (new edition) that we had managed to paste together during the week.

"Good evening, Mr. Fisher. Sorry for making myself at home—your colleague was sure you'd be back."

Oh. Yes. Be my guest. And other noises.

"I've been glancing at your guidebook, hope you don't mind." Not at all. "Quite interesting, an improvement on last year. Though I couldn't help noticing, why it's printed in Birmingham. Considering all the number of printing firms in Shepford."

Oh, indeed, indeed. Almost as many printing firms as secondhand shops and I haven't got your golf clubs and I'm in a hurry.

Try to *look* as if you're in a hurry, and he mightn't ask about the golf clubs.

"Look, I'm sorry—" I began, reaching for my coat.

"Am I keeping you, Mr. Fisher? Am I holding you up?" I didn't like his tone, but on the other hand, I did. He was trying to sound snide and not quite succeeding. He was young,

110

like me, trying to be grown-up, like me, but making nearly the same kind of hash of his efforts. You're playing at detectives, Carpenter, but you can't persuade yourself you're a real one. I hope. No—I don't hope, I know. I recognize the tone of voice, the hackneyed adult phrases, the wooden mannerisms. It's like calling to like.

"Do you think I could possibly—?" Another unfinished sentence from me, this one left uninterrupted. Do you think I could possibly never meet you again? Do you think I could possibly just leave, go, and assume that all this golf club nonsense had been a bad dream? Do you think I could possibly ring you tomorrow? was what I really meant to say, but I was afraid of entering the falsetto register.

He's better at it than I am. He has more nerve or can see himself in a mental mirror looking as if he has more nerve.

"I'm sure it's inconvenient, Mr. Fisher," said Detective Constable Carpenter, plodding on like Councillor Drummond as if I'd never opened my mouth. "I was wondering if you could spare five minutes or so for a quick drink."

"Well, it *is* a bit short notice—" I had hit top C.

"It's not about your golf clubs, Mr. Fisher, that can wait. It's about another matter."

"Oh, yes?" Top G, if there was such a note. "What's that exactly?"

"If you *did* have time for a drink. Just a private conversation."

My God, he's come to blackmail me.

Chapter Nine

Helen and I, with Detective Constable Carpenter between us, sat in our favorite booth in the Heritage Motor Lodge bar, and Helen did not seem best pleased, for tears were trickling down her cheeks.

Grotesquely embarrassed myself, so that there was a pain in my diaphragm as the result of hunching myself up so tensely, I was glad to see that our plainclothes gooseberry was equally discomfited. His solution, or attempted solution, to this novel social dilemma was to avoid looking at Helen, to pretend indeed that she was not among those present and to address his entirely desultory remarks to me. My own policy was to follow his example.

The conversation with Detective Constable Carpenter as I drove him to the Heritage Motor Lodge had been of the what-fine-weather and they're-making-a-cockup-of-these-roads variety, the kind of chat you would expect to have with the bank manager before he opened your file. I had been in a state of great apprehension ever since leaving the Civic Center and was growing increasingly fearful that he was about to get down to brass tacks, whatever those would turn out to be. (Perhaps he was waiting for Helen to leave, in which case he would wait a long time.) But I was growing more than increasingly fearful, I was increasingly fancying Helen. I always did when she cried. I wanted to lick the tears away, savoring the salt taste on my tongue, then ask her how she felt about a quick bunk-up in London. If we got the first commuter train in the morning we could be in Euston by breakfasttime, find one of those hotels where they make you pay in advance so they don't know or care whether you're staying overnight or not, and crawl back on our hands and knees for the slow train at half past midnight. Allowing five minutes off to ring the *Nationwide* program, to ask how they felt about covering a boring children's dog show, this would give us thirteen hours and twenty minutes in bed, thus extending our golden June of shagging into a glorious July.

Whatever Detective Constable Carpenter wanted of me, he was certainly enjoying his vodka martinis. He and I were nearing the end of our second, while Helen, whose dejection had not affected her thirst, had finished her third (assuming, as I could not assume, that she had had only one before we arrived) and was now toying pitifully with her empty glass.

"I don't know what they put in these," said Detective Constable Carpenter, "but they certainly carry a kick. Or is it because I'm not used to them?"

That's a trick question if ever I heard one. Has Purchase been on to him, I wondered? Has Detective Constable Carpenter cast his no-doubt eagle eye over my swindle sheets?

Another tear trickled down Helen's cheek. Don't, my love. Or if you have to, do it in private when you've wiped your eye makeup off and your bum is nicely settled across two hotel pillows.

Censoring my words very carefully, I said in my best Publicity Club of Shepford voice, "They're a very bad habit to get into, I can tell you. I'm afraid I've been led astray by certain of our American guests."

"What—dragged screaming to the bar, are you? Spending all your hard-earned cash on forced entertaining? You can't tell me! The old swindle sheet —*I* know!" Here it comes.

Not licking my lips, but wanting to, I said as if offended by the roguish innuendo: "It's all very well, but all these visiting firemen have to be fed and watered, you know." The pompous mixed metaphor was borrowed, with gratitude, from Pisspot. "*And* in our own free time," I added.

"Get away!" joshed Detective Constable Carpenter with the off-duty familiarity that he had begun to slip into with his second martini. "You enjoy every minute! Expense account, civic lunches, receptions, trips to Prague and back—I wish I had your job!"

He thinks I'm more senior than I am. But I can't tell him I'm more junior than he thinks. That means he's going to blackmail me for more than I earn, if he's going to blackmail me at all. I wish he would get on with it, one way or the other.

I badly needed another drink but didn't know whether I ought to order another round. For motives too obscure to analyze, I had been trying to put myself over to Detective Constable Carpenter as a two-drink man: probably something to do with the wish to present the image of a solid, upright citizen. I would have been helped in this effort if the solid, upright citizen's mistress could have seen her way to stop weeping into her empty glass.

"What about one for the road then?" cried Detective Constable Carpenter, rubbing his hands briskly, and that settled it. I made a twirling finger motion to Harry, the barman, who I was pretty sure would have a substantial batch of martinis already prepared in anticipation of another evening with his couple of lovebirds, as I had once overheard him describing us to one of his clients.

"And then I must go." What I meant, for Detective Constable Carpenter's benefit, was that whatever he had to say to me he had better get it said, and for my own benefit, that I intended to leave when he did, on the pretext of continuing our conference in the parking lot. This would be a shitty thing to do to Helen, but then I had often done shitty things

114

in my life, and I might as well behave in character. Besides, she was sniffling quite noisily now, and her nose was reddening, and I had stopped fancying her.

Detective Constable Carpenter, either to hide his embarrassment at her performance or because he was getting to the point of our interview at last, said heartily, "So you'll be missing your game of golf on Sundays?" And upon this Helen delivered herself of a hiccuping wail and sobbed: "He doesn't *per-per-per-play* golf, and I wish you'd go *away!*"

"Napkin, madam?" This was from Harry, who had just very smoothly served the drinks. He handed her the tea-towel affair that waiters carry over their arms, and she buried her face in it. Harry continued to hang around, evidently hoping for the return of his property. I signaled to him to piss off.

It was impossible to keep up the show of ignoring Helen's distress. I took her hand across the table and repeated, "Helen, Helen, Helen, Helen," in what was meant to be a soothing tone, although I failed at keeping a tinge of exasperation out of it. Detective Constable Carpenter assumed a sickly, lopsided grin and, in a fairish replica of the heartiness that had kicked off her outburst, observed, "You'll be watering your dry martini, carry on like that!"

Helen put the mascara-stained cloth aside and dabbed at her nostrils with the crumpled Kleenex that had served her during the trickling-tears period. She took a few deep breaths and seemed to compose herself. She would have been less composed had she known that her face now looked as if she had been delivering coal.

"I'm sorry. I'm all right now."

"Go and wash the mascara off your face."

"Yes. In a minute."

"Never mind, love," said Detective Constable Carpenter. "Worse things happen at sea."

She favored him with a weak smile and attacked her martini. After some down-the-hatching and first-todaying and all-the-besting, Detective Constable Carpenter did the same.

"No," he said, to indicate both a change of subject and the dismissal of the painful Helen interlude from his mind. "You were saying about Councillor Drummond the other day. Quite a character, isn't he? Our future mayor? I expect you see a lot of him?"

My last excuse to Detective Constable Carpenter for not setting off on my long-promised exploration of Shepford's secondhand shops had been that I had a lunch engagement with Councillor Drummond. I might even—for there had been no one in the office to eavesdrop when he telephoned—have expanded on this a little, suggesting that appointments with Drummond were taking up much of my time lately. A little name-dropping, I had reasoned, could do no harm, particularly as Drummond was chairman of the Watch Committee and presumably in a position to get nosy plainclothes coppers put back on the beat.

I could understand his interest in Drummond—any man of ambition in Shepford had to be interested in Drummond, and I had no doubt that Detective Constable Carpenter had dreams of promotion when the Case of the Missing Golf Clubs was finally cracked. But I couldn't see why he thought this an appropriate moment for vicarious social climbing, when Helen had just told him in so many words to shove off.

He's been tailing me, and he knows I didn't have lunch with Drummond.

"Well, you know what Drummond's like—always busy-busy, rushing about, doing fifteen things at once, canceling appointments at the last minute," I said. "So I don't see all that much of him these days, no."

"Oh. I somehow had the impression you more or less lived in each other's pockets."

Yes, I know you did, you snide bugger, and if you fancy yourself as Inspector Hawkeye, give me your theory on the sound we can both hear as of water dripping into a zinc bucket. It is Helen tapping her foot rhythmically against the central metal column supporting our table, and what it means is that if you do not state the purpose of your visit very soon and then clear off, there will be an ugly scene.

"No," he plowed on. "I just wondered, what he's like, that's all. I mean I've *seen* him, to look at, but never to speak to. Just wondered what he's like."

I gave him some shorthand impressions of Drummond, omitting that I thought he was a self-important twat who made me feel like an office boy, and then I added, in the hope of placating Helen by dragging her into the conversation, "You should talk to our friend on the right. She used to work for him."

"*Did* you? Did you really?" He made it sound as if this were very interesting. "That's very interesting. Very interesting."

The repetition of the phrase made me suspect that Detective Constable Carpenter was half pissed on three vodka martinis, but there was no time for speculation on this theme. Helen's foot tapping came to an end with a crescendo that rocked the table, and she put down, or rather slammed down, her empty glass.

"Tom—is it?"

"Jack." He had introduced himself to her by his first name, which I remembered thinking had removed any need for calling him officer from time to time.

"Jack. I'm going to be very rude. It must be painfully obvious that you've walked into the middle of a family row. Anyway, a personal row. But you're sitting there, and sitting there, and it's how's your golf and how's Councillor *fucking* Drummond, and this, and that, and I'm very sorry but it *must* be obvious, so why . . . won't . . . you . . . *go!*"

117

"Helen!"

"No. No. No. The lady has spoken. Never let it be said that J. Carpenter Esquire cannot take a hint."

"I'm sorry," said Helen. "And I must look a mess. I'm off to wash my face."

Detective Constable Carpenter, who, despite his protestations, had shown no other signs of leaving, now rose in the kind of ape crouch he must have learned at Police Federation annual dinners with his lady wife. I did the same, feeling more of a fool than he seemingly did, and as Helen stalked off toward the ladies' and my eyes followed her retreating bum, fancying her, I had an idea that I had seen a figure flitting across the archway connecting with the hotel reception area and that the figure had somehow looked as if it had been hovering there for some few seconds; moreover, that the figure was that of my colleague Hattersley.

We resumed our seats, I puzzled, Detective Constable Carpenter looking less disconcerted than I thought he would have been.

"Quite a lady."

"Yes. Sorry about all that. She gets a bit hysterical."

"Oh—!" followed by some deprecatory noises made by the tongue against the roof of the mouth, indicating that he had come across more of these scenes than I had had hot dinners.

What the bloody hell is Hattersley doing here?

"By the way," I said, "you won't, er—?" With a jerk of my head in what I judged to be a roughly southeasterly direction, embracing the scuffed lawns and weed-grown paths of my home environment, I signified my anxiety about Jeanette learning of the tempestuous assignation just witnessed.

"Oh—!" An identical set of noises, this time accompanied by a screwing up of the face suggesting that we were both men of the world and that for his own part he was having policewomen and meter maids rotten every day of the week.

Producing a wallet even more wafer-thin than Purchase's,

Detective Constable Carpenter now made another sound: "Ar—?" to ask if he was right in thinking that he would not be pressed too hard for his share of the bill. A succession of "Tuh-tuh-tuh-tuh!" sounds from me reassured him on that point, whereupon, as he tucked his wallet away and seemed ready to leave, I thought a return to the Queen's English might prove useful.

"So. This has been very pleasant, but I'm still not sure what it's all about."

"Not about anything. Just thought it'd be nice to have a drink and a chat. Oh, and before I forget—*golf clubs*."

Shall I tell him the truth? No: He would arrest me for wasting police time or something. I bet he enjoys arresting people, this one. I bet he watches himself doing it. *This is me being a real detective and apprehending a tea leaf.* A snapshot for his album of adult moments, to remind himself that he has really experienced them.

Reverting to the cough-and-grunt method of communication, I acknowledge the urgency of the golf-club question.

"Just where you got them from, that's all, so I can get a proper description from whoever sold them. Sorry to nag, Bill, but out of twenty-nine items nicked out of that Fairfields estate, there's only one that I couldn't identify if I came across it and that's your fizzing golf clubs. 'What make?' *'Don't know.'* 'What type of clubs?' *'Ooh, don't know.'* 'What kind of bag, is it zip-up or what?' *'Ooh, think so, but can't remember.'* God blimey, Bill, had you been knocking back these dry martinis when you bought them, or what?"

I murmured something about my notorious vagueness when it came to personal peoperty. What was uppermost in my mind was that now that he had started calling me Bill, I would have to start calling him Jack as soon as possible. And why was I flattered to be called Bill by the police, since it was common knowledge that they always put themselves on first-name terms with criminals?

119

"But taking your point, *Jack,*" I said doggedly, having acknowledged his lecture, "you can't tell me you've come all the way down here just to talk about my golf clubs, *Jack.*"

"I didn't come to talk about anything in particular. Told you—I wanted a drink. Even coppers are human, though it may take a bit of believing."

"But it was about *something,* Jack, wasn't it?" Too many Jacks.

"It was about nothing!"

"Excuse me, gentlemen." This was Harry, the barman, whom I had vaguely noticed approaching us after answering his internal telephone. He retrieved his mascara-stained napkin, glanced at me with a sigh and an upward roll of the eyes to convey a wide mutual understanding of the female temperament, and said to Detective Constable Carpenter, "Was you expecting someone, sir?"

"Yes, I was," replied Detective Constable Carpenter, to my surprise.

"He's waiting in the Polo Lounge, sir."

"I'm on my way."

Detective Constable Carpenter got to his feet. I was gratified to note that I had been right about him not being able to hold his martinis, for he lurched slightly while maneuvering his way around the table.

"Duty calls," he said mysteriously, playing at detectives again. Then, having turned away, he turned back, revealing a foxy expression signaling that he was about to take me into his confidence at last.

"For what it's worth, Bill, I'll tell you what it was. *I* thought you knew Councillor Drummond better than it seems you do. And *I* thought if you *did* know him at all well, and you *did* get the chance to throw a word in— No, the thing is, Bill, you mightn't think it in my type of job, but my type of job's the same as any other, when it comes to getting on. A word in the right ear—you know? Still. Forget it."

120

You're a cheeky cow, Carpenter.

Seemingly even more pissed than I'd thought he was, he staggered off, waving aside my relieved but generalized assurances about words in right ears. Not only a cheeky cow, Carpenter, but a twat, and not only a twat but a fraud. A juvenile lead masquerading as a heavy.

This choice of metaphor pleased me, and I ruminated on its wider implications as, mildly puzzled about something, I crossed to the bar where Harry was polishing glasses. If Detective Constable Carpenter was a juvenile lead, what was I? A juvenile lead, too, that went without saying. Helen was a juvenile lead, but my mother and Jeanette were heavies. Drummond was a heavy, Purchase was a heavy, my rat-faced neighbors were all heavies. Hattersley was a heavy trying to look like a juvenile lead. Pisspot was a juvenile lead who could have played the heavy if he'd wanted to. And we were all typecast in these roles, and nothing that we could do, or resolve to do, could alter the way we played our parts.

"Harry, who did you say was waiting in the Polo Lounge?"

"No idea, Mr. Fisher. He just asked for your friend. 'Tell him I'm in the Polo Lounge,' that's all he said."

"Did he ask for him by name?"

"No, he didn't, come to think of it," said Harry with an air of excited mystification that I found too conspiratorial for my taste. Harry was a heavy who would have liked to have been a juvenile lead. "'The gentleman with Mr. Fisher,' that's what he called him. 'Tell the gentleman with Mr. Fisher I'll be waiting in the Polo Lounge.'"

"Thanks, Harry."

He looked at me as if he expected me to slip him a quid for the information, or was it that I would have enjoyed the gesture of giving him one? Anyway, he didn't get it. Behind me, Helen was resuming her place at our table. I told Harry to provide more drinks and headed for the men's room but made a slight detour once I was out of Helen's eyeline, so that I could peep into the Polo Lounge. Hattersley and Detective Constable Carpenter were sitting in the far corner, both of them crouched over a low coffee table, and they were studying some documents.

One of my problems, Helen, is that whenever I have a problem to face, I always have another problem concurrent with it, which seems to take precedence. So bear with me if I seem abstracted. I cannot give my full attention to anything, because too many things need my full attention. My life has chosen to arrange itself on ramshackle lines, like a badly wrapped parcel about to burst open; I can secure one corner of it only by disturbing the others, which then must be secured in turn.

"You never told me you played golf."

"I don't play golf."

"He said you did."

"He thinks I do."

After this exchange from the Shepford Little Theater production of *Private Lives,* all was silence again until Helen dampened a finger and ran it meditatively along the rim of her glass, producing a piercing hum that, as it was meant to do, hastened Harry to our table with my fifth and Helen's sixth, martini. I was more sober than I deserved to be at this stage of the evening.

"I reckon Harry's making these to a new formula. One part vodka to six parts ice water."

"There's some people at the bar. He doesn't want a scene."

"If it comes to that," I said, observing, as Helen hadn't, that the people mentioned were Jack Dance and a woman who didn't look very much as if she were Mrs. Jack Dance, "neither do I."

"You needn't worry. There won't be one."

How did Hattersley know where to find Detective Constable Carpenter? Straightforward enough: a message scribbled on his deskpad while I was out of the office having a pee. But why didn't he come into the bar, instead of lurking about like the Phantom of the Opera, then making cryptic phone calls from the Polo Lounge? And why hadn't Carpenter told me who he was meeting, instead of all that "duty calls" stuff? And if they didn't want me to see them together, why meet here? Or was I *meant* to see them together?

Detective Constable Carpenter is playing at detectives, that's what it is. The juvenile lead is playing at detectives. But what's the heavy doing? I would like to know what Hattersley is playing at.

Come on, Helen. Say your piece.

I wonder if Jeanette wonders where I am? Yes, because what with the shock of finding Detective Constable Carpenter sitting at my desk, I forgot to call her to say I was visiting Pisspot in hospital. She must think I am now sitting in a bar somewhere with the author of *You Do Not Yet Know All the Things I Can Do with My Tongue.* I ought to ring her. I could say I'm in the Heritage Motor Lodge with Jack Dance, discussing a children's dog show.

You have to speak first, Helen.

She didn't take a deep breath, as I thought she would, or start any kind of speech; she came in at a tangent, speaking in a far-off voice.

"We were so close."

Yes. We were. We were so close at times that no population census could have categorized us apart.

"Yes. We were."

"We were one." She was very calm and articulate and so direct and reasonable in her approach that anyone who didn't know her might have thought she was talking sense. "You were me, and I was you. We were each other, whenever we made love. We didn't know who was which, it was as close as that."

Yes. Well. You say these things, Helen, and you're listening to your own voice saying them, but what do they mean exactly? We were very good in bed, and on tables, and in the backs of cars, and in haystacks and fields and woods, and we could have been very good on the roof of the Civic Center, if I'd fancied you, but we were by no means one and by no means close on that particular occasion. Are you sure this isn't simply another miracle of the age of technology—that we are two mass-produced parts, separately drawn from stores, which just happen to interlock to an accuracy of one-thousandth of an inch?

"Yes. It was."

"Then what's gone wrong?"

Jeanette asked the same question, and I couldn't tell her because I can't tell her things. I can tell Helen anything except the things I don't know, and this is one of them.

"Playing silly buggers, for one thing."

"'Would you say you slept in twin beds or not in twin beds?' Answer: not in twin beds."

I gave her a flinching smile, acknowledging this kick in the balls, and she put out her hand and added, "*I'm* sorry, Bill."

"I asked for it."

"I mean I'm sorry about that night. I was very drunk. And I panicked when your wife answered the door. I *had* to say something."

"You could have said good-night."

"Bill, you *know* I'm sorry. And all right, I'm life president of the Gone Too Far Club. But that's not where it all went wrong, is it?"

"That and other escapades. Bogus phone calls. Careering up and down the walls of the Civic Center in workmen's cradles."

"And following you about like a shadow and being a nuisance. Bill, all that was to attract attention because you were avoiding me. I only behave like that when you *are* avoiding

124

me. So how can you say you don't want to see me because of the stupid things I do when you *have* stopped seeing me?"

You're a logical little devil on the quiet, aren't you, Helen? But there's a flaw in there somewhere.

"I don't know," I said. "But it's got to end."

"What has? Our relationship or my behavior?"

"Both."

"All right." She drew a deep, resigned breath as if she accepted this ultimatum, which of course she didn't. (Nor did I, at heart, and that was why it all had to end. I had to stop seeing her because I couldn't stop seeing her: another of life's paradoxes.) "Then tell me *why* it's got to end and I'll go away, and you won't have to worry because I promise I won't do anything silly."

That's a tempting offer, Helen.

I said nothing, having nothing to say, and she went on: "Look. Bill. The last time I was supposed to meet you here, and you'd gone, and I went and made that scene at your flat, you were going to tell me something. Tell me now what you were going to tell me then."

I can't, because I wouldn't have told you anything that night, when it came to it. We would have drunk our martinis and finished up in the back of the car on that old disused road near the brickworks. "The lay-by," as we have come to call it. That's why it has to end.

Jack Dance and his mistress had finished their drinks at the bar and were going into dinner. He glanced in our direction and must have recognized us both, although he pretended not to. I wondered if Helen had been his mistress when she worked for him, since having mistresses seemed to be a habit with him.

"Can I ask you something, Helen?"

"That's why we're here, isn't it?"

"While there's been us, has there been anybody else?"

She smiled, too enigmatically for my liking.

"Does it matter?"

"Yes."

"But I thought our relationship was all over?"

"It still matters."

"Then whatever you say, it's not all over."

No, I can see that. And if there *was* somebody else, as it might be Hattersley (what's he up to with Detective Constable Carpenter?), and I found the pair of you at it, I would have to see you again, for the last big scene, and so that you could prove that it wasn't all over.

"Bill. Listen to me. When I fell in love with you, I'd had three affairs, and you were the third one. That was all it was going to be; it was fun, it was exciting, and I needed it—not you at first, *it,* the affair—because there was something missing in my life and it was a kind of topping-up process, like the others. And I went through the usual spectrum of emotions—anticipation, pleasure, gratitude—and it should have stopped there, but it didn't. I sometimes wish it had, but it didn't. Because I'd found my missing piece. You complete me, Bill. I'm wildly in love with you."

Thank you. And now I can answer the question, Helen, about what's gone wrong. It's because you sound as if you mean it, and even worse, as if you are not mistaken in what you say. I complete you and you complete me, insofar as I will ever be complete, and perhaps all that other stuff is true as well, about you being me and I being you and how close we were and are. And that's why I shy away. I shy away from Jeanette because she never gets near me and from you because you get too near.

"And no," said Helen, "there hasn't been anybody else. And won't be. And couldn't be. And I'm not going to say there's only you because that wouldn't be enough to keep me faithful. There's only *us.*"

Upon which my spirits rose considerably, and I leaned forward and kissed her on the mouth, out of gratitude, for she was lying.

Had there been a witness present—had Harry, for example, been able to overhear all that we had been saying (and he was trying hard enough as he pottered from booth to booth in his empty bar, distributing and redistributing nuts and pretzels)—he would have found it impossible to detect where the truth ended and the lie began. She spoke in the same level, sincere, serious voice that had pronounced the disturbing testament of her love for me; she spoke in the same style of subdued passion; and nobody who didn't know could have guessed by even the flicker of an eye that here was a married woman who went home each evening to her husband, who enjoyed a normal marital relationship, and who if asked to explain these contradictory roles would say, "I can't help appetite."

I knew very little about Helen's husband, except that his name was Geoff, that he was an executive with a pet-food firm, and that he was often conveniently away on business trips. Helen's policy was not to talk about him, at all, ever. If he had to be referred to for any reason, it was in the passive voice: "I'm expected home early . . . I'm being taken out to dinner." So the picture I had comfortingly (but unconvincingly) formed of an ineffectual and probably impotent rat-face faded, as it was meant to fade, into a picture of nothing, and I stopped asking myself, as again I was meant to, why a woman like Helen should have married an ineffectual and probably impotent rat-face, which plainly she hadn't. And the only remaining clue was, "I can't help appetite," now recycled as "There's only *us*."

We were juvenile leads after all, and it was light comedy we were playing after all.

"I know what you're thinking, Bill. Do you want me to leave him?"

Quintuple Christ.

No, you don't know what I'm thinking, Helen, you've got your wires crossed. You know what I was thinking a fraction of a second ago, but I've moved on since then. We're juvenile leads. It's comedy.

"I'll tell you what I do want," I said, "and that's a drink."

And I'll drink a toast to you, and what I could have had, if I'd wanted it enough. And then you must go.

I made a tippling motion to Harry and took her hand and squeezed it, and a jaunty voice exclaimed, *"Still here, then? I'm surprised to see you two upright!"*

Detective Constable Carpenter took his light overcoat from the peg where he had left it under the influence of three martinis. "Don't take that the wrong way, will you? Good night."

Judging rightly that we were on our last drink, Harry had restored the vodka quotient, and the first sips flooded me with warmth. Helen dug her nails into my palm and laughed as if we'd been having a happy evening. "I'm surprised to see us upright myself. We're not usually, by this time."

I'll tell Jeanette I've got to have dinner with Jack Dance. It was only to have been a drink, that's why I've not rung before, but now he wants to make it dinner.

"It's no use, Bill. You still want me, don't you?"

Yes. And need you.

"Yes."

"What's worrying you?"

"What to tell Jeanette."

"No, it's something else."

"Helen. When you used to work for Councillor Drummond, did he always keep his golf clubs in his office?"

128

Chapter Ten

"Mrs. Fisher for you."

"Jeanette? How many times do I have to ask you not to call me at the *ahffice*?"

"Oo thoo oo coo roo oonoomoojoosoo!"

"What? What?"

"Son, this is your momma, so pay attention. I'm speaking on the extension. Your wife says she thought it was OK to call you in an emergency."

"So hang up, Momma, and let Jeanette explain her problem her*self*!"

"She can't do that, son. She trapped her big nose in the vacuum-cleaner nazzle."

"Bill? This is Oscar. I'm speaking on the extension."

"You can't be, Oscar. We don't have that many extensions."

"Bill, I don't know how to tell you this, but I'm speaking on the extension that Jeanette was speaking on when she fainted just now."

I had made frantic moues to Sheilagh to say I was out: Jeanette's phone calls were always about domestic matters such as the radiators blowing up, and tended to be tedious. But Sheilagh kept her hand over the mouthpiece.

"It's not your wife. And it isn't you-know-who. I think it must be your mother, she's phoning from a call box."

What the hell does *she* want? My mother had a morbid fear of telephones and never rang me. Perhaps Jeanette has trapped her nose in the vacuum-cleaner nozzle. Or taken an overdose.

"Hello?" There was a chill in my stomach as I lodged the receiver on my shoulder.

"Hello, Billy! This is your mother speaking. I'm ringing up from the bus station."

She sounded as if she was ringing up from a tramp steamer in the North Sea, on what she thought was a bad line.

"What's wrong!"

"Oo, there's nothing *wrong!*" Of course there bloody is, you think the phone is like the old telegram service, to convey bad news, and it's to do with Jeanette, or you would have rung me from home before you came out. It's serious. And I wondered: how can I talk to my mother in what she thinks is my normal speaking voice, when Patsy and Sheilagh will think I'm putting on a broad northern accent?

"It's nothing to be alarmed about, Billy," she went on, sounding very much as if it was. "Only I wondered if you could meet me for five minutes, while I'm in town."

You're not in town, Mother. The bus indicator said "Shepford Central" but it didn't mean that; it meant "Central Bus Station." Meaning the center of bus control. Get on the 15A, out there in your tarmac wilderness, and go back home.

Whatever she had to say I didn't want to hear it, and I wanted to say, "Mother, I'm sorry, but I'm up to my neck in work." But that would have meant a windfall of flat vowel sounds for Patsy and Sheilagh to pick up and laugh at. So I said, "All right. Where?"

"Isn't there a caffy where they sell morning coffee?"

The Café Billard? The Café Sport? The Relais des Voyageurs?

Mother, there are no cafés anymore in Shepford. There

130

are no tea shops, supper rooms, chop houses, grills, fish-and-chip saloons, oyster bars, inns, or coffeehouses. Where do you think you're living? England?

"There's that Pizza Parlor in Castle Street. They might serve coffee."

I arranged to see her there in half an hour, the time it would take the infrequent Green Arrow to shuttle her from the Central Bus Station, and rang off.

"What are you lot grinning at?"

"Eee, bah goom, lad, oi nivver knew yow cum from t' Yorkshire," mocked Hattersley, in a teeth-grating amalgam of Black Country, West Riding, and Mummerset. Even more excruciatingly, Patsy attempted, and botched, a snatch of "Ilkley Moor Baht 'at" while Sheilagh, whose own Midlands accent could have cracked glass, proceeded to gibber incomprehensibly until told by Hattersley to pack it in and get the mail sorted out.

Feeling like an office boy in front of Drummond was one thing, but feeling like an office boy in my own office was not on. I said curtly to Sheilagh, the first time I had ever spoken to her that way, "And when you've done that, I want these notes typed up."

"Ooh! Ar! Nay! Ee!"

"They never know when to stop, do they?" Hattersley sighed.

And *you* can mind your own business for a start, Hattersley. But even while getting tight-chested about this assumption of his that he was number one in Pisspot's absence while I was number two, whereas the reverse was true, and about the fact that it was he who had started the girls off in the first place, I felt easier in my mind after his ee-bah-goom bit of ribbing. If you were going to shop someone to the police—grassing, as I believed it was called—you wouldn't make jokes with them, or even about them in their presence, unless you were a professional informer and you were hardened to it. But I still had to know what Hattersley was doing with Detective Constable Carpenter last night.

I was still hanging about the office ten minutes after I should have set off for my mother's coffee morning at the Pizza Parlor when at last Sheilagh and Patsy, acting as though they had corporate intelligence like ants, rose simultaneously and took themselves off to the ladies'. It was the first chance I'd had of speaking to Hattersley alone.

I decided on the bold approach.

"You should have come across and had a drink with us last night."

"Oh. You looked busy." He tried to look busy himself, not wanting to talk about it.

"It was a bit embarrassing," I said, without knowing why. Perhaps it seemed an adult-sounding thing to say, implying an instinctive grasp of adult mores. The phrase had floated, like "dog show," into my mind from nowhere.

"Why should it have been?"

Yes. Why should it have been?

"Well. After all, if you're meeting Bloke A, and he happens to be sitting with Bloke B, who's shared the same office with you for years, the least you can do is sit down and have a drink."

"As a matter of fact, I thought I was doing you a favor. I thought you and Helen would want to be on your own."

Helen? How does he know that name?

He interpreted the question, although I hadn't asked it aloud.

"I have met her, you know. At that party. And it's not exactly a secret, is it?"

Of course he's met her, at the same party where she was standing on her hands and showing off her panties, all that time ago. He wouldn't have forgotten that, but I had—meaning I'd forgotten he'd been there. And he's said next morning that she was a "character," and I'd thought that he had missed the point about Helen because that night I had driven her home, or rather homeward, and talked with her for hours, and started her third affair and my first one, and she was not a "character" as I already well knew, she was Helen.

And he knew about her all this time, and had pretended not to. And she knew about him, and pretended not to.

"Anyway," I said, "what was all that mystery about?"

This is inadmissible evidence, Fisher. All you can pin on Hattersley is a suspicion that he is having it off with somebody. All you have on Helen is that when she says, "There's only *us,*" the statement must be expanded to include her husband, wherefore you have a feeling at the back of your mind that it may also have to be expanded to include a third party.

"What mystery?" asked Hattersley, stonewalling.

A further thought was swimming against the tide of my immediate anxieties. *"And it's not exactly a secret, is it?"* No, and how have I been able to delude myself for so long that it is? Scores of people must know about Helen. Purchase knows about her. Jack Dance saw us together only last night. There have been occasions without number when we've been recognized, if only fleetingly at traffic lights; and I've always thought, absurdly, it doesn't matter, no one is going to put two and two together.

Shepford was a small town, no matter how desperately it tried to masquerade as a big one. I now faced the reality that there must have been gossip, of which, now that I *was* facing reality, Harry, the barman, was probably a prime distributor. How far, then, had it gone? Who knew and who didn't know? Had it reached the ears of Helen's husband? Or Jeanette's? No, not Jeanette's, she did not move in informed circles. All Jeanette knew was that I was acquainted with someone who could do peculiar tricks with her tongue.

133

"You and that tame detective," I said. "What did he want you for?"

"Nothing, in particular. Just wanted a chat."

"Yes, well, he wanted me for nothing in particular as well. But you were showing him some papers."

"Was I?"

My mother would be on her second coffee by now, and I was growing irritated by Hattersley's wooden attitude.

"Look, I haven't time to play Twenty bloody Questions. All I want to know is, was it something that concerns me?"

"Not directly."

"What do you mean, not directly?"

"It was something concerning the office."

"Then it does concern me. At least, while Pisspot's away. Look, mate, I'm *sorry,* but I think I'm entitled to know." If you're going to be pompous, Hattersley, let's both be pompous.

"And *I'm* sorry, but he told me not to discuss it with anybody."

"I don't care what he told you. Those papers he was looking at. Did they come from this department?"

"Yes."

"Right. Who is in charge of this department in Pisspot's absence?"

"You are."

"Right. Who authorized you to remove those papers?"

"Pisspot did."

Oh.

My involuntary hissing intake of breath must have sounded to Hattersley pretty much like wind being taken out of sails. I continued, lamely, laboriously and pointlessly, "You rang the hospital, did you?"

"I did."

"And Pisspot said it was OK?"

134

"He did." A note of amused patience had crept into Hattersley's voice. The bastard was humoring me. I rallied myself for one last despairing canter on the high horse.

"So Pisspot knows what it's all about, and *you* know what it's all about, and I'm the only one that doesn't?"

"I can tell you what it's *not* all about, if it's worrying you," said Hattersley, with the air of throwing me a tid-bit. "It's nothing to do with the swindle sheets."

You condescending sod. If you'd told me that in the first place, I wouldn't be standing here now, utterly humiliated, wondering how to get out of this confrontation with some rag of dignity. "Thank God for that," I could have said, and departed for the Pizza Parlor light of heart.

"I don't want to know what it *hasn't* got to do with. I want to know what it *has* got to do with."

"Sorry. It's confidential."

"Then bugger you."

I stormed out of the office, furious with Hattersley but more furious with myself. Any curiosity I felt about his transactions with Detective Constable Carpenter was subordinated to my frustration at being beaten. I suppose I should never have tackled him in the first place, not in that way, anyway, not by trying to come the heavy when it was plain to everybody, even the office girls, who thank God had not witnessed the contest, that I was a juvenile lead. Hattersley had taken me on with one hand tied behind his back, and whatever it said in the internal telephone directory about who was Pisspot's Number Two and who was his Number Three, and whatever the differentials in salary, and whatever the dates on our birth certificates, it was now sickeningly, depressingly clear who was really senior to whom.

I put the whole scene out of my mind by starting up an animated conversation with Oscar on our plans for launching an Olde English Tea Shoppe franchise, and after that a chain of cafés, chophouses, grills and oyster bars, but people began to stare at me and I was miserable again as I turned into Castle Street. Entering the Pizza Parlor, I resolved to think seriously about growing a mustache.

I found my mother perched incongruously on an aluminum-and-leatherette mushroom too tall for her dumpy legs, at a kind of circular plastic shelf that served as a table. The shelf was supported by a central column of flexible looking-glass mosaic which made a jigsaw reflection of her unhappy face as she picked diffidently at a tomato-smothered concoction the size of a dustbin lid.

The town of Shepford shouldn't be doing this to my mother.

"They won't serve coffee by itself, Billy. You're forced to have something to eat."

A slightly built, rat-faced juvenile lead in a blue-striped waistcoat affair put a cellophane-covered menu in front of me.

"Just coffee."

"No. Am sorree. We don' sairve jus corfee."

"Why not?"

"Why not, why not? Beycus, iss not possibler. You ave to ordair some food."

Don't wave your arms around at me, short-arse. I pointed at my mother's doughy-looking pizza. "We've already got enough food to feed ten people."

"Iss separate owder. You mus choose sometheen yourselv."

"I want a cup of coffee," I said, with the deliberation I had observed in others. "And if you can't or won't get me a cup of coffee, get me the manager."

"Ees not ere, but ee tell you same thing. Iss cormpenny policee."

136

"Listen. I'm with Shepford District Council. Are you tel- ling me it's your company's policy to refuse my order?"

"You jus wan' corfee. Notheen elz."

"*Correct.*"

He shrugged, picked up his menu and retreated. My mother murmured, "You show me up, you do, our Billy," but I could see that she was pleased and proud, and that she was filing the incident away in her compendium of anec- dotes. I wished that she had numbered Hattersley among her acquaintances.

Now then, Mother, what's all this about?

She composed her face into the solemn, formal expression that was brought out only when she had important tidings. She moistened her lips, following this operation by an ex- pectant pause, like a TV newscaster waiting for his cue.

"I've got to go up to Stradhoughton. Mrs. Lacey's passed away."

Mrs. Lacey. Mrs. Lacey. Oh, yes. My ex-fiancée, Barbara, would have been acquainted with a family called Butterfield or Liversedge or something, and these Butterfields or Liver- sedges would have spent a day at the Ideal Home Exhibition where they were sold a fridge by a man connected by mar- riage to a Mrs. Lacy back in Stradh—

"You'll remember, Mrs. Lacey, Billy. Her that was ever so kind to your Auntie Polly when she had that long illness. She had nobody of her own, poor soul. So I've got to go up, like it or not."

Not only did I not remember Mrs. Lacey, I could not place Auntie Polly either, or indeed any of my relatives except my grandmother, who was dead. A substantial and previously undistrubed nest of kith and kin was flushed out for the fu- neral, and I could not pick six faces out from the whole pack of them. They posed in front of me in turn, heads cocked whimsically to one side, eyes twinkling, lips pursed. "See, he doesn't remember us," said these people of my own blood, and they were right, I didn't, I had been too occupied for their meat teas on Sundays. Now I sometimes wished that I'd tabulated them all when I had the chance: uncles on the beer, aunts with their illnesses, nephews and nieces, great-uncles gone to ruin—I'd had the makings of a rich full family.

"You're a loner, Bill," Oscar said.

My mother wound a skein of congealing melted cheese around her fork, then abandoned the experiment and pushed her plate aside. She seemed nervous about something.

"Still, that's not why I've taken you away from your work."

I should bloody hope not.

Her voice was pitched higher when she spoke next, and the words came out in a rush. "I'm thinking of moving back to Stradhoughton for good, our Billy. So now you know."

You and me both, Mother. We could pick up the car and set off now up the M. 1, and I could be chasing you around the Town Hall by midnight. But you don't want to go back there; you just want to go back, to some ordered existence you think you had once. So do I. And the Town Hall would be there, and the market hall if they haven't pulled it down, and the arcades, and all those blackened buildings, and I'll be so pleased to be back that I'll marry a typist from the Rates Office and emigrate back to the moon.

"Well, lad, don't you want to know why?"

"I should think you're about to tell me, aren't you?" I revolved slightly on my aluminum mushroom. "That coffee's a long time coming."

"It's no use blaming the waiter, our Billy, you're forced to have something to eat. You heard what he said, it's the company policy."

I could go and pick a row with the rat-faced juvenile lead

138

in the striped waistcoat and put off my mother's forthcoming address by about two minutes. But it wouldn't be much use. I knew, as accurately as if I had a typed transcript in front of me, what she was about to say.

"All right then, why? Why do you want to go back to Stradhoughton?"

"Because I've got eyes in my head, our Billy, and I can see what you can't see, or your won't see, more like. Your marriage is in great danger."

Great danger. Not an accustomed phrase of hers. Like *taking things,* one that she'd had to borrow from somebody else's vocabulary. It must be more serious than I'd hoped for. Perhaps Jeanette's leaving me. She has found Helen's letter, and she's leaving me.

"Why do you say that?"

"Why do I say it, why do you think I say it, because it's true." Speaking in a half whisper, her usual volume in any public place, she found it difficult to put across the effect of snapping angrily. "Because you won't look at a thing till it's pushed in front of your face! You won't, Billy! You haven't the faintest, foggiest idea what's going on in your own home, now have you? Admit it."

Jeanette hasn't found the letter. It's a more generalized complaint than I can deal with.

"You might well say nothing, but I've got plenty to say, and it should have been said years ago. Your Jeanette's very unhappy, our Billy—you *know* she is, you've only got to look at her."

Very unhappy. Another one from the library book of words and phrases. I never knew that my mother required happiness as a condition of life, or even that she thought anyone entitled to it. A cowlike contentment, that's all she's ever aimed for. Perhaps it's what she means by happiness.

"And why won't you talk to her! I mean to say, if something's wrong, it's got to be put right. *Has* to. It won't go away, it'll just get worse and worse until you've *got* to do something about it."

"I *do* talk to her." I was annoyed to find that I sounded sulky.

"You *don't* talk to her. *You* know what I mean, our Billy, so don't try to look as if you don't. And I'm not putting all the blame on you, it's Jeanette as well, it's both of you. You just won't communicate, and that's half the trouble if you want my opinion."

Communicate.

I was growing uneasy. She was making sense, so far as her half of the world was concerned, but her half of the world was trying to invade mine, and I'd always thought we had some kind of territorial treaty about that. She was making it sound, with all this talk about *happiness* and *marriage* and *great danger* and *communicate* and all the rest of it, as if other people's lives were somehow my business, as if what I did affected them in some way, shaped them even, as if my actions had consequences. I'm a juvenile lead, Mother. Can't you discuss all this with Jeanette and keep me out of it?

To change the subject as far as she would permit it to be changed, I said: "I don't see what all this has to do with you going back to Stradhoughton."

"Well, it isn't because Jeanette wants to get shut of me, so you can get that idea out of your head for a start. We get on very well together, your wife and me does, and if you'd framed yourself and made a proper go of that marriage, you'd have had your mother for a free baby-sitter. As it is, you'll have one to pay for, and it's not fifty pee an hour they're asking these days, it's a pound an hour. That's if Jeanette doesn't walk out first."

"Jeanette isn't going to walk out, nobody's going to walk out," I said recklessly, even while appreciating what a straw she'd given me to clutch. If Jeanette's thinking of walking out, how much easier to give her an encouraging shove. "And you're not going back up to Stradhoughton."

"Oh, but I am. My mind's made up."

"A minute ago you were only thinking about it."

"Yes, well, I've thought about it."

"Where would you live?" I knew she meant it, my mother meant everything she said, but I wanted to keep my verbs conditional. I had always found that a good way of staving off the future.

"There's plenty places. Your Uncle Herbert, for one—he's got room, and there's nobody looking after him these days."

Never heard of him. And even my mother had brought him to mind only because he represented a spare bedroom. She must have gone through the list of relatives, rejecting them in turn, not only because she couldn't stand the sight of them, but because they would have no room for her, and she would have settled on Uncle Herbert not because of any personal qualities he possessed, but because of the spare living room he controlled and the fact that nobody was looking after him these days. It was only one step removed from advertising for companionship, light hsewk & cookg in retn for rm, in the evening paper.

I, Bill Fisher, have done this thing. Actions have consequences. She had been quite happy with Jeanette and me in her cowlike-contented way, sucking her sweets and writing her letters and knitting matinee jackets for children she had never met, and now her suitcases would be coming out of the cistern cupboard and she would be soliciting my forgotten uncles like a commercial traveler. I have done this thing. I am responsible for this action which is the consequence of the consequence of an action. I have changed her life. I have adult, godlike powers which I do not want.

"Anyway, wherever I go, I shan't be in nobody's way, like what I am in yours."

"Rubbish." Unconvincing, trying to sound convincing.

141

"It's not rubbish, Billy. It's ever since you got married, I should have seen it years ago. You've never had a life of your own, the pair of you, I mean to say not as a couple. You've never even got started! I mean to say, you can't even have a proper blazing row, not with me living there."

Agreed, and it's been a very convenient arrangement.

"Rubbish," I said again. It was as good a catchword as any.

"You can say rubbish till you're blue in the face, but I'm telling you. It's time you were on your own, with your own wife, in your own home, and sorting out your own future, with nobody else to bother you."

Future.

That's a large order, Mother. That's a very large order indeed.

Twisting uncomfortably on my aluminum mushroom I caught the rat-faced waiter's eye and gesticulated angrily toward the place where my coffee should have been had he brought it when asked. For her part, my mother pushed aside her tomato-and-anchovy circumference of goo to indicate that she had lost her appetite. It was a purely histrionic gesture, since only a starving navvy could have finished it. She suddenly looked old and tired, a trick that she used to pull on me even in the days when she was neither. It meant she was about to say something disturbing.

"If you could only see that lass of yours, in this last few weeks, after you've gone to work. Crying her eyes out she was, yesterday morning. She was, our Billy! She was sobbing like a baby."

Don't tell me things like that. I wasn't there, so it didn't happen.

"And *I* know what's wrong, and *you* know what's wrong. Or I hope you do, anyway."

Yes, I can't tell her things.

"She wants loving, our Billy. Any wife does. Just give her a bit of love."

142

Love. Loving. The last time I had heard my mother employ that verb had been fifteen years ago, ten minutes after my grandmother died, and she had said it then as if the word had just been invented, like Terylene.

It's more serious than I thought. It's out of my league.

My mother had embarrassed herself by using one exotic expression too many, and to cover her confusion, she began to assemble the accumulation of paper bags and packages that seemed to attach themselves to her like barnacles whenever she ventured into town. As she was drawing on her gloves, the rat-faced waiter plonked two bills down in front of her. I picked them up.

"What's this thirty pence? *I* didn't have anything!"

"Iss onna menu. Meenimum sharge, thirty penz."

"Nay! That doesn't seem right! That doesn't seem right at all!" my mother exclaimed quite loudly. One of the other customers turned round and looked at her.

"Leave it," I muttered. "I've no time to argue. I have some business to do."

I had some business to do. One of the ratbags on the Festival Committee had put me in touch with her ratbag sister who ran a pet shop in Cripplegate and who had volunteered to organize the children's dog show. As everyone seemed to be taking this event seriously, I had thought it was perhaps time I started doing something about it, and so I had made an appointment to see her. I had ninety minutes to kill, but I wanted to get rid of my mother and do some thinking, or avoid doing some thinking. I left her at the corner of Castle Street, headed purposefully toward the nearest car stack, then, once out of sight, slackened my pace and began to meander aimlessly through the streets.

Most of them were lined with furlongs of bile-green builders' fencing, behind which, in the words of *Pageantry with Progress* (new edition), a forward-looking town was ridding itself of the mantle of a bygone era. The construction cranes were more numerous on the horizon than steeples had once been: the noise of drills and pile drivers was so familiar by now that it had become an unnoticed backcloth of sound, like waves lapping the breakwaters in a seaside town.

The familiar trademark of Creative City Consortium, the demolition gang headed by Jack Dance, was everywhere: three C's linked together like a piece of broken chain. If they could only dismantle and redevelop human beings, I could have offered them a fruitful contract.

Love. Loving. I love, I loved, I have loved, would that I could have loved.

I didn't love Jeanette. I didn't love Helen. I didn't love anybody. I fancied Helen, and we completed each other, and she was me and I was her, but we were juvenile leads, so it didn't count. Juvenile leads make love and talk about loving, and they experience the sensations of love, but they don't love.

In my new circumstances, it was going to be very tricky to keep the arrangement with Jeanette going on an even basis, unless I put a bit of effort into it. There would have to be conversations: two-sided ones instead of three-sided ones. Long silences, I supposed, would become more noticeable: I would have to cut down on private thoughts. When I was out, Jeanette would be alone, and it would make the hours seem longer, so she would become depressed and might even cry in my presence. She would demand attention and other luxuries that I could not afford to give her. It would be like being married, properly married instead of playing at it. Was it shrewdness, intuition, or what that had inspired my mother to place me in this dilemma? Or did she, as she had always claimed, know something about the human condition that I didn't know?

Oscar and an associate of his who had shown interest in the

144

Tea Shoppe franchise idea were waiting for me outside the offices of the Shepford Building Society, so I did not have to think about the prospects of Mortgagedene. We strolled along together, talking business. "One thing we insist on in all our tea shoppes: no minimum charges." They left me as I turned into Cripplegate, where the hoardings had come down to reveal a rust-stained edifice like a gigantic, mildewing replica of an architect's model of a shopping precinct. I glanced at my watch and descended, via an escalator that did not work, into the subterranean arcade where the pet shot was located.

For want of specially ordered materials, so apologetic notices told me, the arcade was not yet completed. Its aerosolscrawled concrete pillars lacked their tiles, its rough cement floor awaited its finish of old brick, its panelless ceiling was as yet a confusion of wires and junction boxes, like the inside of a very large transistor radio. I walked along a gangway of planks that led me to the pet shop, where there were kittens playing in the lighted window. The idea crossed my mind that I should perhaps take one home for Jeanette, telling her that Mr. Pussy-paws had given birth. It would be company for her on long evenings when I was absent from home, not loving Helen. But the picture of Jeanette weeping quietly to herself as she poured out saucers of milk in the quiet, fluorescent-humming kitchen made me dejected. I dismissed the kitten notion as unworthily sentimental and entered the shop.

A beefy girl in jeans and a sweater that looked as if it were the top layer of fifteen other sweaters was sorting out mice, or doing something with mice that involved transferring them from one sawdust-covered seedbox to another.

"Mr. Fisher. Oh, yes! I'm frightfully sorry, Mr. Fisher, but Mrs. Mackintosh has had to go down to the kennels rather urgently. I did ring your office, but you'd already left."

I murmured something about not worrrying, I would drop in again when I was passing.

"But there *is* someone here who'd like to see you. Mr. Lightfoot. I should think he's interested in your dog show, it sounds a marvelous idea."

Lightfoot. I know that name. But I never use it, which is why it didn't register at once.

"Mr. Fisher?"

There was a door leading into what looked like a tiny office at the back of the shop, and he had opened it and was standing there: a stocky man of about forty-something in a good suit. Pink, well-shaved face. Not a rat-face and certainly not an ineffective, impotent rat-face. Not a juvenile lead, either. A heavy.

"Would you come in for a moment?"

I went in, and he shut the door, remaining with his back to it.

"Now. You've been having an affair with my wife."

Chapter Eleven

Real things are happening. Not promised, not threatened, they are happening now, in the present tense, and to me, in the first person singular. Actions have consequences. I am experiencing a consequence.

I had imagined this moment from time to time. "I ought to knock you down, Fisher," he would say, and my reply—offhand, underplayed—would be, "Go ahead if it makes you feel any better." But in that scene, Helen's husband, Helen's nothing husband, had been played by a juvenile lead, like myself. It was light comedy. This was drama. I had opened a door and wandered onto the wrong stage, into somebody else's play.

If he said, "I ought to knock you down, Fisher" (and he looked as if he well might before our interview was over), I would not know how to respond. The line I had rehearsed was the wrong one, and there was no prompter to tell me what the right one was. I would lick my lips and avoid his penetrating, decent gaze. That would be the moment when I was exposed as a sham, a shit even, and I would be exposed not only to him, but to myself. I didn't want that moment to arrive.

I was afraid: not physically but morally afraid. The knocking-down threat, although it might be delivered, was unlikely to be executed, at least, not here, for the windowless little office was no bigger than a stationery cupboard. The question of what he was doing in it anyway had flickered in my mind and then been extinguished as the least relevant of all the questions I had to find answers to: Helen, when not talking about her husband, might at least have mentioned that his firm owned a chain of pet shops, as a pet-food firm well might, and that the absent Mrs. Mackintosh was only the manageress.

I was afraid of being afraid. "Nothing to fear but fear itself"—well, I feared it. I had much experience of panic, but little of real fear. I wished that I had been frightened more often in my life, that I had been involved in a war or some similar event, where you pick up supplies of moral fiber.

Lightfoot remained with his back to the door. I had my back to a paper-heaped desk. There was two feet of space between us. I leaned back, half perching on the edge of the desk, to expand this neutral zone to about two feet three inches.

"You've been having an affair with my wife," he had said. Not, "I believe you've been having an affair with my wife?" Such niceties had to be taken note of. No question had been asked or implied, so no answer was required. I said nothing and did not lick my lips. But my heart was pounding, and my mouth was dry.

"Well?"

The question had now been posed. I would have to speak, but before I spoke I would have to clear my throat. I did so, then aimed at basso profundo in the hope that whatever came out would be somewhere in the alto range.

"Is that what your wife tells you?"

Of the hundred or so imbecilic answers that must have flashed through my brain like a computer feedback, I had probably selected the most imbecilic of them all. My thinking, insofar as the jangling sensation in my head could be called thinking, was that it was of the first importance to know how much Helen had told him, if anything. If nothing, then he could only be working on rumor, conjecture, and the possible evidence of Harry, the barman, and a few minor witnesses, in which case I would stand a fair chance of bluffing it out. So to that extent, "Is that what your wife tells you?" was less imbecilic than, say, "What are you going to do about it?" which had been considered and rejected.

What I didn't take into account, and should have done, was the effect that such a question would have on a man of his obviously middling-public-school background and intensive training in honor, decency, and not mentioning ladies' names in the mess. I had already been fascinated to observe that a vein was throbbing in his forehead—the first time I had ever come across this phenomenon outside the pages of Bulldog Drummond—and this alone, never mind his whitened knuckles and the fact that I was clearly dealing with the owner of a cravat and blazer, should have warned me.

"What the *devil* do you mean by that? Are you suggesting that my wife is a liar?"

My brain-computer was issuing a correction. Erase "Is that what your wife tell you?" and substitute "What gives you that idea?" Good thinking: a parry on those lines might have evoked a similar berserk response, but at least it could have yielded some badly needed information.

But it was too late for that, so I had to make do with: "I'm not suggesting any such thing."

"Then what are you suggesting?"

I wished he would stop passing the initiative to me. I tried volleying back with: "I think we might keep our voices down a little, don't you?" I nodded toward the wall, behind which I had no doubt that mouse-sorting activities had been suspended. There was, I was in process of discovering, no such state as total anxiety; it was as capable of infinite expansion as

149

mother-love is supposed to be, and one of my supplementary anxieties was that when this was all over, I would have to make some kind of exit through the shop past the beefy girl in the jeans and sweaters. Would I say "Good morning," or nothing, or what?

"You think that, do you? You'd rather no one else heard about your squalid little adventure, would you? I'm afraid you've left it a bit late for that, Fisher, I should think the whole of Shepford knows by now."

Nevertheless, he had taken up my suggestion and lowered his voice, a difficult adjustment to make while indulging in Bulldog Drummond rhetoric; so I surmised—anyway, hoped—that he was exaggerating the Shepford grapevine angle.

He relaxed his knuckle-whitening grip on the door handle and looked as if he would very much like to pace the room, had it been big enough. When he spoke next, in the absence of any further word from me, it was in a deliberate, discoursing manner.

"Last night I had an anonymous telephone call. I was informed that my wife was having drinks with a William Fisher at the Heritage Motor Lodge." *Hattersley.* "You won't deny that, I suppose?"

"No." Bloody *Hattersley.*

"I may say that I've had such telephone calls before. I've chosen to ignore them. I work long hours, I'm frequently away on business, and I see no reason why my wife should be deprived of her social life. She has her own circle of friends, her operatic society activities and so on, and whom she chooses to have drinks with is entirely her business."

He paused, perhaps wondering, as I often had, why he had never had the simple wit to check up on Helen's almost nonexistent operatic society activities. He paused for so long that I thought it was expected of me to come in with some harmless-sounding interjection. With the name *Hattersley* ringing in my head, I did not select carefully enough. I said, "Quite," which I should not have done.

"Just keep your bloody mouth tightly shut, Fisher, until I've finished. I say I've never objected to my wife meeting her friends. I know that she's met you on several occasions, and I know in what particular bars and restaurants you've been seen. I took no steps to prevent it. I gave both of you the benefit of the doubt until last night."

A suspicion was dawning on me, driving *Hattersley* gradually out of my swirling thoughts. Hattersley can wait; this is more important. *Helen's husband had known all along.*

"Apparently last night there was some kind of scene between you. And in bloody public! Is that true or not?"

"I wouldn't say a scene, exactly. It's true that Helen was a little—"

"*What did you say?*" Suddenly it was vein-throbbing time again. He took a step toward me, his face jutting close to mine, and I could see that it was getting perilously close to I-ought-to-knock-you-down-Fisher time also.

What *had* I said, anyway, to provoke this reaction? I succumbed at last to the temptation to lick my lips, and he supplied the answer.

"Don't you *dare* use my wife's Christian name to me! Do you hear? *Do you hear me?*"

"All *right*—I *won't!*"

My initial fear had peeled away, but only to expose an onionlike structure of other layers of fear beneath it. What I was presently afraid of was that I would burst into a nervous snigger, as children sometimes do when harangued by teachers. Helen's husband, although unquestionably a heavy, was coming across as an absurd and even pathetic figure, one who belonged in comic opera rather than straight drama. But it was straight drama we were playing, and I had better

151

not forget it. I sank my teeth into my lower lip to discourage any inclination for it to quiver. Lightfoot, for his part, was doing some work on his cheek muscles with the object of regaining his elusive self-control.

"I say a scene in public, with my wife, in front of a witness. A police officer, if you please! Good God, man, do you know the reputation of the police in this town for gossip and scandalmongering? The way certain councillors' names have been blackened, for instance—all that comes from your police friends, perhaps you didn't know that! And then you stand there and look bloody astounded when I tell you this story about you and my wife's got round the whole of Shepford!"

Yes, he's known all along all right, but he's chosen not to know, like a Somerset Maugham remittance man whose bridge partners look at him in a certain way when he gets back to his hot-blooded wife after a month upcountry. And like the same character, he wouldn't face the truth until he thought he heard sniggers from the club veranda.

"I drove to the Heritage Motor Lodge at eight o'clock last night. My wife was no longer there, as you well know, but her car was. I waited in the car park until you brought her back there a little after eleven. I shan't dwell on the rest. I shan't ask where you took her, because I know where you took her. I know the whole sordid story. We were still discussing it at four o'clock this morning."

Poor Helen. And I was surprised to realize that this was the first time I had given any thought to Helen since entering this small and increasingly stifling room. We had discussed Helen, or rather he had, and I had ill-advisedly spoken her name; but all the time I had been thinking of her not as Helen, but as this man's wife, and I had been thinking of him not as Helen's husband, but as *a* husband, an aggrieved husband, the cuckolded husband of any wife with whom I might have chanced to have been shacked up at some point.

Looking at him now as the substance of the shadowy figure who gratified Helen's self-confessed appetite, I was conscious that as the layers of fear had continued to peel away, a small core of relief had been revealed. I could identify it now: it was relief that Helen's husband was the man he had turned out to be. He had known about us all along but had done nothing until the fear of public ridicule forced him to take action. If I was the amateur psychologist I thought I was, this would indicate that while not rat-faced and ineffectual, as hoped for, he was almost certainly impotent or near impotent, as also hoped for. That seemed to fit together nicely enough, although there was one piece of the jigsaw unaccountably left over: what did Helen do with that appetite of hers?

Lightfoot (as I could not imagine myself calling him, for all that he called me Fisher) seemed to have reached the end of the narrative portion of our interview. The vein in his forehead had been brought into play again, and he had begun a process of looking me up and down as if I were a crossbred dog he was thinking of buying or having put down, or a headmaster wondering how to cure me of nose picking.

"God, you're a swine, Fisher, aren't you?" he now said, or more accurately spat. I felt the nervous snigger fighting for survival behind my clenched teeth, and I clenched them more tightly so that my mouth tingled.

"Aren't you?"

I didn't know what to say to that, and a reply was plainly expected. I could not bring myself to mumble "Yes," and I could not think of any suitable form of words, of the type I would normally use, that would be acceptable. What I very much wanted to do, and what I had to restrain myself from

153

doing, was to copy Lightfoot's own speech patterns, as I always did with stronger personalities than myself. But that would have meant saying something in the order of, "Now look here, Lightfoot, we're both men of the world," and he would have hit me in the mouth.

I struggled for expression and finally came up with: "I'm certainly not proud of myself, if that's what you mean." I felt ashamed of myself for saying it and was uneasily aware that I had got pretty close to the sham/shit self-exposure point, but I knew that he would not settle for much less.

The groveling admission, or what he accepted at face value as a groveling admission, seemed to please him, yet it did not seem to mollify him, for he now went on to pose an even more difficult question: "Do I have your word that you will not see my wife again or attempt to communicate with her in any way?"

Here again I was in difficulties. The only safe formula was: "You have my word." But it was impossible. I tried to speak, but my tongue felt swollen.

I would have to get around it somehow, as I always got around saying "Pouilly Fuissé" when ordering wine.

A muttered "I shouldn't worry about that, it's all over anyway" was the best I could do, and it was not good enough.

"What the hell do you mean, it's all over?"

"It's all over. It's finished. Look—" I could just about spit the phrase out if I put a coarse "Look" in front of it. "Look, you have my word that we won't be seeing each other again. All right?"

"Never mind that for the present. It's your use of the word 'all' that I'm querying. *All* over, you say. *All.* You make it sound as if it's been going on for bloody months!"

Quintruple Christ. How long does he want it to have been going on for, then? Weeks? Days? Helen, why didn't you ring me this morning with my side of the story? Or perhaps you did, and I was sitting watching my mother eating pizza and grizzling on about matters of no importance whatsoever.

"Well? How long *has* it been going on?"

The same heaven-sent inspiration that had given me "dog show" came to my rescue, and I heard myself saying in curt, clipped tones not unlike my inquisitor's, "I imagine your wife's already informed you on that point." *Now* who's calling her a liar? Neat.

He took the point, although not in the way I had expected. I was now interested to see that as well as being a master of the vein-throbbing trick, he could also curl his lip.

"You know, of course," he said—not said: sneered—"that you're by no means the first one, don't you?"

I felt a vein throbbing in my forehead. The words "That's a caddish thing to say about any woman" were actually forming on my lips. I swallowed them hastily, but I could feel my knuckles whitening.

"I don't think that's any business of mine, Lightfoot," I said stiffly.

"No, I don't suppose you do. Get what you can while it's going, that's your motto! But don't delude yourself that you've been enjoying exclusive rights. You're the fourth one in three years, to *my* knowledge."

You bloody fool, Lightfoot, *they were all me!* All your anonymous phone calls were about *me!*

In that case, they can't all have been from Hattersley, who appears to have mentioned me by name. Very well: they were from other people, who didn't mention me by name.

I can't help appetite.

At any rate, she has not been having appetites with Hattersley. You don't knock somebody off, then shop her to her husband, even if you're a convoluted sod like Hattersley.

155

There's only us.

I'm sorry, Helen; I ought to have knocked your husband down, hadn't I?

I experienced a tremor of hope as Lightfoot consulted his watch. Was he timing this, then? Was he fitting me in between appointments? Was it nearly over?

Evidently he still had a few moments in hand, for after wrinkling his brow as if consulting mental notes for anything left unsaid, he asked abruptly, "You have a wife, don't you?"

"I do."

"Fine thing if your wife gets to hear about this." Good. He's not going to tell her. He's not going to do anything, in fact. The incident is almost closed.

"Let's hope she doesn't," I said. The last onion-skin layers of fear had fallen away. I examined my emotional condition, warily, and discovered that I had pulled through to a state of cautious elation. It was nearly over. Today would pass, and tomorrow would come, and the day after, and in a few days this real thing happening, this consequence of an action, would no longer be raw in my mind. It would take its place in my memory bank as an experience I once had, an anecdote to tell myself, with all my present embarrassment skillfully edited out. The day would even come when thinking about it would make me feel cocky. It's not every man who has such a tale to tell.

The recurling of Lightfoot's lip informed me that I had been premature in my diagnosis, or rather in the symptoms of lightheartedness that the diagnosis had explored. He seemed to have taken exception to my last remark.

"It'll be no thanks to you if your wife *doesn't* hear about it," he said puzzlingly. Yes, it will: I shan't tell her. "No thanks to your behavior, I should say. You should be damn well ashamed of yourself."

I am. I'm ashamed of having said, "I'm certainly not proud

156

of myself, if that's what you mean," and I'll try to forget that I ever said it.

"Shouldn't you?"

No, I'm not going to repeat it.

"Aren't you going to say *anything*, man?"

"What do you want me to say?" That was easy enough.

"Aren't you going to apologize? Aren't you man enough to say you're sorry?"

I wished I could tell him. I wished I could say, Captain Lightfoot—for I had begun to think of him as Captain Lightfoot, even though it was improbable that he had ever been more than a conscript second lieutenant—Look, Captain Lightfoot, where I come from there are certain words and expressions that we have difficulty in using. "Love," "Loving," "taking things," "communicate," and "happy" are examples of these. Another is "sorry." We may use it in the casual form, when we bump into people in the street, for example, and as an expression of sympathy, when we say, "Oh, I *am* sorry," to someone who has been bereaved; but we have great difficulty in pronouncing the word in its formal, apologetic sense, especially to strangers. We do not say, "I love you," we do not kiss our mothers, and we do not apologize. I'm very sorry.

But I would have to get something said, and I was thinking up ways of saying it when Lightfoot, uttering an expression of contempt that might well have been *Tchah!,* flung open the door, turned back to face me, and in full view of the beefy girl in the jeans and sweaters, who was now brushing a dog, very unexpectedly spat in my face.

Chapter Twelve

Helen and I were in bed together, or lying across a bed together, and she was doing things with her tongue that I had not previously known she could do, but we were not very much afraid.

We had taken fantastically elaborate precautions. Both of us had independent, cast-iron, watertight, private-investigator-proof, later-checking-up-by-husband-or-wife-proof, legitimate, infallible excuses for being in London.

She had not been working for six months now, and at last she had got herself another job. This, so I was informed now that her husband had entered the realm of our common speech, was approved of; he thought another spell in employment would keep her out of mischief.

It was an interesting post, not that it interested me much beyond the scope it gave us for meeting again. The suburb-village or village-suburb of Mayfield where she lived, and where Jeanette was still pressing me to lay down roots, had been steadily expanding to embrace a suburb-village-suburb or village-suburb-suburb of brick bungalows deployed on carved-up, hard-earth, chicken-wire-separated segments of unadopted half-moon crescents following the natural curvature of the earth, or moon. Helen would be a kind of hostess-receptionist, directing the technicians, junior executives, and dental mechanics whom Shepford was trying to lure into its concrete web toward the place where they might vainly try to train roses while reflecting on the error they had made in moving from their university towns or pleasant industrial valleys.

But everything in Shepford that did not belong to Jack Dance and his Creative City Consortium was a branch or subsidiary or offshoot of some company or consortium in London; and the headquarters of Mayfield Properties was in London; and it was there that Helen had to go, and went, cutting two hours off our golden-June-into-glorious-July extension, for the interview that would confirm her appointment. A further two hours would be lopped off this evening, when she had arranged to visit her brother in St. John's Wood. But that gave her a valid reason for staying in London all day. Cast-iron. Watertight.

As for myself, I had put it about that I was in Birmingham. It was, if anybody cared to check, all down in black and white in the minutes of the last Festival Committee meeting:

> Mr. Fisher was asked what progress had been made in regard to the possibilities of coverage of the Festival by the *Nationwide* television program. Mr. Fisher reported that he had made preliminary contact with a Mr. Hellicar of *Nationwide,* who was most anxious for discussions to take place. Since Mr. Hellicar would be in Birmingham on the seventeenth in connection with the BBC training scheme, it was agreed that sooner than incur unnecessary expense by traveling to London, Mr. Fisher should arrange a meeting in Birmingham on that date.

Not only had I put it about that I was in Birmingham, but I had been observed departing for Birmingham and had actually set foot in Birmingham. The rendezvous with Helen coincided with my mother's final departure from Shepford to take up residence with Uncle Herbert. I had persuaded

159

her that rather than see her off on the West Riding express from Kings Cross, which would have meant us traveling up to London in the same buffet car as Helen, it would suit my busy schedule better if I drove her to Birmingham where she could catch a not-much-slower train, changing at Leeds. There had been a painfully tear-sodden farewell scene with Jeanette, and my mother had shaken hands with sundry rat-faced neighbors, all of whom had been informed that I was now driving her to Birmingham; I had dumped her at New Street Station and then belted down the M. 1, to establish myself in a large, modern, anonymous hotel in the Euston Road under the pseudonym of Midgeley.

It was the first time Helen and I had seen each other since her husband had spat in my face three weeks ago, although there had been three telephone calls of varying degrees of guardedness.

The first was immediately after the pet-shop confrontation when, in a fairly traumatic condition, I returned to the office to hear from Sheilagh that the switchboard appeared to be going mad, since the telephone kept ringing every ten minutes and when she answered it there was nobody there.

It rang again as I took my coat off. Hattersley, I was glad to hear, had gone across to the town planning office and would not be back today. I would have had to sit opposite him, seething, the bile rising in my throat as I gathered courage to have it out with him, the chill settling on my stomach as I came to terms with my own cowardice.

"There it is again, you see," said Sheilagh, hanging up. "Phone rings—I answer—*click*. Don't suppose by any remote chance it's that friend of yours, is it?"

"I haven't got any friends, Sheilagh," I said haggardly. I saw her exchange an amused pout with Patsy and regretted making such a pretentious remark.

I contrived to spend some time at Sheilagh's desk, ostensibly correcting the notes she had been typing up and probably giving her the impression that I was mesmerized by her nipples producing intriguing indentations in a very marketable new cotton sweater. When the telephone rang again, I picked it up, happening to be near at hand.

"Yes? Information and Publicity?"

"Bill!"

"Oh, good afternoon, Dr. Hagerty! I was hoping you'd ring."

"Did he find you?"

"Yes indeed. We had a most interesting discussion."

"I'm dreadfully, dreadfully sorry I couldn't warn you. He locked me in the bedroom and took the living-room phone off the hook. I couldn't get out until the cleaning lady came."

Poor Helen.

"I can quite understand that, Dr. Hagerty. Perhaps we ought to meet again and talk about it further."

"We can't meet yet, darling." Pang. She only ever called me darling in bed. "We've got to be so, so careful. Can't you arrange to be in the office alone some time, so I can ring you privately?"

"Nine o'clock tomorrow morning. Yes, Dr. Hagerty, that would suit me perfectly."

"He doesn't leave the house till nine. Make it a quarter past. And Bill, I love you desperately, and I want you desperately."

"I look forward to that, Dr. Hagerty. Many thanks. Goodbye, Dr. Hagerty."

It was the first time I had ever heard Helen sound hysterical when sober, as she presumably was at that hour. It suited her, and I fancied her strongly. As I put down the receiver my eyes lingered on her surrogate breasts, straining provocatively against Sheilagh's acceptable cotton sweater.

I got to the office at a quarter to nine the next morning and

161

swiveled restlessly in my chair until the telephone rang at twenty-one minutes past. That left us only nine minutes before Patsy and Sheilagh arrived for work. We invested the time in a hurried examination of possible meeting places, discarding all of them as too hazardous and finally settling for London on the seventeenth, when Helen, as she had just learned, would be up for her interview. It meant waiting three weeks, but we agreed that it would be a useful Caesar's wife period, during which Helen could lead an ostentatiously pure life of hen parties and operatic society meetings, thus not only calming her husband's suspicions that she might still be seeing me, but also clocking up credit for future assignations when the heat was off. We also agreed that there had better be no more of these early-morning telephone calls, in case the switchboard girls became intrigued by my revised office hours and began listening in.

But there was one more call. It came one evening when I was working late, frantically correcting the final proofs of *Pageantry with Progress* (new edition) which was supposed to have been in the printers' hands at the end of the previous month. Sheilagh had suffered a fresh outbreak of "Phone rings—I answer—*click*" trouble during the day, and I trusted on telepathy to tell Helen that it would be worth her while ringing after the girls had gone home.

The message finally seeped through to her at six thirty. I snatched up the receiver almost before the bell had started to ring and tried to cradle it on my shoulder. Retrieving the instrument from the wastepaper basket I heard Helen's voice crying, "Hello? Hello? *Is* that extension three nine seven?"

"Helen! Hey—did you know we're telepathic? I've been sitting here, willing you to ring!" No harm in fostering a bit of mystique.

"Oh, *there* you are. May I speak to Mrs. Chalmers, please?"

It's all right, Helen, you don't have to speak in code. The switchboard girls have knocked off and we're on a direct line.

"We can talk, love. Everyone's gone home."

"Oh, it *is* you, Maggie! Darling, I didn't recognize your voice! I'm so glad I caught you and I've got lots of news, but I can't talk now because Geoffrey's just walked in and he wants his dinner. Don't you, Geoffrey?"

Sextuple Christ! Not only is she ringing from home, but her husband is in the same bloody room!

You're getting a tremendous kick out of this, aren't you, Helen? I hope you are, because I certainly aren't. And for God's sake watch what you're saying because you sound half pissed to me.

"And what if he picks up the extension?" With the receiver close to my mouth, I whispered the words at obscene-telephone-call level. "Look, Helen, I'm going to ring off."

"Yes, well, I shan't keep you a minute, darling. I just *had* to let you know that I've got you those plants."

Plants? Plants?

She's getting a kick out of calling me "darling" too. And isn't she overdoing the gushing a little? I wondered irrelevantly if Helen always talked to her women friends like that.

"What plants?"

"*You* remember, darling. Those sweet little red things we saw growing near the golf course and then you saw them again in Councillor Drummond's window box and you said you *had* to have them."

Councillor Drummond's golf clubs. Septuple Christ, I had forgotten all about them. Helen had worked out a scheme for purloining them, insisting on carrying it out alone. It was, she had assured me, child's play: all she had to do was loiter on the stairs during Drummond's lunch hour, wait until his secretary came out to the ladies' on the landing, walk into his office, scoop up golf clubs, and make her retreat down the back stairway that led to the mews where her car would be waiting.

But I had thought the plan had been abandoned in the

163

light of our recent troubles. In any case, I was no longer sure that golf clubs were the priority they had once been. Detective Constable Carpenter had stopped pestering me lately, and I had every hope that he had given me up as a bad job.

"Yes, all right, Helen, I'm with you."

"Well, it turns out that they're a very rare type of peony, darling, but I've *got* them. Aren't I clever? Now I must ring off because Geoffrey's pacing the room. What do you want me to do with them?"

Why not stick them up his—

"Can you hang onto them?"

"Yes, of *course* I can, darling! They'll be quite safe with me. And we'll meet up very soon. Bye-bye, darling, and lots of kisses."

Osculatory sounds reached my ear as she put down the telephone. That had been four days ago. And now here we were, in our afternoon hotel, and I was experiencing osculatory sensations of a type new to me.

Little had been said in the first ninety minutes, although many sounds had been made, and a conversation had been held, full of inner meanings and subtleties, as if we had newly discovered and then quickly mastered a sign language so intricate and comprehensive that it superseded the spoken word.

We lay back exhausted, too exhausted even to reach for a cigarette, and after a long while tried to resume our dialogue, but were too exhausted, and Helen, at last, reverted to standard English.

"Do you want an inquest, Bill?"

"No."

If she meant an I-was-there account of the night her husband waited for her in the Heritage Motor Lodge car park: no. I had closed that book.

164

"Thank God. I've been enduring inquests for the last three weeks."

Poor Helen. But don't tell me about it.

I groped for my cigarettes and succeeded only in brushing the packet to the floor. Lacking the initiative for further movement, I let my arm hang limply over the side of the bed and closed my eyes.

"Who do you think told him, Helen?"

"I've thought about it and stopped thinking about it. I don't *want* to think about it."

"It was Hattersley."

"It can't have been. He wouldn't do anything like that."

I opened my eyes again and wanted to look into Helen's face to see what expression was accompanying this interesting remark. But I didn't. Don't, Fisher, no inquests, she's had enough. And her face will reveal nothing, except love, which is a very effective mask.

"Did he give you a rotten time, Bill?" Her husband, she meant. She was changing the subject.

"Not particularly."

"I don't know what he said to you, and I don't think I want to know, but did he tell you I was promiscuous?" She was not changing the subject after all. Thank you, Helen.

"He said I was the fourth in three years, to his knowledge."

"Did you believe him?"

"No."

"I'm glad."

We reached out simultaneously and clasped hands across the bed. It was a good moment, and I was sorry to destroy it.

"That operatic society of yours. Sometimes you told *him* you were going to it, and sometimes you told *me* you were going to it."

"Well?"

"Well what?"

165

"You mean, well, was I lying to him, but not lying to you? Yes. I *had* to go there sometimes just to have been seen there in case he ever checked up, and whenever I did go, I always got him to pick me up afterwards so he'd know I'd been there. So that on the other nights, when I was out with you, he wouldn't start worrying himself about where I was."

You must be a very proficient liar, Helen. I bet you could give me lessons. But are you proficiently lying now?

"And Hattersley?" I said.

"I don't know Hattersley."

"You said he couldn't have made that anonymous phone call. 'He wouldn't do anything like that.' How do you know he wouldn't, if you don't know Hattersley?"

"Oh, *Bill!*" She rolled toward me and raised herself up slightly, putting both hands on my shoulders and looking into my face. "I mean I didn't *think* he'd do anything like that, you goose! Someone you work with, someone you've known for years, someone who's got to sit opposite you the next morning and pretend it wasn't him. Impossible."

Convincing. I smiled at her and said wryly, "You don't know Hattersley."

"No, I *don't* know Hattersley, but before we drop the subject—yes, Geoff *does* think I've had four affairs in three years. However careful I was, he was bound to be suspicious sometimes, and on four occasions I made some silly mistake, told him I'd been where he knew I hadn't been, or whatever, and he knew I was having an affair. But Bill, he thinks they were four separate affairs, and they weren't—they were all with *you!*"

My own interpretation exactly, Helen. And I should have knocked your husband down.

"And if I didn't say anything to you about all this," she went on, answering a question I hadn't asked, "it was because I didn't want you to worry and perhaps stop seeing me, for fear of—well, for fear of what finally happened three weeks ago. And I *let* him go on thinking there'd been four different men because if he'd ever found out there was only one, he would have known it was serious and done something drastic about it." That was the other unanswered question on the rota.

"And is it *still* serious, after all that's happened?" This one was not on her list. She knew it didn't have to be asked. But I didn't bargain for her answer, which I expected to be as rhetorical as the question.

She looked at me very steadily, cupping my face in her hands. "It was a game when it started, Bill, and I sometimes behave as if it's still a game, but it hasn't been one for a very long time. I love you, and I want to live with you. I want to be divorced from Geoff and married to you."

I waited to hear myself say *octuple Christ* and it didn't happen. Very well: then if I was not alarmed there must be some other sensation present—euphoria, perhaps. Helen and I often shared a euphoric five minutes, when we would make impossible, practical, daft, detailed plans to go on holiday together or permanently rent a secret pied-à-terre under an assumed name. We enjoyed those moments, and I could have done with one now, but euphoria had not happened either. All I could feel was a pleasant numbness, as if I had been lying for a long time under something like a very heavy mattress which had now been removed. But my mind was not affected, and it seemed to be functioning with surprising clarity.

Although I had thought often about leaving Jeanette—or more desirably, about Jeanette leaving me, as half promised by my mother at our Pizza Parlor tête-à-tête—I had never got very much further than the suitcase-packing stage in my planning. Euphoria gave me either a visa to the United States (if I was not fancying Helen) or (when I was) a book-lined suite of rooms in the turret of a nonexistent block of Victori-an-Gothic mansion flats overlooking the cafés and brasseries of the Cornmarket, and there Helen would visit me when she was able; but when euphoria wore off, I was left with a bed-sit over a fruit shop in a condemned terrace, all I could afford if I still had to support Jeanette—but at least Helen would still visit me, and after the golden June had become glorious July, and July August, and August September, she might one eve-ning put on a butcher's apron over nothing else and fix scrambled eggs, before September became October.

"Boy! Does Helen know how to scramble an egg!" Oscar wanted to say, but I wouldn't let him. He had no part in this.

I had never considered being married to Helen, except in the euphoric moments. If the thought ever came into my head at other times, I pushed it out quickly, drawing away in-stinctively from the sticky preliminaries: the private inves-tigagors and the solicitors' letters, *Fisher* v. *Fisher*, and the di-vorce judge's disapproving comments, and Jeanette very possibly breaking down in the witness box, and above all, "I ought to knock you down, Fisher." That would be the worst moment—and yet that moment had already been and gone. We were *past* that moment.

It was possible to marry Helen. Such arrangements were being made all the time, by people far more mature than I, who presumably knew what they were doing. We would have to move out of Shepford: that was possible and even desir-able, and that too was being done all the time. I would need a job, wherever we went. Washer-up—anything. No, not wash-er-up, anything: I was being practical now. I had fifteen years' experience in local government; I would see what was being advertised in the *Municipal Journal*. So we would go to Birmingham, or Leeds, or Swindon, but not Stradhoughton, and Helen would work too and supplement my income; but I would have to support Jeanette at her present spin-drier level, out of guilt, so we would live in a bed-sit over a fruit shop, on supermarket plonk and pasta, but our marvelous October would become November. And people, adults, did all these things and changed their lives in this way, and so would we.

"I shouldn't have said that, should I?" Helen had misinterpreted my silence.

Her face was resting on mine by now, her body resting on my body. I began to stroke her hair, but it reminded me of the way I had stroked Jeanette's hair (*Brief Encounter, Lassie Come Home*) when I couldn't tell her why I couldn't tell her things. So I stroked Helen's face, instead.

"We'd have to move out of Shepford," I said at last.

"Promises, promises." It was a more lighthearted response than I'd expected. I felt euphoria tingling through her. I rocked her in my arms and started to speak, then stopped myself, and started again, and stopped, and then spoke.

"Helen. I'm going to leave Jeanette."

"Don't tell me that, Bill. Don't tell me what you mean to do. Don't tell me anything, until it's done. But whatever you do or don't do, I can cope."

"Can you?"

"I always have. I always will. I can cope with anything except losing you."

It seemed like twelve hours later, although it was only half an hour or so, that I was pulling on my underpants by the net-curtained window. Helen was still lying on the bed, looking cherished, and half asleep from contentment, not from tiredness, for it had been a very gentle half hour. Across the Euston Road I saw the late sun reflecting on the western curve of the glass roof of King's Cross Station. "I was going to live here once," I said, for no particular reason: only that I had been reminded that I was going to live here once.

"Mm?"

"When I was about eighteen. I was going to live in London. With a girl."

"Oh, *were* you?" Not half asleep after all.

"It seems light-years ago."

"Were you in love with her?"

"I thought I was, but I couldn't have been."

"Why not?"

"Because we never got here, did we? She did, but I didn't."

"That's a non sequitur, Bill."

Chapter Thirteen

I was taking a vicious delight in sending Hattersley on petty errands. Festival week was drawing near. The inspiration that had given me "dog show" had provided me with several other ideas and gimmicks, and these had won the approval of the linen-suited Jack Dance, with which was automatically bracketed the approval of Councillor Drummond and his sidekick Councillor Hopkinson, and so I had been given responsibilities. One of them was to plan the route for the procession of bands, scout troops, old comrades' associations and assorted rat-faced legions that would converge on the Cornmarket in the last throes of the festivities. Routine tasks such as traipsing round the shops with posters could joyfully be unloaded onto Hattersley. Serve the bugger right.

Sheilagh and Patsy were munching apples at their desks, and I was eating sandwiches and poring over the planning office's latest amended amendments to the one-way traffic scheme, and I was fairly well content. My affair with Helen had not become the scandal of the town, as projected by her husband; I got the odd knowing look from time to time, but then I had become used to getting knowing looks during my time in Shepford. Helen's new job had given her mobility, and so we had begun a pattern of weekly meetings near an old windmill by the county border, later to be stepped up to twice a week if there were any unforeseen snags about leaving Jeanette. Jeanette was behaving well; since my mother's departure for Stradhoughton she had been surprisingly cheerful, imagining, perhaps, that we were in for a new regime. I had been far less tense than anticipated in our newfound privacy. Knowing that I had at last made up my mind to go had relaxed me; I felt quite affectionate toward her, as I might have done to Mr. Pussy-paws had there ever been such a cat. (Last night we had even played Scrabble and then made what passed for love, back in the squeaking bed again.) I had rehearsed my abdication speech many times, and now I had but to deliver it and face her sensible tears.

"Oscar? Oscar? We were *happy,* Oscar. You, and me, and Momma Winklebaum, and—and *Bill.* And then—pow. Like a sock in the *jar!*"

Studio silence.

Small voice: "He'll come back, Oscar? Won't he?"

"Honey, I—Jeanette. Honey? Were you ever smashed out of your mind?"

"I don't think so, Oscar."

"Can a real friend introduce you to a noo experience?"

There were recognizable sounds of commotion somewhere out in the clinical corridors of the Civic Center, and soon the glass door of the office was flung open and in staggered, or half tumbled, Ron Casey of the *Evening Mail,* his crime-beat colleague Jack Wilmott, and Pisspot. Ron Casey was half pissed, Wilmott was three-quarters pissed, and anyone who didn't know Pisspot would have said that he was entirely pissed, but I could tell that only slimline-low calorie-Indian-*tonic* water had passed his lips. He clutched a walking stick, although he seemed to have little need of it except for brandishing purposes, and under his arm was carrying—or thought he was, though in fact it was by now lodged precariously under his elbow, and in danger of falling to the ground—a familiar green file.

172

"Pisspot!"

"Arsehole!"

"*Mister* Rainbell!" Patsy and Sheilagh combined their gleefully shocked welcome with a rattling of the tea-money tin in my face. I happily shelled out my fivepenny fine, while Pisspot fished into various pockets and eventually dug out what looked like his entire wealth in coins, which he flung in the general direction of Patsy's tin.

A sustained hollering of "Tea! Tea! Tea! Tea!" sent the girls scurrying off with their in-tray of mugs and milk cartons, and after a report on Pisspot's health—the burden of which was that he had never felt better and that the Karl Marx Hospital (as he chose to call it) should be renamed the Karl Marx Health Farm—flung out an arm to call my attention to the condition of Ron Casey, who had flopped in Patsy's chair, and Jack Wilmott, who was lying on Hattersley's desk.

"You will observe that our confreres have been celebrating. I, of course, restricted myself to carbonated aitch-two-oh."

"Reggie, why didn't you let me know you were out and about? I would have come and had one with you"

"I am not out and about, my dear Arsehole, I am passing through. I suffer from convenient bouts of dizziness which seem to attack me whenever I think of the Shepford Festival. In fact, when I see all that bumph on your desk, I believe I can feel one coming on now."

"In other words, you're going to skulk at home till the Festival's over. I don't blame you. So what was the celebration in aid of?"

"We were drinking the health of our new director of finance. In his absence, needless to say."

"I didn't know we *had* a new director of finance."

"You know now," said Ron Casey. "Three guesses."

The present rat-faced director of finance's rat-faced deputy, I supposed, but I couldn't remember his name.

"No—I give up."

"The incorrect answer!" boomed Pisspot. "Your three choices should have been James Purchase, James Purchase, and James Purchase."

"Purchase!"

I looked suitably mind-boggled, as indeed I was. Purchase! Worth a quadruple Christ at least.

Then, even as I mused bewilderedly on Purchase's general inability to run even a rats' Christmas club, a fresh wave of incredulity washed over me.

"But I always thought—"

"You always thought, my dear Arsehole, that he was plotting and scheming for my own exalted position. As indeed he was. But if you are offered a plum, the gooseberry loses its flavor."

"Yes, but even so, Reggie. The phantom nose shaver of Shredded Wheat Towers?" Don't imitate Pisspot, Fisher. He doesn't intimidate you, he's on your side.

A polysyllabic groan floated up from Hattersley's desk, which the crime reporter Jack Wilmott had transformed into a fair replica of a mortician's slab: *"Drummerswungerfurrer."*

"Drummond swung it for him," translated Ron Casey.

"Upon which subject," roared Pisspot, flinging down on my desk the green swindle-sheet file which he had several times dropped and several times picked up and which I had been hoping he might be getting around to mentioning, "compliments of the management."

"Thank God for that. Did you get these back from Purchase?"

"Let us say they were rescued from Master Purchase's pending tray. Your lying swindle sheets have ceased to pend."

I flipped through the file. *To hospitality at the Heritage Motor Lodge for Mr. Oscar Seltzer of Time-Life, Inc.* . . All present and correct.

No, not quite all present and correct.

"Do you notice anything, Arsehole?"

"Yes. *Your* dockets are all here, and *my* dockets are all here, and Hattersley's are, but—" I looked up at Pisspot with a diplomatic swiveling of the eyes, meant to take in Ron Casey and the comatose Jack Wilmott.

"We are among friends, my boy! Why do you think the cream of the *Evening Mail* is here? What you observe, and what Mr. Wilmott there would love to print but alas would not be allowed to by the craven *bar*stard who calls himself an editor, is that Master Bulldog Drummond's swindle sheets are missing."

It was true. Drummond, as chairman of about seven thousand council committees, all of which seemed to be forever welcoming visiting industrialists and other freeloaders, had long ago established a precedent for extracting part of his entertainment allowance from our department. Diversification, Pisspot had once laconically called it, while initialling Drummond's docket. But now his swindle sheets were missing.

"I believe," continued Pisspot, "that the trick was invented by the editors of the *Great Soviet Encyclopedia.* Read Master Orwell."

Patsy and Sheilagh, pink from steam and the pleasure of seeing Pisspot again, returned to distribute mugs of tea. It was curious, I reflected as Sheilagh stretched forward over my desk to stir in the required three lumps, that I fancied neither of them, even as stand-ins for Helen, when Pisspot was present. He seemed to reduce them, or perhaps elevate them, to the status of daughters.

He cut short their twitterings about who else took sugar

and who didn't with a roar of "Ladies! We thank you for your hospitality. Your luncheon awaits!"

"We've had lunch already, Mr. Rainbell." Patsy giggled. He reduced them to giggling too.

"Then have a second lunch! Have a third lunch!" And with a thwack of his walking stick at Sheilagh's bottom, at which she took no offense at all but merely uttered a schoolgirl shriek, he dismissed them.

"What I can't work out," I said, feeling like the character in the detective play who says, "But there's one thing I don't understand, inspector," "is how the odd twenty quid on Drummond's swindle sheet makes Purchase director of finance."

"You don't think that's all there is to it, do you?" said Ron Casey, with a rather pitying worldly sneer that I didn't much go for. "He's been covering up for Drummond for years, hasn't he?"

"Has he? How?"

"You're aware, my dear young innocent Arsehole, that Drummond is about as straight as the proverbial corkscrew?"

"So I've always heard, but has anybody ever proved it?"

"We live in hopes. We live in hopes."

"*Sollertahnaw!*" This street cry came from the otherwise senseless form of the *Evening Mail's* crime reporter. The mug of tea which Patsy had thoughtfully placed by his limp right hand had been twitched over and was dribbling over some quite important files.

"What?"

Ron Casey translated again. "He's sold the Town Hall."

"He's done *what?*"

With a monumental effort, as if he were about to make a dying confession, Jack Wilmott raised himself up on one elbow. He spoke with exaggerated clarity.

"He has *sold* the *fuck*ing Town *Hall*."

Christ and the square root of Christ! And I felt resentfully innocent among these people—my dear young innocent

176

Arsehole, Pisspot had called me, and I deserved the epithet. Ron Casey, who was six years my junior and who had begun to look even younger as my gullibility was exposed, knew things I didn't know. Jack Wilmott, who had never been known to stand upright after three in the afternoon, knew things I didn't know. Pisspot, dear old bumbling myopic Pisspot, who you would have thought never looked much more beyond his nose than the *Guardian* crossword, knew things I didn't know.

"How do you mean, he's sold the Town Hall? How can anyone sell the Town Hall?"

Wilmott, having got this far on his road to recovery, forklifted himself up to a half-sitting position. Unaware of spilled tea seeping into his trousers, he pronounced in the same spelling-it-out-to-idiots manner: "He *sold* the fucker to Jack fucking *Dance,,* didn't he? Who else would you sell a fucking town hall to?"

"The conference center of the future, Arsehole! The Tower of Babylon rising on the ashes of Hatter's Castle!"

"But how can he? It's not his to sell!"

I detected pitying glances between Jack Wilmott and Ron Casey. They went Pisspot's way, too, but he did not respond, and I felt grateful.

"My dear Arsehole, if in this life you sell only what is yours to sell, you will never dine at the Ritz. We are not speaking of contracts exchanged between solicitors. We are talking about what I believe is technically known as *backhanders.*"

Yes, of course we are. Stupid of me not to have realized. And Ron Casey now looked about nineteen.

I tried to cover my confusion by mimicking Pisspot, which I did clumsily.

"Yes, I'm aware of that, my dear Reggie, but you'll agree that the Town Hall is hardly in the same class as a corner sweetshop. There is such a thing as a Preservation Order."

"You can't have a Preservation Order on a dangerous

structure," said Ron Casey, aged seventeen, and still my senior.

"Who says it's a dangerous structure?"

"Jack Dance does."

"Or rather, " came in Pisspot, "Mr. Dance's knowledgeable and independent advisers, who have delivered their report to the District Council, copies to the Department of Environment, and are now refreshing themselves in Bermuda. At Mr. Dance's expense, I need hardly add."

No, you hardly need.

"And Purchase comes into all this, does he?"

"That's what we're working on, sonny boy," said Wilmott. I remembered the last time I had been called sonny boy, in the back room of a pet shop in an unfinished arcade that looked like a boiler room, and felt myself flushing. But Wilmott, I told myself in self-defense, only spoke like that because he was a heavy and not a juvenile lead, for all that he was drenched in tea and didn't even know it.

Getting the image of Helen's husband out of my head meant putting another image into it, and the one that arrived was of Hattersley and Detective Constable Carpenter, poring over some papers in the Polo Lounge of the Heritage Motor Lodge. I said to Wilmott, "Do you happen to know a plain-clothes man called Carpenter? Detective constable?"

"Carpenter. Carpenter. Oh, *Carpenter*. *Cunt*," observed Wilmott, and as if exhausted by his three-minute excursion into coherent English, collapsed across Hattersley's desk again, his final utterance being, "Noyeytoyla."

"Noddy in Toyland," explained Ron Casey. "He means PC Plod. Carpenter. He's a joke, isn't he?"

Yes, he is, you bloody boy scout, and that was my diagnosis the first time I ever met him, so don't look at me as if you were my sodding patrol leader.

I addressed myself carefully and exclusively to Pisspot.

178

"Reggie, what I'm trying to get at is if any of all this has anything to do with him, joke though he may be. Because you know he was sniffing around here while you were in hospital and Hattersley showed him some documents?"

"I don't wish to speak ill of a colleague, my dear Arsehole, but Hattersley is a — No: I contain myself. I do not speak the word. We are in Shredded Wheat Towers; we are not privileged. The expression 'cunt,' so freely flung about by our somnambulant friend, has not been used."

I glowed. I hoped that Ron Casey would transmit Pisspot's testimonial to all his shepherd's-pie-scoffing colleagues, and that all his colleagues would spread it throughout Shepford, and that it would eventually get back to Hattersley's burning ears.

"Detective Constable Carpenter is, however, a female organ par excellence. I know the man. I know him well. He once attempted to arrest me for disorderly conduct. I told him that if my conduct was disorderly, his was bloody outrageous, and we left the matter at that."

Yes, very amusing, Pisspot, and I'd like the full story one day when I have three days to spare, but what's between him and Hattersley?

"Our flat-footed friend's misfortune is that he is permanently behind the times. Long after it had become common knowledge, he made the blazingly obvious discovery that *Pilgrim's Progress* over there"—(his name for *Pageantry with Progress* (new edition), advance copies of which had just been delivered—"was being printed by Bulldog Drummond's brother-in-law. Having relatives of his own in the print, he already knew of the connection between Drummond and brother-in-law, but not of the connection between brother-in-law and *Pilgrim's Progress*. I believe the revelation came to him in a blinding flash in this very office."

Yes. And that was why Detective Constable Carpenter was

so keen to get me out for a drink. *"I somehow had the impression you and Councillor Drummond more or less lived in each other's pockets."*

"Going on to put five and five together to make eight, Detective Constable Carpenter then suspected a slight case of hanky-panky, of course knowing nothing of the very large case of hanky-panky already being investigated by his superiors. Friend Hattersley, as one female organ to another, assisted him in his ludicrous investigations by digging out the printing contract, a Xerox of which I happen to know has been in senior police hands for the last six months. since I gave it to them myself. . . ."

All this swirled in and out of and back in and around my mind, as I tried to pinpoint my reactions to Pisspot's story. Delight: I was delighted that Detective Constable Carpenter had been confirmed, by a higher authority than mine, as a female organ. Satisfaction: I was well-satisfied that Hattersley had been taken in by a female organ, had been defined as a female organ himself by the same higher authority, and was thus relegated from heavy to juvenile lead. But anger: I was angry that all these machinations had gone on above my head, had gone on somewhere outside the realm of all the busy thoughts I had to think each day; that I hadn't been considered worthy of, or fit for, or adult enough to hear about, such semipublic confidences: even by a juvenile-lead female organ like Carpenter who had preferred to put his trust in a juvenile-lead female organ like Hattersley. *I* could have shown him that printing contract, if he hadn't written me off as useless that night at the Heritage Motor Lodge. I would have been delighted to assist the police in their inquiries.

Except that Detective Constable Carpenter's inquiries were six months behind everybody else's. Pisspot was so indiscreet and so free with secrets, but he never told me anything.

I said thickly, thinking to myself that this must be what authors mean when they say someone speaks thickly, "So what you're saying is that he was wasting his time with Hattersley?"

Pisspot rolled his eyes in a God-help-us manner, and I was sorry to see this time that he rolled them in Ron Casey's direction. Casey, reduced in my eyes to about junior prefect age, piped up: "PC Plod of the Flying Squad is just about fit for writing out parking tickets. *Every*body knows about that printing contract. What Carpenter doesn't realize, and nobody at Shepford Central dare tell him in case he goes blabbing it around, is that they're hoping to get Drummond on about thirty-five other charges."

"At least," I said lamely, not knowing why I was defending Detective Constable Carpenter, "he's shown a bit of initiative."

"Initiative bollocks. They're just letting him get on with it to make Drummond think it's a minor inquiry with a schoolboy detective who couldn't even solve a crossword puzzle."

At this moment Jack Wilmott, who had fallen asleep, rolled off Hattersley's desk and landed on the floor. Cursing richly to himself, he staggered to his feet, and Pisspot took the opportunity of this natural break to invite his guests to leave.

"Well, gentlemen, you have your information about the Phantom Nose Shaver. Let us hope that one of these days the dam will burst and our investigations will see the light of day. Meanwhile, we all have our routine duties to perform, so as the poet has it, *piss off.*"

They pissed off, and the two of us were left alone. Still wearing the fairly new overcoat that had looked secondhand since the day he bought it and still clutching his stick, Pisspot was sitting at his desk, which his girth seemed to reduce to the size of a bedside table. It was an absurdly small, drawn-from-stores utility desk for a man in his position. There was an empty paneled room beyond our office, which could have been his own private office had he wished it, with Grade I furniture and a carpet according to his status, but he had never bothered. I would have had that office had I been him or if I had had his job.

"Well, Bill."

When we were by ourselves, he rarely called me Arsehole. Nor did he talk as if he were on a convention hall platform. Anyone overhearing Pisspot's private conversation would have thought he was addressing quite a small gathering.

"Well, Reggie."

We chatted for a while; he asked after Jeanette and I wanting to tell him we were splitting up, but not daring to, for fear of some sage advice coming my way. Partly to change the subject and partly because I genuinely wanted to know, I reciprocated by asking after Mrs. Pisspot. I liked his thin, weather-beaten, gardening-gloves wife who treated him like a very old dog that she was still fond of, one that had won prizes for her in its time but had now grown incontinent and daft. She looked and talked and behaved like a Festival Committee ratbag but wasn't one, because she had occasionally had Jeanette and me to dinner and had not been patronizing to either of us.

The interval for civilities over, Pisspot humphed and grunted through his accumulation of mail for a minute or two, then peered at me over his half-moon spectacles and asked abruptly, "How would you like to go to Prague?"

My heart should have jumped and I should have seen myself in Prague even before the words had left his mouth: drinking schnapps or vodka or whatever they drink there, with my gorgeous interpreter, in the great reception chamber of the Hall of Culture, under the chandeliers.

Yet all I thought was: that trip's a long way off, and I may have pissed off with Helen by then.

182

And a stray aside: if I haven't pissed off with Helen, could I take her with me? She could tell her husband she was exporting English bungalows to Czechoslovakia.

"Do I have to answer that, Reggie? I'd jump at it. Why—can't you go?"

"One of us has to. But the question is, should it be the dir*ect*-ah of information or the dir*ect*-ah of publicity? Is it our role to inform the benighted foreigner of the delights of this ancient market borough or to publicize the ceaseless quest for knowlege of building methods by our hardworking city fathers?"

"I'm not with you, Reggie."

"Then you ought to be with me, young man, because I've given you the broadest of broad hints. The dir*ect*-ah of information, or the dir*ect*-ah of publicity? Hmmm?"

Both of which hats are worn by you, Pisspot. Do stop talking in riddles.

He gave me a weary, petulant sigh, as if feeling put upon because I had failed to read his mind.

"Bill. Or may I call you Arsehole, since we're alone? You know that Bulldog Drummond starts his mayoral year next week, assuming the *bar*stard isn't in Shepford Jail by then. And you know that Hopkinson takes over as chairman of the Senior Appointments Selection Board. You are with me so far?"

"Go on, Reggie."

"*One.* Master Hopkinson has had his eye on you at those Festival Committee meetings. He is impressed. God knows why he's impressed, but impressed is what he is. *Two.* Master Hopkinson brought grapes to my bedside last week, and we discussed my future."

I followed what he was saying clearly enough, but none of it was registering. "About your staying on? Isn't that all settled?"

"It is all settled, but when a man of my age and build skids arse over tit on some blasted female's blasted beads and lands up in hospital with buzzing noises in his head, he begins to consider his position. Whither Pisspot? is the question. Bill, I can still do my job blindfold, and I shall bloody well *have* to do it for the next five years, if Beatrice and I aren't to live on bread and scrape. *But.* I could do it a bloody sight easier without bumph like *this* to cope with."

He picked up between two fingers, and dropped into the wastepaper basket, the latest copy of *Shepford Events,* an ill-produced publication put out by our department and subsidized by advertisements from Chinese take-aways. It involved a surprising amount of work, which Pisspot reluctantly supervised.

"Bill, I don't know what you think of Hopkinson. The man is a female organ, of that there is no doubt. He is certainly not an out-and-out crook like Drummond and Company, and he means well; but he comes high on my list of gullible buggers. He has allowed his head to be stuffed with all that crap and balls about Shepford being the up-and-coming town and Europe-in-a-meadow and suchlike codswallop. And he very much wants to make his mark. So it was not very difficult to persuade Master Hopkinson that an expanding, forward-looking shit-heap such as this should have an expanding, arsehole-creeping Information Department such as the world has never seen. Which, following the usual amoebalike pattern of such operations, would involve splitting my job in two or if you like hiving half of it off. I would remain dir*ect*-ah of information and you would become dir*ect*-ah of publicity. What do you think of that? And I'm glad to say he jumped at the notion, which of course will be presented as his very own to an astonished district council."

No Christs, no euphoria. The same numb feeling as I had felt with Helen. The same clear thinking.

184

Reggie, if you'd told me all that just over a week ago, you would have seen me standing on my hands. But I shan't be here for your expansion and arsehole-creeping, Reggie. I'm getting out of it with Helen. And even if you *had* told me that just over a week ago, and I'd rushed out into Bell Park yelling that I was going to be the new dir*ect*-ah of publicity, it wouldn't make any difference now, because things have happened since that day and I would still be getting out of it with Helen. I'm growing up, Reggie, though you may not have noticed yet. I'm too grown up to accept your grown-up job.

"Well, say something, Arsehole, even if it's only thank you very much!"

I shook my head and grinned, to prove that I was just coming out of a daze.

"That's bloody fantastic, Reggie!"

"I should jolly well think it is. Not that I expect thanks, mind you, since my motives are basefully selfish. And not that you've got the bloody job yet, so don't count chickens. And if you do count chickens, don't expect them to lay golden eggs. Hmmm?"

Pisspot examined me quizzically over his glasses, as if assessing my ability to recognize good sense when I came across it.

"Don't fool yourself that this is a plum job, Bill. It is not a plum; it is a gooseberry. If you had any sense, you'd turn it down. This is not repeat not a town with a future, and if you ever fall for that expanding Shepford crap, I will kick you up and down this office until your arse turns blue. It's a glass and concrete excavated ruin we're living in, and if I were your age, I'd be out of it on the next train. Except, of course, that after the next train whisked you two hundred miles north or a hundred miles due nor' nor'west or wherever, you'd walk out of the bloody station and find yourself back in bloody Shepford. Perhaps the whole country's had it, I don't

185

know. This town certainly has. But don't let the *bars*tards get you down, Bill. And don't let them con you, and don't let them turn you into a piss ar*tiste*. Here endeth the first lesson."

Thanks, Pisspot. Thanks for everything, Reggie.

I saw an indistinct but definitely female shape appear behind the frosted glass door. Not Patsy or Sheilagh; it could be a chit of a messenger girl with the afternoon post. There was a timid knock, suggesting that it was a chit of a messenger girl who had just left school.

"Enter!" roared Pisspot, and Jeanette, my future ex-wife, nervously poked her head around the door.

Chapter Fourteen

"Is it all right? Are you busy?"

"Madame Fisher! Come in, dear lady! Take a chair! Have a cup of exceedingly cold tea!"

I was surprised not only to see Jeanette, since visits to the Civic Center were discouraged and this was only about her third in eight years, but also by her demeanor. She looked flushed and excited, with a sparkle in the eyes that suggested she was on the verge of some mad adventure such as buying a pair of new shoes. Definitely perky.

After "He never told me you were out of hospital, Mr. Rainbell" and "You're *looking* well, Mr. Rainbell, are you *feeling* well?" and "How's Mrs. Rainbell, Mr. Rainbell?" and "I hope you don't mind my barging in like this, Mr. Rainbell" and "Will you excuse us, Mr. Rainbell?" she finally turned to me.

"Bill, you know those new bungalows they're building over in Mayfield?"

Yes, and I know how you came to know about them, too, my flower. Helen, bloody Helen, of Mayfield Estates Ltd., had sent us an illustrated brochure about them. The envelope had been in her handwriting, and I had uttered some multiple Christs upon finding that it was addressed to "Mr. and Mrs. W. Fisher." "I thought it was a nice way of telling you I was thinking about you on my first day at work," she had said when we met by the windmill on the county border.

187

"Yes?"

"Well you know they're opening a show bungalow, completely furnished, where you'll be able to walk round and see what it will be like to live there?"

Not what it will be like, Jeanette. What it *would* be like.

I'm going to tell you tonight, and I'll be gone tomorrow.

"Well?"

"And you know Mr. Richardson?"

Do drop this tiresome style of interrogation, ducky. No, I do not know Mr. bloody Richardson.

"Who's Mr. Richardson?"

"Did you hear that, Mr. Rainbell? Who's Mr. Richardson, he says—he's only lived next door but one to us for eight years!"

The fit of asthmatic coughing induced by Pisspot to register dutiful mirth died down, and Jeanette continued. "Well, Mr. Richardson's left Carmichael and Sons, and he's started working in that new office that Mayfield Estates have opened up in Castle Street, and—ooh, Bill, I must tell you this! Do you know who I saw there, this morning? That lady that came round from the Bedding Council that night, and we all thought she was squiffy. I'm *sure* it was her, Bill. She was just coming out of the office as I was just going in."

And what was she wearing, and did she look happy?

"Did she recognize you?"

"I don't think she even saw me. Anyway, to get back to Mr. *Rich*ardson. He's been in charge of getting all the carpets down in the show bungalow, apparently, so of course, he's got his own key. And it's not open to the public until Monday, officially, but Mr. Richardson, he said if we didn't tell anybody and we promised not to disturb anything, he'd lend us his key and we could have a look round it this afternoon!"

Big deal. "What would we want to do that for?"

"Oh, Bill, you are thick sometimes! Isn't he, Mr. Rainbell?

188

I'll tell you what we want to do it for—because once the show bungalow opens, that estate's going to be sold like hot cakes! They're going to be showing whole parties round it, Bill! And we could get in first and get our names put down and plonk down a deposit! Don't you see?"

I'll definitely tell her tonight. "I'm not sure about this key-borrowing lark," I said, playing dispirited hesitation against her persuasive enthusiasm—a reversal of our usual roles. "We might get your friend into trouble—you shouldn't really have asked him for it."

"I didn't ask him, Bill! I just went into the office for another brochure, to send to your mother, and it was Mr. *Richard*son who made the suggestion. So what do you think?"

"Well, I couldn't get down there this afternoon, for a start. I've got a lot of—"

"*Hogwash!*" Thank you, Pisspot, a fine friend you are.

"No, honestly, Reggie, it's only a few days to the Festival, I've just *got* to—"

"Bugger the Festival! My dear Mrs. Fisher, I beg a thousand pardons! You see the effect your husband has on me—he reduces me to a fish porter! Take him away, madame! Lead him from my sight! And don't bring him back until he has bought you all the bungalows you desire." Thank you *very* much.

I'll tell her this afternoon then. In a furnished show bungalow, as we peer into its fitted wardrobes and inspect its fitted kitchen, to see what it would be like to live there.

No, that would be cruel. I'll tell her in the car, before we've even picked up the key.

Jeanette's happy prattle about sink units and underfloor heating took us down the lift and into the lobby of the Civic Center. A burly, public-house-landlord type was standing by the inquiry desk while the rat-faced commissionaire was ringing through to some extension or other on his behalf;

189

the possibility of his being no more a public-house landlord than I was, but a plainclothes detective of the heavy rather than the juvenile lead division, was suggested by his general demeanor and also by the bag of golfclubs slung across his broad shoulder.

The rat-faced commissionaire spotted me as I hurried Jeanette toward the revolving doors. Pointing what looked to me like an accusing finger for the non-public-house-landlord's benefit, he shouted in stop-thief tones, "Mr. Fisher! Just a minute!," and I turned reluctantly to greet my visitor as he lumbered across the lobby toward me and dumped the golf clubs at my feet.

"Mr. Fisher?"

"Yes?"

"I'm Detective Constable Reid, Shepford Central. This is Detective Constable Carpenter's inquiry really, but he's on day off. I believe you've had some golf clubs stolen?"

"That's right." If I talk like this all the time, he'll think I have a naturally high voice.

The well-worn bag of golf clubs looked very much as if it had been jumped up and down on and slung down a quarry. But they were not Councillor Drummond's golf clubs. His were practically new, and in any case they were safely locked away in the boot of Helen's car.

"Do you recognize these, Mr. Fisher?"

"Er—I'm not sure. I believe so. In fact—yes. I recognize the grass stains on the bag. And that broken zip."

Why had I said that? Surely, as far as I was concerned, the case was closed except for tidying up loose ends. All I had to do was jump up and down on Drummond's golf clubs and throw them down a quarry.

"And Mrs. Fisher? It *is* Mrs. Fisher? Do you recognize them?"

"No, I'm afraid I've never seen them before."

190

Silly bitch. "I'd only just bought them," I said, or quavered, hastily, hoping that Detective Constable Carpenter hadn't told him to ask me where. "So she *wouldn't* recognize them. But they're definitely mine."

I knew why I'd said it. So he would just get me to sign something, give me the bloody golf clubs, and let us get off. So I could tell Jeanette I wanted a divorce. One problem no longer superseded another in my mind; I was growing up.

If the real owner turned up, would this count as technical theft? Or even nontechnical theft?

"Only we raided this flat on the Fairfields Estate—next block to yours, I believe. And it was like Aladdin's Cave in there. Electrical stuff he'd got, radios, fruit bowls, bedside teamaking equipment, you name it. And do you know what he'd the cheek to say, Mr. and Mrs. Fisher? He said he was opening a secondhand shop, and it was all stock that he'd bought!"

What a pity I hadn't known sooner. He could have sold me a set of secondhand golfclubs.

Detective Constable Carpenter's heavy stand-in guffawed.

"Opening a secondhand shop! I laughed! Anyway. It appears no one else has reported golf clubs missing, so we assumed they must be yours. So you can formally identify them, can you?"

"Certainly."

"Only there's one or two items of gear—well, naturally he's got all his own stuff in there as well, his own household effects—and there's one or two items that we don't know whether he's thieved them or not. And what he's claiming is, these golf clubs were given to him by his brother."

Christ multiplied by fifteen.

"I see. Well, I'm pretty sure they're mine, but I *could* be mistaken. You see, I'd only had them a day or two before they went missing."

"Only his brother's in New Zealand, so it's going to be a long job checking up."

Can't I sort this out later, officer? It would be so much simpler. Just leave it for the moment, let me get Jeanette in the car and tell her I want a divorce, then Helen will leave her husband and we'll jump up and down on Councillor Drummond's golf clubs and throw them down a quarry, then I'll come around to the police station and tell you I've made a mistake, this isn't my property after all because there should be a dent in the No. 3 iron, and then we'll bugger off out of Shepford and live happily ever after.

"Oh, dear," I said. "We don't want to get anyone into trouble, do we, Jeanette?"

"He's in trouble enough already, Mr. Fisher. But if you can't be absolutely certain this is your property, we'll have to send a telegram to New Zealand."

Which is the most serious charge? Wasting public funds and police time or making a false accusation?

I bent down over the battered old bag of golf clubs and made a great show of scrutinizing it closely.

"Ah. Wait a minute. No, they're not mine. It didn't have this cigarette burn."

"That could have been made any time, Mr. Fisher. He could have made that burn himself."

Detective Constable Carpenter would never have thought of that. Why does he have to have days off?

"Ah. These irons. I should have looked at these before. There's six irons in this set. Mine has only five, that's why I got them cheap. I can't remember the numbers, but there were definitely only five. It wasn't a complete set."

When we throw Councillor Drummond's golf clubs down the quarry, we'll have to take out one of the irons and put it in a suitcase, and take it with us when we bugger off out of Shepford. Then we can take it to a golf course and throw it in some bushes.

192

"You're sure about that, Mr. Fisher?"

"Absolutely."

"I think we'd better check with New Zealand just to make sure. He could have found a spare iron and added it to make a complete set, couldn't he? We'll inquire further, Mr. Fisher, and let you know what transpires."

You mean the episode isn't closed? But it must be closed. I've grown up now, and this episode belongs to the days when I wasn't grown up.

I am not thinking about golf clubs. I am thinking about Helen. I am going to tell Jeanette. I am going to begin telling her before we reach the telephone box in the distance.

We had picked up the key to the show bungalow, and now we were on the long straight road that led to Mayfield. I had not told her yet because they had altered the one-way traffic system again and I had been having to concentrate on my driving. But I was going to tell her now.

I had the scenario in my mind, long ago polished into final draft form. It would begin with a discussion of Helen's letter, when the identity of she who could do with her tongue things that a certain person did not yet know about would be formally revealed, as would that of he to whom these things were to be done. I no longer wondered why Jeanette had never said anything about finding the letter. She must have thought about doing so during the weeping period that precipitated my mother's departure for Stradhoughton, and my mother would have counseled her to keep her tongue between her teeth and let this passing infatuation blow over. I could almost hear my mother giving her this advice. "He's not the first one to go off the rails and he won't be the last. But they never leave home for their fancy women, Jeanette, not unless you make it so they've got to. And then they wish they hadn't, and you've all the palaver of taking them back."

Had my mother read the letter for herself? When admonishing Jeanette to keep her tongue between her teeth, did she possess newfound knowledge of other uses to which tongues might be put? I was momentarily struck with horror, and momentary horror took me past the telephone box that was my landmark.

I would tell her before we reached that telegraph pole. That second one. That third one. I would tell her now.

"Jeanette, do you remember finding a letter of mine, ages ago?"

"A letter?"

"It was in the inside pocket of my blue suit, when you took it to the cleaner's, and it was still there when you brought the suit back from the cleaner's. Then it vanished."

"Oh. That letter," said Jeanette flatly.

We've started. There's no going back now. And I'm more relieved than scared.

"What happened to it, then?"

"Bill." She drew a deep breath. It was her we've-got-to-have-a-talk deep breath, the one that always heralded the periodic overhauls of our marriage, when she would take it methodically to pieces and lay each part out as if it were a machine stripped down for greasing. Well, this would be the last time.

But then she went on in a small voice: "I'm afraid I've got a confession to make."

Yes? *What?* You read it, you didn't read it, you showed it to my mother, you burned it, you kept it, you lost it, you posted it to a sex magazine? *What?*

"It *was* in your suit when I brought it back from the cleaner's, because it fell out of your pocket when I was trying to unstaple the cleaning tag. And I was horrified."

You must have been, but you don't sound horrified now. Continue.

"It was about three or four pages, wasn't it? And written in

194

pen. And all the ink had run, and it was all blurred and soggy and horrible. It must have been the chemicals they use or something, reacting to the ink, because the envelope was quite all right."

I had not looked in the envelope. I'd felt the envelope to check that the letter was still in it, and I'd kept on feeling it from time to time to see if it was still there, but I hadn't looked at the letter because I knew it by heart. Continue.

"And I felt quite guilty about it, because I should have gone through the pockets before I took the suit to the cleaner's, if I'd had any sense. And it might have been an important letter for all I knew."

"Yes. It was. That's why I'm asking about it." Continue.

"Well. I left it in your inside pocket, thinking you'd be bound to find it and blow me up about it. But you didn't, and you wore the suit two or three times, and you still didn't say anything about it, so I knew you hadn't looked at it. And I felt even more guilty for not telling you."

Poor Jeanette. And I thought it in almost the same way as I sometimes thought, poor Helen. Loving sympathy. Warm, affectionate sympathy anyway. To worry so much about nothing, in such a dutiful, wifely way! It was touching and sad.

"Anyway. You remember that night you went to that big dinner with Mr. Rainbell, and you came home a bit squiffy? You threw your jacket over the chair next to the wardrobe, and it slipped off, and the letter must have fallen out of your pocket again, because I found it under the chair next morning."

"What did you do with it?"

"I'm sorry to say I threw it in the dustbin. I'm sorry, Bill, I know it was a stupid thing to do, but I thought if you saw what condition it was in, you'd be mad at me for not going through your pockets before the suit went to the cleaner's,

195

and you would have said *that* was a stupid thing to have done. Which it was. And I suppose I must have panicked, and I'm very sorry."

Don't apologize, Jeanette, for Christ's sake. We *don't* apologize where we come from, you should know that. And it's so touching, and sad, and even tragic, that you worry about nothing in your dutiful, wifely way.

"Was it a *very* important letter, Bill?"

"Not all that important. Just some stuff about the Festival. Why—didn't you read it?"

"I told you—all the ink had run. It was illegible."

"It can't have been illegible from beginning to end. Didn't you even *try* to read it?"

"Of course not," said Jeanette with great wifely dignity. "I wouldn't dream of reading your letters."

I wanted to stop the car and hug her, but I couldn't do that; it would give a false impression. But I wanted to so something for her now, some impulsive thing, to show how moved I was and how much I appreciated her worrying about nothing in her dutiful, wifely way and how touching and sad and tragic and heart-aching it all was.

We were on the outskirts of Mayfield, passing a row of pink and blue houses that had once been laborers' cottages. On the doorstep of one of them sat a handsome young black and white cat, washing itself with a white-tipped paw. I stopped the car, leaving the engine running, jumped out, scooped up the cat, flung it in Jeanette's lap, and drove off, reaching forty in second gear in less than ten yards and praying that the angry householder reflected in my rear mirror had not got my number.

The cat and Jeanette were staring at each other, both equally astonished.

"It's Mr. Pussy-paws!" I gasped as we screeched around a corner. "They've been looking for him everywhere!"

"Bill! Are your sure?"

"Of course I'm sure! I've *seen* him often enough! So have you!"

"But how did he get all the way down here?"

"They used to live here, years ago. And you know what cats are—they always go back to their old haunts."

We were speeding along Mayfield's reconstructed High Street, with its village launderettes, its village Electricity Board showrooms, and its village secretarial employment agencies. I came back down to forty.

"Who's a naughty Mr. Pussy-paws?" Jeanette was asking the bewildered cat. "Who's run away from home, den? But oo'll be *glad* to get home, won't oo, because oo'll have a nice big saucer of milky-wilk."

God, is she going to talk like that to the bloody animal? Still, it makes no difference to me, I shan't be there to listen.

"Ah, well that's just it," I said. "You see, the whole point is, they've moved. They've gone to Norwich."

"What—and left him behind?"

"Well, he'd vanished, hadn't he? What could they do? I thought you'd heard about it."

"No—I knew *some*body had moved out of the flats, but I didn't know who it was. Didn't they leave their address with anybody?"

"Not that I know of."

"Poor Mr. Pussy-paws. And such a pretty little thing. Who's doeing to look after oo, den?"

"I suppose he'll have to move in with us."

"Oh, Bill! Honestly? Could he?"

She hugged the wretched cat to her bosom, whereupon, after an initial struggle and probably because it had been deprived of affection by the rat-face lately observed in my driving mirror, it eventually settled down and began to purr.

You'll get on very well with Mr. Pussy-paws, Jeanette.

197

When I'm gone, you'll have long, daft conversations with him.

And I can't tell you now, but I'll tell you tonight.

We had reached the suburb of the moon where the new bungalows were set out like computerized dots on a map put together from information fed by an unmanned TV satellite. The contours and craters all had names, perhaps given to them by the discoverers who had been here long ago and who had long since left: Milking Green, Meadow Path, Tithe Barn Close, Church Close, Farm Close, The Common, Nettlewood Fold, Bramble Fold, Bluebell Fold. There were, of course, no milking greens or meadows, no tithe barns, churches or farms, no common, no woods where there might have been nettles, brambles, or bluebells. We were in a child's construction-kitland of crescents and cul-de-sacs with green construction-kit roofs and red construction-kit chimney stacks; every bungalow had a construction-kit porch and a construction-kit gate and a construction-kit white fence, and there were new young trees, protected by tubes of wire mesh, growing not far away from where the old trees had been felled, their stumps cleverly converted to accommodate litter bins. And Jeanette, cradling the purring Mr. Pussy-paws in her arms, loved it all, uncritically, and so did he.

The show bungalow was at the end of a frying-pan-shaped dead end called Shepherds Croft, without the apostrophe. We walked up its crazy-paving path of imitation quarrystone to the front door of reinforced glass and wrought-iron vertical bars, suggesting an enlightened Borstal. I turned the key that had been lent us by Jeanette's rat-faced friend, and the door wouldn't open.

"That's funny!" And she didn't know it, but I meant that literally.

"Don't tell me after all this he's given us the wrong key!"

198

"No, it fits all right. But it won't go all the way round in the lock. It seems to be double-locked from the inside."

"Are you sure it isn't the back door key? Because he didn't say, did he? He just said, that's the key, and be sure to bring it back."

An extension of the bogus quarrystone paving, which I now saw was more pink in texture than I had previously feared, led us to the back of the bungalow. There did not seem to be a back door, and I had the vaguest idea that we had passed some affair of stripped-pine planks, which we had taken to be the entrance to a fuel store or laundry room, which might turn out to be the side door. But there was a back window all right, of the picture variety, and looking into it and noting the tasteful bedroom furniture in mainly white painted wood with dull gold fitting, I saw Helen and Detective Constable Carpenter sprawled naked across the candlewick-covered king-sized divan bed.

I registered, before Jeanette gave a little shriek and the boggle-eyed Mr. Pussy-paws meowed his interest, and they looked up and saw us, that there were still things Helen could do with her tongue that I had not known about. Even though the pain in my left side was excruciating, I couldn't help wishing that she had done them with me when the opportunity was still there.

Chapter Fifteen

The bunting, which even at the beginning of the Festival had looked like something strung up around the Cornmarket to frighten the starlings, was a sad sight after a week of rain. Last year's plastic replicas of the Shepford coat of arms had been lost, and the dog-eared, paint-streaked substitutes, hanging by string from every lamp standard, had not weathered well. The substantial balcony of the Old Town Hall, where my lady wife and I were guests of the new mayor, had been shored up with tubular scaffolding, a precaution against the recently discovered shifting of the granite foundations.

The pain in my left side had remained with me in varying degrees all through the week; I could chronicle the progress of the Festival by referring to a mental graph of these degrees of pain. It had been a dull, continuous throbbing all through the gymkhana and display of children's physical training that had started the week; a series of vicious, searing jabs or stabs during the floodlit tattoo; a long, mournful ache, more sorrow than pain, at the exhibition of arts and crafts in the foyer of the *Evening Mail* office; a nagging gripe, like a serious attack of wind, as Old Folks' Day degenerated into mutinous chaos; anguish during the hundred-meter dash in the combined schools sporting events; agony during last night's Son et Lumière at Shepford Castle. And the pain was with me still, it wouldn't leave, as I sat in my canvas chair among all the Festival top brass, rubbing the left of my chest, my fingers brushing against Helen's letter in the inside pocket where Jeanette would never find it.

> I'm sorry, Bill, I'm sorry I'm sorry I'm sorry I'm sorry. Will you see me again? Just once? Please? Please? So that I can explain properly?

Of course I will, Helen, eventually. The scene must be played out, mustn't it? Even juvenile leads are old troupers: the play's the thing, the show must go on.

> I *had* to do it, Bill. You've no idea. He was practically blackmailing me.

No. If what Jeanette and I and Mr. Pussy-paws saw was blackmail, Helen, then I'll take up blackmail myself as a living, and my rat-faced, lip-licking victims will hand over their life savings when I've only asked for twenty-five pounds in used notes.

> There was nothing else I could do, Bill. He has been pestering me ever since that night at the Heritage Motor Lodge—he kept "happening" to bump into me & wanted to ask questions about Drummond & Jack Dance. I *told* him there was nothing I could tell him but he was so persistent, he began making sly comments about you & us & talking about obstructing the police in their inquiries & how he could make serious trouble for us both. I was so frightened I agreed to have a drink with him—I met him in the Old Bell at Mayfield because it was convenient for me, he asked me a lot of questions about Drummond & then asked was I going into town & could I give him a lift.
> Bill, please please please believe me. I was driving him

back to Shepford & we ran over some glass or something & found we had a flat tire & had to change the wheel. I forgot all about Drummond's golf clubs in the boot & of course he saw them—Drummond had reported them stolen so he knew about them from the police list & there was no use saying they were mine because they were an American make, Jack Dance brought them back for Drummond from New York & you can't get them in this country. I was terrified, Bill. I tried to pretend it was all a silly practical joke & that I meant to return them & he pretended to believe me & said what a "character" I was & was I going to be "nice" to him. I cringe as I write this down & I shan't write any more of it, you know the rest.

Yes. Do I bloody well not?

Bill, Bill, Bill, darling Bill, forgive me, it wasn't what it must have looked like to you, I was acting, I was doing what he asked me to do because I was terrified & I hated it. Please please let me see you, Bill, meet me by our windmill again—we've only been there once & already I think of it as our windmill. Will you see me there? I know you'll be busy with the Festival but after that I shall drive there every evening & hope & hope that you'll come. Will you? Will you?

I'll be there, Helen. I'll give it about four or five days, I think, to keep you waiting. Or three days, or two, if the pain has gone by then, so that I can see you and talk to you and get the pain back again. And we'll go on meeting and talking and exhuming those four affairs that you never had; it'll give our relationship a new dimension, a kick, a bit of zest that it never had before. I look forward to it, you probably look forward to it yourself, it's our big chance. Such fat parts for two juvenile leads, and such thrilling, unexpected twists in the light comedy. "Will run and run and run"—*Evening Mail*.

202

"Rain keeps off, should be colorful occasion," barked His Worship the Mayor, adjusting his unaccustomed chain of office for the fiftieth time. Knowing Drummond, he was probably assessing its troy weight and wondering if he could get away with reporting it lost.

Next to him sat his ratbag wife, and next to him the new director of finance, whose beautifully clean-shaven nose was disfigured only by a small surgical dressing held in place with Elastoplast; then came Purchase's ratbag wife, then the rat-faced Town Clerk and his ratbag wife, then Councillor Hopkinson of the Senior Appointments Selection Committee, and his ratbag wife, then me, and then Jeannette in her silly little hat and nice new clothes. On the mayor's left, and behind us, were various other rat-faces and ratbags of some standing in the town. There were two empty chairs: Pisspot's wife preferred to stay at home pottering among her roses, while Pisspot himself was probably sipping slimline—low-calorie-Indian-*tonic* water in the King's Head Lounge Bar across the Cornmarket, where the *Evening Mail* gang, having written their accounts of this last afternoon of the Festival some hours before, were taking advantage of the all-day extension.

There was a fair number of people in the Cornmarket, thronging the sidewalks and roadways behind the rope barrier that cordoned off the square itself. Two roads, Cripplegate on the west side of the square, and the meandering shopping-center access road on the east, had been left clear—the access road for the procession of old comrades, boy scouts and other rat-faced patrols that must by now have just about set off from its rallying point at Shepford Castle; and Cripplegate for the triumphal march into the Cornmarket of the Shepford Police Silver Band.

The police band, if the schedule I had arranged continued to work like clockwork, should be arriving any minute.

Meanwhile, those with a taste for music had to make do with the Shepford and District Traffic Wardens' Steel Band, which was playing something of a calypso nature while the gin-gargling ratbag of Festival Committee fame judged the Spottiest Dog contest.

I was somewhat uneasy about the number of dogs in the Cornmarket, although the protracted event in which they were contenders had been going smoothly enough so far. The children's dog show had produced a remarkable response, yielding a turnout of some five hundred mongrels, Alsatians, Dalmatians, terriers, bulldogs, and other breeds and half-breeds, all of which, as they strained at their leads or scrabbled frantically in their makeshift orange-box kennels, were kicking up a fair amount of row. It had been my idea to stagger the dog show throughout the afternoon, my theory being that once, say, the Ugliest Dog class had been judged, all those with ugly dogs would then depart the arena, and so on with other dogs in other classes, so that the canine proportion of the crowd would be steadily diminished as the day wore on. This had not worked out in practice. A rat-faced steward was bawling into the PA system: "Can I appeal to all you little boys and all you little girls again? Once your dogs have taken part in their particular section, will you please remove them from the Cornmarket? Please remove your dogs from the Cornmarket; then come back without your dogs to enjoy the fun." But no one took any notice. For one thing, many dogs would have been entered in more than one class. For another, most of the dog-escorting children were hemmed in by the great press of adults behind them. But apart from the excessive yapping and the strong smell of unwashed dog that wafted across the square, there had been no trouble so far.

To the cacophony of dogs and steel band, which was ill-rehearsed, there was now added another sound—that of a

204

Sousa march being played rather better than the traffic wardens' rendering of "Ob-La-Di, Ob-La-Da."

"Ooh, look, Bill, the police band's coming!" cried Jeanette, clutching my arm in great excitement, as if the police band were making their arrival by parachute.

I craned over the balcony and looked across the Town Hall side of the Cornmarket toward Cripplegate, where I could see the glint of sounding brass.

"Don't they march splendidly!" a county ratbag was saying. "And then one hears that our police are ill-disciplined! Nonsense!"

I looked at my watch. Spot on time. A rat-face wearing an armband, who had been standing at the end of Cripplegate waiting for the band to approach, signaled to the traffic wardens to cease their racket and clear off.

"Wait a minute! They're turning left into St. Peter's Street! Why are they turning left into St. Peter's Street?"

I craned forward again. Directed by their drum major with his mace, the police band was indeed wheeling into St. Peter's Street, about two hundred yards short of the Cornmarket.

"Of course!" exclaimed Purchase. He had unfolded the street map in his copy of *Pageantry with Progress* (new edition), which had been handed out to the mayor's guests along with the souvenir program and other bumph. "Cripplegate is subject to the revised traffic scheme. There's now a compulsory left turn into St. Peter's Street."

"Damn blast it," spluttered Drummond. "Doesn't apply special occasion, surely God!"

"If it applies at all, then it is applied *to* all, surely," croaked the county ratbag. "If the police take no notice of restriction signs, then who will?"

I had been poring over my own street map. "You do realize," I said, leaning across to Purchase and speaking as if it were his fault, "that if they're going to obey every road sign they come across, there's a no right turn in Castle Street, so they'll have to fork left as far as the no-entry section, then take a compulsory right into Hill Street, which should get them on to the Route Four expressway, and depending on which way they turn there they'll finish up either back where they started from or in Wolverhampton."

"I'm afraid I'm not responsible for the traffic regulations!" snapped Purchase.

"Well, *I'm* certainly not. I worked out this route from the map issued to me by the Festival Office."

And brought to me, I now recalled, by Hattersley, whom I had dispatched on this little office-boy errand. It would not have been beyond him to palm an out-of-date map on me deliberately.

"Surely a steward can run after the police band and point out that the regulations don't apply to pedestrians?" someone was saying, and someone else was saying, "At least let the steel band play on a little. We ought to have *some* music, if only to drown the noise of all those blessed dogs!"

But it was a little late for request encores from the steel band. The traffic wardens had arranged themselves in straggling lines of three and were now shambling off to their next engagement, a concert at the old people's home.

As they headed toward the shopping-center access road there was another diversion. An old Ford van, painted in psychedelic colors and traveling at speed, came tearing out of the access road into the Cornmarket, scattering the battalion of traffic wardens in all directions, steel drums jangling, in fear of their lives. The van screeched to a stop at the edge of the square, its back door was flung open, and two young men in denim suits stitched over with gold and silver stars began to unload amplifying equipment. The legend on the side

206

of the van read in Art Nouveau letters, THE MADISON—a combination of talents which had achieved a certain amount of fame in Midlands discotheques and other centers of opinion. I could have told The Madison for nothing, however, that they were in the wrong place and should have been unloading their gear twenty minutes ago in a disused coke compound—or Street Theater, as it was now known—on the industrial side of the town.

Though presumably the hard core of The Madison's following would be waiting impatiently at the coke compound, many of the teenagers present in the Cornmarket were sufficiently impressed by the sight of them to break ranks and dash across the square brandishing bits of paper, pairs of panties and lipsticks. More important, The Madison's arrival seemed to have interested the small television unit that had descended on us from Birmingham. (When I had finally got around to ringing *Nationwide,* a nice lady had said that it sounded a super idea, but unfortunately it clashed with open day at Battersea Dog's Home, which they'd already arranged to cover, and if only I'd let them know sooner.) The TV camera zoomed in on our visitors just as the scattered traffic wardens recovered their corporate composure and, with their polished, sawn-off oil barrels still hanging around their necks, converged on The Madison's van with pencil stubs and pads of parking tickets at the ready.

The effect of the disturbance on the Shepford's Silliest Dog class, which was at that moment being judged, was not a good one. Such silly dogs as had been commanded to sit at their young masters' feet while being examined for cross-eyes, lolling tongues and other points, came lolloping up to join the melee surrounding The Madison. The silliest dogs, which could not be trusted off the lead, strained and pulled, barking furiously, in their efforts to join in the commotion.

The TV crew, with an escaped Norwich terrier worrying their ankles, panned the camera to take in reaction shots of the set faces on the Town Hall balcony.

"Hm, I wouldn't describe *this* as very good publicity for Shepford," grumbled Councillor Hopkinson.

Rat-faced stewards were restoring something like order, mainly by seizing teenagers by the scruff of the neck and frog-marching them back to the rope barriers. Several unleashed dogs were still frolicking about the square, but they were gradually being rounded up by their infant guardians. The driver of The Madison's van was now receiving instructions on the best way to the coke compound from several of the traffic wardens, who were gesticulating to him to drive up Cripplegate and turn off at Bank Street. This would be a mistake, since Bank Street was now a dead end.

The traffic wardens reformed themselves in threes and resumed their ragged march toward the access road, one of them peeling off to pursue The Madison's van and point out that as Cripplegate was a one-way street, they could not drive up it but would have to reverse as far as Bank Street.

The crisis more or less over, I sank back into my canvas chair in some relief. At least, I was able to tell myself, it had stopped me thinking of Helen for about ten minutes.

Perhaps feeling that his dignity as mayor precluded his witnessing such a shambles, Councillor Drummond had studiously ignored the incident involving The Madison and was browsing through *Pageantry with Progress* (new edition). Even as I lit a much-needed cigarette and inhaled gratefully, I heard him explode: "Good—*God! What devil this!*" Eyes popping, face purple with indignation, he shot out an arm so viciously that it would have sliced the bosom off his ratbag wife had she possessed one, and thrust the guidebook, open at the page that had encouraged this reaction, to Purchase. Purchase looked at it with distaste, exclaimed, "Inexcusable!"

and passed it on. Councillor Hopkinson stared at it without a word and passed it to me.

The guidebook was open at an obscure back-pages section, an industrial and commercial directory whose closely printed text had been broken up with single-column photographs of factories and office blocks. The offending page showed a picture of the new chemical laboratory that had been built where the old Assembly Rooms used to be. The caption should have contained some information about the debt owed to the laboratory by the aluminum powder, paper coating, and polyurethane paint industries. Instead, it read:

> RAT-FACE HOUSE: where the screams of human guinea pigs may be heard nightly while plastic-surgery technicians carry out vivisection-type experiments to produce an improved, forward-looking rat-face for a go-ahead, forward-looking new Shepford.

Christ on crutches.

Bloody Hattersley. I had definitely screwed that bit of nonsense up and thrown it in my wastepaper basket. And just in case I hadn't definitely screwed it up and thrown it away, I had checked that caption specifically when going through the final proofs. And it had not been in the final proofs when they were handed over to Hattersley to sort out and return to the printers.

"Any explanation of this, at all?" asked Councillor Hopkinson coldly.

"None at all," I said blankly, restraining the impulse to call him sir. "I simply don't understand it. There must have been a slipup somewhere."

"I should just say there has been a slipup. Have these things been publicly distributed?"

"I'm afraid so."

"When you see Mr. Rainbell, tell him there'll be an emergency meeting of the Council Publicity Committee tomorrow morning. You'd better come too."

"Yes, sir."

Further discussion was prevented by the sounds of commotion from the shopping-center access road. The Shepford and District Traffic Wardens Steel Band, which should have been halfway to the old folks' home by now, was shambling back into the Cornmarket, playing an approximate version of "When the Saints Come Marching In." In a moment it was possible to see the reason for this unscheduled portion of the afternoon's entertainment. The band was being pressed forward—or, from its own point of view, back—by a great procession of old comrades, nurses, ambulance men, and hordes of other uniformed figures representing a cross section of the Shepford community. The procession had become hopelessly disorganized somewhere along its winding route and was marching about twenty deep, with half the Women's Voluntary Service contingent shoulder to shoulder with half the Red Cross contingent, and the other halves of both contingents pretty evenly distributed among the serried ranks of police cadets, choristers, firemen, nonmusical traffic wardens, commissionaires, and sundry others who appeared to be taking the cross-section idea pretty literally.

Concurrent with this, the rat-face in charge of the public-address system was announcing the grand finale of the children's dog show: " . . . the moment you've been waiting for, the Disobedient Dog class. Yes, children, we are looking for the most disobedient dog in Shepford. Now let's have all those disobedient dogs in the center of the arena."

A rat-face with more knowledge of children would have taken care to say, "Let's have all those disobedient dogs, *with their owners,* in the center of arena." This important rider was omitted. Several of the smaller children, imagining that the disobedient dogs were required to frisk independently into the arena and demonstrate their bloody-mindedness, let go of their leashes. At this example, other children, who had been coming forward with their dogs firmly under control, hesitated in the belief that they had misunderstood the instructions just announced, then unleashed their dogs or merely let go of their dogs' leads. The Disobedient Dog class was a popular attraction, and nearly all the dogs present seemed to have been entered for it. As the traffic wardens' band led the limping army of cross-representative, cross-sectionalized, cross-fertilized Shepford citizens toward the square, hardly an inch of it was visible for the seething mass of yowling, growling, snapping, yapping and, above all, fighting dogs.

Also concurrently, The Madison's psychedelic van had been observed—by Jeanette, and more important, by such teenagers who had not thrown themselves joyfully into the sea of dogs—to reemerge from the dead-end Bank Street into Cripplegate, where, its driver presumably having forgotten whether Cripplegate was one-way going west or one-way going east, it reversed at speed into the Cornmarket.

The TV camera had been knocked off its podium by now, so it was unable to record the great procession entering its final stages of disintegration as, pushed on from behind as in some mad general's battle in the First World War, wave after wave of the cream of Shepford's decent, God-fearing, law-abiding, uniform-wearing youth was thrown into the snarling, slavering pit of dog flesh to which the Cornmarket had been reduced; while the dregs of Shepford's less decent, non-God-fearing, un-law-abiding and non-uniform-wearing youth, some with small terriers attached to their lower limbs, had put The Madison's van in a state of siege and, in their anger and disappointment at their idols' refusal to mingle among them and sign autographs, were on the verge of tip-

211

ping it over. Meanwhile, such members of the Shepford and District Traffic Wardens' Steel Band as were not fighting off Alsatians with their drumsticks, were offering a spirited attempt at "Cricket, Lovely Cricket."

Not concurrently, but only fractionally consecutively, there was a kind of subdisturbance at the corner of the square nearest the Town Hall, where the road had been closed for the benefit of the spectators. The sound of "Speed Bonny Boat Like a Bird On the Wing," scored for brass, fragmentarily clashed with the calypso-tinted baying and howling of five hundred dogs. I saw several policemen clearing a path through the crowds, incidentally pushing them back into the mass dog fight from which they were trying to escape, and the Police Silver Band came into view.

"Speed Bonny Boat" was naturally arranged as a slow march, and the police band were indeed slow-marching toward their doom, for it had been agreed in correspondence with the Festival Committee that this would be a most spectacular way of entering the Cornmarket.

Even more spectacular than the well-disciplined slow march, however, was the fact that the police band had been joined, since last sighted in Cripplegate, by some very senior officers. Walking, rather than marching, several steps ahead of the drum major, but keeping in step, and maintaining the proper pace, were the chief constable of Shepford, uniformed but carrying his gloves; a uniformed superintendent and a uniformed inspector; and someone in a dark overcoat and trilby who, although he reminded me somewhat of the man in the Civic Center lobby who had turned out not to be a public-house landlord after all, was plainly his senior by very many ranks.

As a berserk Dalmatian attempted to seize the lead trombonist by the throat, and a nondescript breed that seemed to have a trace of greyhound in it leaped up at, and partly

212

through, the big drum and the police band ceased to play "Speed Bonny Boat"—some of its members attempting to restore order, others fleeing in terror, others heading for The Madison's now overturned psychedelic van with the object of making arrests—the deputation headed by the chief constable peeled off, and with eight or nine mongrels chasing after it, made briskly for the steps leading up to the Town Hall balcony.

Councillor Drummond had already gone white and was fingering his chain of office as if telling beads. He ceased to be white and became the color of putty as the chief constable and his party, still trying to walk in some kind of formal manner, but having to edge their way through a row of canvas chairs, approached and crowded around him.

"Mr. Mayor, are you Mr. Percival Walter Angus Drummond?" asked the chief constable, at the same time leaning slightly backward so that his hand could reach and conceal from the ladies' sight the jagged tear in the lower part of his trouser seat.

"Am," muttered Drummond, eyes downcast, avoiding those of his ratbag wife, who was looking as if she feared public rape.

"And do you reside at The Mill House, The Lane, Pontsford St. Mary's, near Shepford?"

"Do."

"I am the chief constable as you know, sir, and this is Superintendent Grout, who has warrants for your arrest under certain sections of the Public Bodies (Corrupt Practices) Act, 1889. Will you come along with us now to Shepford Central Police Station, where the charges will be read to you?"

"Would have thought neither time place, surely more suitable occasion," Drummond, with a new change of hue to that of cigarette ash, was blustering, but the chief constable had

213

already turned to Purchase, whose clean-shaven nose, I was fascinated to see, had grown damp and pink as if it, and it alone among his features, had just emerged from a Turkish bath.

"Are you Mr. James Henry Purchase, sir, of Number Forty-seven Castle Park, Shepford, and are you the director of finance of the District of Shepford?"

"I am James Henry Purchase of that address, but my appointment as director of finance has not yet been promulgated," replied Purchase, punctilious to the last.

"I am the chief constable of Shepford, Mr. Purchase, and this is Superintendent Grout, who has warrants for your arrest under certain sections of the Public Bodies (Corrupt Practices) Act, 1889. Will you come along with us now to the Central Police Station, where the charges will be read to you?"

Drummond and Purchase, heads bowed, were led away, accompanied by their tight-lipped, blood-drained, ratbag wives and one or two sympathizers or relatives among our little group. The hum of excited or astonished or indignant chatter was cut into by Councillor Hopkinson, who, as a lost Afghan hound howled piteously up at him from below the Town Hall balcony, said with hoarse urgency, "First things first, I think, Fisher. I've seen crowds panic, and this crowd's panicking. Do something."

"What can *I* do?"

"It's your show, Fisher. Get to that microphone and appeal for order. *Move!*"

I pushed my way reluctantly forward to the microphone from which, in happier times, Councillor Drummond would eventually have made the speech of thanks to all organizers worked so hard make Festival first-rate tiptop success been this week. "Ladies and gentlemen," I began, without any no-

214

tion of what I meant to say; but the microphone was not working, and so I was relieved of that responsibility.

I stared out glassy-eyed at the maelstrom in the Cornmarket and was somehow able to isolate two clear details, as I remembered being able to pick out details in a crowded picture of hell that I had once seen in the Stradhoughton Art Gallery's collection of Victorian paintings. The first of these was a child of about five, who was being dragged in the direction of Cripplegate by the very large sheepdog which had been number two runner-up in the Silliest Dog class; the child clutched grimly on to the length of rope that served as a lead, but such was the speed and energy of her pet that she was now traveling mainly on her back, like a thrown rider whose foot has caught in the stirrups.

The other details was Pisspot, who was emerging from, or rather being ejected from, the Kings Head Lounge Bar on the far side of the Cornmarket.

Swaying, shouting, and keeping dogs at bay with his stick, Pisspot disappeared into the morass of fighting, pantie-waving, arrest-evading teenagers in the vicinity of The Madison's overturned van; emerged again, and kept his head above, a fifty-yard heaving slick of small children and dogs; vanished into the tightly defended human fort that had been formed by the Shepford and District Traffic Wardens' Steel Band; reemerged; and was now staggering up the steps leading to the Town Hall balcony, bawling, "Justice has been done! Justice has been done this day!"

The recently vacated canvas chairs were pushed aside and fell over as Pisspot, drunker than I had ever seen him before, weaved toward me. Scandalized ratbags shrank back; Councillor Hopkinson buried his face in his hands; Jeanette gave Pisspot a nervous, inquiring smile, and I saw her mouthing "Good afternoon, Mr. Rainbell."

215

"My dear Arsehole, why you're not elcebrating auspacious day, whorror you, blurry lily-liller teetotaller? Donyouunstan, Arsehole, my dear ol'Arsehole, we have won we have won we have fucking WON! The *bars*tard Drummond is in chains!"

He seized my arm, as a master of ceremonies would seize the arm of a winning boxer, and raised it aloft.

"An nother thing, dear ol' Arsehole, must give assemble olpupace goo news."

He blew like the north wind into the microphone, which had miraculously begun to work again, and steadying himself with one hand against the rock-firm balustrade of the buttressed balcony of the dangerous structure that was the old Town Hall of the ancient Borough of Shepford, he drew breath; and Pisspot's stentorian voice, drowning even the barking of dogs and the crying of children and the general racket below and beyond us, boomed over the pandemonium of the Cornmarket.

"Ladeez and gennel*men!* May I present to *you!* For the first time in Shep-*ford!* The new, reigning, shit-heap champeens of the British Isles, the firm of Pisspot and Arsehole! Or, if you prefer it, Arsehole and Pisspot!"

Chapter Sixteen

"That's a pretty little street over there," Oscar said. "Yeah, that's real pretty. Now in the Uneye-ed States, you'd never come across a street like that."

I couldn't see it with his eyes or even with my own; it was my third day of walking aimlessly about, and I was exhausted. I remembered dimly what the street had been like, two years or three years or four years ago, when I'd last seen it: more of an alley, really, with some little houses, a very old timbered pub, a village-looking post office and one or two villagy-looking general stores. The narrow roadway had been cobbled, like the Cornmarket. There had been a "Save Green Street" Society which had sent circulars to the Department of Information and Publicity, among other influential bodies, and they had been thrown away unread.

It was all gone now, it was a gap, a rubbled space, with bile-green builders' fencing all around it, but the fencing was half flattened because the consortium that was to have built a Georgian-style square of prestige shops here had run out of money, and the patrolling guards and their guard dogs had been withdrawn.

"Real pretty."

Go away, Oscar, this is serious.

I had not seen Helen yet. This would be her third evening by the old windmill on the county border, if she was still waiting there. I didn't want to see her. It was serious. I was not available for light comedy, nor probably ever would be again.

Hattersley was expected to be the new director of information and publicity. Mr. R. V. O. Rainbell had retired prematurely owing to ill health. I had been given the choice of transferring to the Rates Office or not transferring to it.

There had already been a preliminary interview with the rating officer, whom I had better stop thinking of as King Rat.

"I would certainly plump for Rates if I were you, Mr. Fisher, even if I had any choice in the matter. I believe you do have some experience in the field, and the opportunities are certainly there. Take rate assessment, not that you'd be so high up the ladder to begin with. . . ."

"Lissena what the man *says,*" insisted Oscar. "Oh kay, it's a routine *jab.* That's only because up until now it's been done by routine people, Bill!"

Oscar, I have to say good-bye to you. It's been fun while it lasted, but it isn't fun anymore. You're a bore even, and an intrusion. Good-bye, Oscar. Thanks.

I couldn't quite make out where I was, although the place seemed familiar. I seemed to be in a graveyard, one that had been abandoned. I was in a walled enclosure, although part of the wall had crumbled to reveal the pretty little street that Oscar remembered and I hardly did. It grew high with grass and the kind of weeds that used to be seen on bombsites, and dotted here and there, in no particular symmetry, were statues in granite and marble, some upright, some lying on the ground. There was a long dais on planks, raised up on bricks, with a line of busts upon it—they looked as if they had just been potted out and, if anyone still cared for them, would in time grow torsos, legs, and arms like the other statues lying all about, and in the fullness of the seasons would sprout scrolls and top hats, their pointing fingers blossoming into heroic gestures.

In the center of this disused cemetery or whatever it would turn out to be, there was a kind of truncated Stonehenge of marble plinths and podia from which some of the statues now lying on the ground had clearly been removed. Dominating this area, and out of proportion to all its neighbors, was the equestrian statue of the first Duke of Shepford in blackened bronze, the guy ropes still fluttering like streamers from his broad shoulders and from his horse's mane. When I had first arrived in Shepford, this statue had stood in the center of the Cornmarket, and I could not remember when it had been removed.

Each morning I had set off on one of these long walks that finished up in strange destinations, telling Jeanette that I had another interview at the Rates Office or that I had to attend the preliminary hearing of the Council's inquiry into the Shepford Festival. Sometimes I mooched about thinking of Helen; sometimes I mooched about thinking of myself; and today I mooched about thinking of myself, Jeanette, and one other. Last night I had got home late and stood at the window of my book-lined turret, overlooking the steeples and towers and glass arcade roofs and chiming belfries; the sound of "Tom Bowling" played on the carillon of the covered market died away, and I saw gravel pits, abandoned quarries, rezoned factories, the doomed woods where the new conference hotel would be, the ribbon of wire netting guarding the pollution-free river; and far off at the end of the long, straight road, the village of Mayfield with its flat-roofed maisonettes and its new bungalows.

"Bill? Can I say something to you? Are you in a good mood?"

Jeanette had given Mr. Pussy-paws his evening can of something with liver in it. Eventually I would have to ween it, and her, off pet foods manufactured by Helen's husband: silly, painful reminder of a scene that should have been forgotten. But the cat purred contentedly enough as it scoffed this doubtful product. Jeanette seemed happier than I had ever known her.

"I haven't got much to be in a good mood about, have I, Jeanette?"

"Oh, you'll have to stop brooding one of these days, Bill! It could have happened to anybody! And it'll all blow over, and after all, one thing about working in local government, you've still got a job, and the money's not much less, is it?"

"No."

"Come and sit down, Bill. I've got something to ask you."

"Ask away."

"Sit down first."

"Why—am I going to faint from shock or something?" I'm picking up her argot, or the husbandly equivalent of it, as I never used to. Does that mean I'm staying with Jeanette, after all? And if I'm not staying with Jeanette, where am I going?

"You *might* faint, for all I know. Bill, what would you say if I told you I thought I was going to have a baby?"

Christ. Quadruple, Quintuple, Octuple Christ.

"You can't be. You're on the Pill."

"The Pill isn't infallible, you know. And anyway—" deep breath, confession time, "—I haven't been taking my pill. It brought me out in a rash, and I thought, just for one month, I'll risk it and see what happens. Bill? Is it all right, Bill?"

"It'll have to be all right, won't it?"

Christ in multiples of thousands.

My mother put her up to this.

A baby. A man-child, or perhaps a woman-child. What do you *do* with them?

You give them milk. You take them to zoos and safari parks.

What do you *say* to them?

You tell them stories.

220

Once upon a time, there was a poor woodcutter, who had but one son. . . .

"Are you glad, Bill, or sorry?"

"I'm glad."

I'm glad. It'll be a new experience. I can always do with a new experience.

"You don't sound it."

"I *am* glad. I need to take it in."

"Of course, it's not confirmed yet, but if it is confirmed, have you made up your mind about the bungalow?"

"Mortgagedene."

"*What*-dene?"

"Good name for a house, that, Jeanette. I'll sign the papers tomorrow. Mortgagedene."

"Don't be so daft, Bill Fisher. We'll call it Hillcrest, same as your mother's house. And won't she be glad to hear I've got some news?"

I had walked around the streamered statue of the first Duke of Shepford three or four times, and now I had placed myself, I knew where I was.

The walled yard belongs to the clerk of works' department of the district of Shepford; I had been here once or twice on business, and that was why it seemed familiar, like the cemetery in Stradhoughton where my grandmother was buried.

I don't love you, Helen. I'm becoming a father this year, so I don't love you. I can accept no more juvenile lead engagements.

Once, before the old terraces had been pulled down, there had been a fumigating shed here somewhere, and mattresses and sofas had been put out on this flattened grass enclosure to air before being returned to their owners. Now the terraces, slum or otherwise, had gone; the festering mattresses, as well as accumulated junk and solid Victorian furniture, had been tossed into public bonfires on waste ground before

221

the retreat to the high blocks on the perimeter of Shepford. Whole streets disappeared, whole neighborhoods, and all the statues of aldermen and benefactors, dislodged by demolition or the building of ring roads, were towed to this place and dumped. At first they were cleaned, in the belief that they would be found new sites in the beautiful, rising city; some of the granite statues were scrubbed pink, some half scrubbed. The others were black and covered in bird droppings. Slowly it became clear to anyone who cared to notice that this was to be their last resting place, and as more statues were towed in, this walled enclosure had taken on the appearance not of an abandoned cemetery, as I had previously thought, but of a knackers' yard.

I can cope, Helen had said. I can cope with anything, I always have and I always will.

And *I* can cope.

Except losing you, she had said.

You've lost me, Helen. It's serious, It's not light comedy. It's not even drama. It's life.

I knew where I was and who I was, and I drew in great gulps of air to show that everything up until now, everything up until last night when Jeanette had said, "Can I say something to you, are you in a good mood?" was behind me. I was a heavy at last, or would be, I was grown up, or would be, and it didn't happen by decision, it happened by circumstances.

A telephone message had been taken by Jeanette about some golf clubs. Could I go around and see Detective Constable Reid at Shepford Central? I knew what I meant to do. I would ask for Detective Constable Carpenter, it was his case anyway, and tell him to wind up the matter in any way he chose, or alternately stick his head up his arse.

Feeling pleased, relieved, relaxed, confident and grown-up, I took a last look at the streamer-tethered statue of the first Duke of Shepford.

"Quite a guy," a voice said in my head. I ignored it. It would go away. But it didn't, and so it was mainly to drown Oscar's voice that I said aloud to the bronze figure of the Duke of Shepford on his bronze horse, "Captain Fisher, sir. First Ambrosian Cavalry. We've just got through, sir—it's murder out there."

But I did not salute, as I would have done once. And I walked, not marched, away.